The Tinder Box

H.J. "Walt" Walter

The Tinder Box
Copyright © 2022 by H.J. "Walt" Walter

ISBN
978-1-957378-33-6 (Paperback)
978-1-957378-32-9 (eBook)

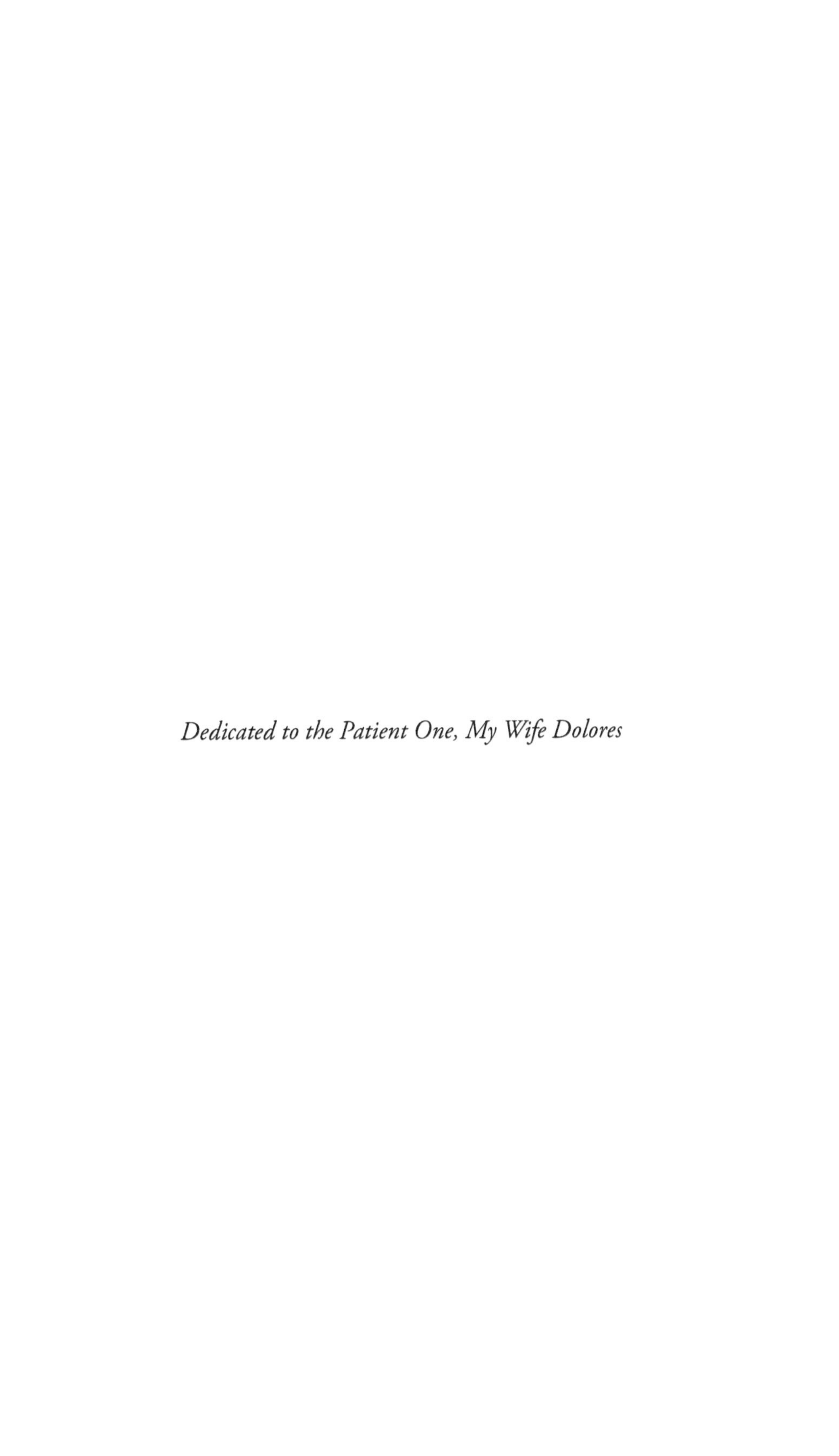

Dedicated to the Patient One, My Wife Dolores

TABLE OF CONTENTS

ACKNOWLEDGMENTS

To my wife Dolores, for always being there when I needed guidance. For being so patient when things went wrong. For always supporting what i was doing no matter how much time it required writing alone in my study.

To a dear friend, Edie Fleeman, for helping in editing my book and making welcome suggestions to improve its content.

ABOUT THE AUTHOR

 H.J."Walt" Walter is a retired naval aviator who served four years in the Antarctic. He spent 22 years flying all types of naval aircraft including single engine props & jets, multiengine props & jets and the turboprop powered C-130. After retirement he earned his college degrees. A Bachelor of Science in Education, Bachelor of Science in Earth Science and Master of Science in Education He also has three years of mechanical engineering at Purdue University and attended the Naval Post Graduate School, Monterey, California. Taught high school Technology Education and Pre-Engineering at Canisius College and was also employed in the engineering department of an aerospace corporation.

1

"THE RECRUIT"

Jolo, Sulu Island, Philippines

The night was warm on the tropical Island of Sulu and the troops were out enjoying the nightlife at a karaoke bar near the US Army headquarters. As the evening was just beginning a bomb suddenly ripped through the bar killing Ross Denanza, a security officer of the US Forces civilian military forces, and Jose Bani, a janitor at the bar, also leaving 25 wounded.

The Philippine National Police responded and reported the incident at the Kamayan Beerhouse, located some 40 to 50 meters away from the main gate of the Army 104th Brigade headquarters in Camp General Teodulfo Bautista.

From a half-mile away the leaders of Abu Sayyaf watched with glee and pride that their attack on the Filipino and American military had been so successful. The result of this attack was a concerted effort to wipe out the leadership on the Abu Sayyaf by any means possible.

The United States responded to this attack by declaring Abu Sayyaf a terrorist organization and issuing arrest warrants for those involved in this attack.

Monterey, California, 5 years earlier

The campus of the U.S. Naval Post Graduate School was bathed in fog with the temperature hovering around 59ºF. It was a beautiful setting on the coast of California. The school was established in the old Del Monte Hotel on some 629 acres back in 1948. Its landscape was basked in coastal cedars and tall white oaks. It was a beautiful place to study Computer Engineering.

Lieutenant John Walker was on his way to his latest computer class. He had been enrolled since transferring from Naval Air Station Corpus Christi, Texas, where he had been a flight instructor in Advanced Training Unit 402. He had been flying "Spads" (AD-3 Douglas Skyraiders), which he really enjoyed.

The days were winding down and John knew he would be returning to the fleet as soon as he graduated in mid-December. It was only September but he anticipated he would be receiving his orders very soon.

The last semester was beginning and his latest class was a new, highly classified ship computer system known as the Naval Tactical Data System (NTDS). John figured this would put him in good stead with the assignment desk back in Washington at the Bureau of Naval Personnel where individual orders were issued. He was hoping to be assigned to an aircraft carrier (CVA) as NTDS officer.

A few days later John was called into his advisor's office. Upon entering, his advisor introduced him to a man who would be known as Commander William Bates. Commander Bates ushered him into the conference room for a little privacy. They sat down and Commander Bates began the discussion.

"John, we have been following your career for the past couple of years and we need an aviator like you in our stable. Should you decide to work with us you would still be in the Navy but would be flying missions for us most of the time. Your job would be mainly intelligence gathering," Bates said.

"What kind of flying would this assignment entail?" John asked.

"We know you have flown the DC-3 before so we have you lined up to fly a DC-3 in Southeast Asia. You will be stationed at the Naval Station Sangley Point in the Philippines. I can't give you any more details at this point until I have a decision from you, if you want this assignment. I don't need your answer today but I am leaving Monterey tomorrow afternoon so I will need your answer by noon tomorrow. Is that alright with you?" Commander Bates asked.

"That will be fine, sir," John replied. "I will meet you in my advisor's office tomorrow around noon, if that's convenient with you?"

"That'll be fine, John. Looking forward to your answer. Tomorrow it is then."

They both arose, shook hands and went their separate ways.

The next day

John met Commander Bates in his advisor's office exactly at noon.

"How are you doing today, John?" Commander Bates asked.

"I'm doing just great, sir," John responded

"Well, have you made your decision?" Bates asked.

"Yes sir I have." John answered, "But I have a few questions. First of all, for whom will I be working?"

"You would be working directly for me," Bates said. "I'll tell you what, give me your answer and then we can go forward from there."

"Well, sir, the DC-3 is not my first choice of aircraft to fly but the assignment sounds interesting so you can count me in," John offered.

Commander Bates offered his hand and said, "That's great, John. Glad to have you on board. Here is the program. In a few days Jim Boyle will contact you. He will be your training officer and will lead you through the steps you will need to take during this assignment. I am sure he will be able to answer any and all of your questions. If he can't he will contact me and I am sure I can fill in the blanks. Your main job will be intelligence gathering and reporting that to me. That's about all for now. The next time I see you will be in the Philippines. Do you have any more questions?"

"Yes, sir, one more question," John said. "What will my status be? Will I be assigned to the base or as a freelance pilot?"

"John, no one will be aware of your assignment with us. You will be a regularly assigned pilot and officer attached to the Naval Station. You are directed not to discuss this assignment with anyone except me, or someone designated by me. Your training officer will clear up a lot of questions. I hope this answers your concerns," Bates said.

"I'll wait and talk with Jim Boyle so I guess that's it for now, sir," John said.

"Okay, John. I will be departing within the hour.

Once again, glad to have you aboard," They shook hands. Commander Bates departed and John went off to his next class.

He was now signed up for the class which covered the history, people, religion, geography and government of the countries of Southeast Asia. It would help him understand the situation he was getting into.

Sure enough, in a couple of days Jim Boyle showed up at the school and contacted John. They scheduled a few days of training, which would be one hour per day during one of John's free periods. They met in the main building in one of the conference rooms so they had privacy. This would allow for open discussions of John's assignment.

During the sessions John learned that his copilot would be Lieutenant Murray Wright, who had already reported to Sangley Point for duty. He would also have a plane captain and a loadmaster whom he would meet when he got to Sangley Point. They were both assigned to the program by Commander Bates. The DC-3 would be outfitted with three cameras with ports with sliding covers which concealed the cameras when they were closed. The loadmaster was a trained photographer and would handle all the film exposed by the cameras.

John was advised that he would be required to keep a daily journal and would make a weekly written report to Commander Bates, the report to be mailed to a post office box in Arlington, Virginia.

In addition, John learned he would have three passports and a special briefcase with three compartments for carrying them. The red passport was to be used for diplomatic immunity and his picture was taken in a dress suit, shirt and tie. The green passport was his official active duty document which pictured him in full dress khaki uniform. Finally the blue passport was to be used when traveling as a casual American dressed in non-descript sports clothes. He was instructed about the situations where each one might be used but was advised that it was always his call based on the country and situation in which he found himself.

Jim was a good instructor and was thorough in his preparation and delivery. He answered all of John's questions and that training went smoothly.

While all this intrigue was going on John still had to keep up his flying proficiency. His flight period was always scheduled for Tuesday mornings. He alternated his flying between the North American T-28 Trojan and the North American T2J Buckeye. The Trojan was a single engine, two place, propeller driven aircraft while the Buckeye was a single engine, two seat, turbine powered aircraft. They were based at the Naval Air Facility Monterey which also served as a commercial airport for the Monterey area. Flying for John was always relaxing, as it was a time away from the rigorous studies required by the postgraduate school.

Time passed quickly for this young naval officer. Transfer orders soon arrived. Thanksgiving was celebrated and then graduation loomed in mid-December. John's complete duty section were all scheduled to graduate together. Among his classmates was Lieutenant Nguyen Quynh, a Vietnamese naval officer. John and Quynh had become great friends, having taken a number of classes together. John judged Quynh to be the smartest naval officer he had ever met. John was no slouch however as he graduated 20th in a class of 84. Graduation was exciting in one sense and sad in another. It meant breaking up a close-knit group of twelve naval officers who had become friends and relied on each other to get the job done. After the ceremonies, goodbyes were exchanged and each in turn checked out with the duty officer who signed orders, each on his way to the unknown in his new assignment.

2

"ACROSS THE PACIFIC"

San Francisco, California

The San Francisco airport was busy as usual. John deplaned from his Delta flight and was headed toward baggage claim. The DC-6 had bumped and bounced for eight hours from Pittsburgh and John was ready for a relaxing drink. It had been a great leave for John. He had visited with his family and spent some time on the ski slopes of Western New York over Christmas and New Years holidays.

John picked up his one bag at baggage claim and walked out to the street to catch a taxi to the Marine Memorial Hotel in downtown San Francisco. He had two days left on his leave so he decided to enjoy the city before reporting to the Naval Station Treasure Island for further transfer to the Philippines.

The Marine Memorial was just as he remembered it. He had stayed there some two years earlier when he first transferred to Monterey. He settled in his room, took a shower and dressed for dinner. As he stepped out into the street from the lobby the taxi starter asked him if he would like a cab. He answered in the affirmative, climbed into the cab and told the driver "Top of the Mark."

This hotel had a great restaurant and a superb view of the bay area. John dined and then returned to the Marine Memorial by 9:00 p.m. He was beat as his internal clock was still set to eastern standard time, so he climbed into bed for a good night's sleep.

It was still dark when John awoke the next morning. His body was still advanced in time; it was already 9 o'clock back in New York but only 6:00 a.m. in San Francisco. John ordered room service for breakfast and was soon dining in his room. He had decided to just roam the city today and end up at Fisherman's Wharf for dinner. After spending most of the afternoon in Chinatown window-shopping, John ended up at the Franciscan Crab Restaurant on Pier 43 ½. He had a great seafood dinner of crab and lobster. After finishing his dinner he remained and had a couple of after dinner libations before heading back to the Marine Memorial.

The next morning he was up early, dined in the Memorial dining room, checked out of the hotel and left by taxi for Naval Station Treasure Island. He reported in with the personnel office and was quickly processed and put on a bus for a 12:00p.m. flight from Travis Air force Base. The ride was smooth and pleasant on a Greyhound charter bus. He thought, that sure was better that the old Navy busses he had ridden before. Maybe the Navy was moving into the 20th century when handling people.

After checking in with the departure desk at Travis Air Force Base he still had another hour, so he walked into the coffee shop for a mid-morning pickup. At 11:30a.m. his flight was called for boarding and he was on his way to Hawaii. The plane was a DC-6 from U.S. Navy Air Transport Squadron 21 but he didn't know any of the crew. They bumped along at 8000' for a couple of hours. He was sitting near the front of the cabin and the co-pilot came back from the cockpit to check on something in the rear of the aircraft. On his return up the aisle he spied John's Navy wings and stopped to talk with him. They chatted about when they graduated from flight training and were designated a naval aviator. After a short time they seemed to be hitting it off and the co-pilot invited John up to the cockpit. John had never been in the cockpit of a DC-6 so he relished visiting one. When he stepped into the cockpit he couldn't believe how spacious it was and all the instrumentation. He was introduced to the Aircraft Commander who invited John to sit in the flight engineers jump seat between the pilots. John accepted and they cruised along chatting for a couple of hours. He received quite an insight into the life of a transport pilot.

They had been airborne about nine hours and were approaching one hour out of Hickam Air Force Base. The pilot recommended John get set for approach and landing so he thanked everyone for their insight and went back to his seat in the cabin. The approach and landing was textbook and after landing on Runway 09 at Honolulu International they taxied over to Hickam. Time on deck was scheduled to be 2 hours. With the 2-hour time change it was only 8:00p.m. in Honolulu. John wasn't very hungry as they had been served in-flight rations so he found a corner in the lounge and settled down for a little rest.

The 2-hours had almost passed and the flight had not been called so he went to the departure desk and inquired about departure time. He was told the flight was in a maintenance delay and word would be passed shortly concerning a new departure time. After ½ hour a passenger service representative came into the lounge and addressed those passengers who were there. They were told that the plane was in a down status and needed an engine change. No other aircraft was available to continue the flight for about three days as an engine needed to be shipped from the Naval Air Station Alameda, California. Passenger service estimated a 3-day delay so passengers were directed to find housing for those days and to call in 72 hours for an update on estimated time of departure. Passenger service found rooms for John and two other officers at the Hilton's Hawaiian Village and provided a staff car to take them there.

John checked into the Hilton and was assigned a room on the 6th floor overlooking Waikiki Beach. Couldn't have asked for anything better, he thought. This should be a couple of pleasant days. The room was very plush with a large bathroom, king sized bed, refrigerator bar, large windows with 2 glass doors opening onto a small patio and air conditioning. In a corner by the patio there was a 25" color TV and a table and chairs. This was great as the government was picking up the tab. He took a long shower and went straight to bed. His internal clock was still on east coast time so it was now five hours later than local time and he was beat.

He slept for some 8-1/2 hours and awoke at 9:00a.m. The hotel had an open snack bar and restaurant on the beach next to the hotel so he decided to put on his swimsuit and have breakfast there. Wrought iron chairs and tables with a glass top and a sun umbrella were the norm. He was seated by the greeter at a table by himself facing the Pacific Ocean. Breakfast consisted of pineapple and papaya followed by eggs over easy with bacon, wheat toast and coffee. John ate slowly and took in the beautiful winter weather. He thought about how lucky this delay was. He could have been stuck in Anchorage, Alaska. After breakfast he moved to a chaise lounge on the beach and took in some rays. He had remembered to bring his suntan lotion to keep from getting burned. After a couple of hours he went back to his room and showered, changed clothes and decided to have lunch. There was an open air, tropical style restaurant on the lower level of the hotel and John figured that was as good a place as any to have lunch. He had a typical Hawaiian lunch, a salad and some fruit with a glass of pineapple juice to wash it down.

He had never been to Ford Island so he planned a trip out there. He took a taxi to the fleet landing where he boarded a Navy launch to the island. Ford Island was located in the middle of Pearl Harbor and was a Naval Air Facility. It had been heavily bombed during the Japanese raid on Pearl Harbor at the beginning of World War II but had been rebuilt and was still used by the Skyraiders off the carriers which pulled into the harbor. This would be a sentimental journey with a visit to the ghosts of naval aviation past. Here is where the planes from the USS Enterprise, USS Yorktown and USS Hornet took off to land aboard their carriers and attack the Japanese in the battle of Midway. John was in awe when he stood on the flight line and took in the history which surrounded him. He visited the tower and some of the hangars before he was ready to depart for the main island of Oahu. After taking the ferry back across Pearl Harbor he caught a taxi to the hotel. It was approaching dinnertime so upon arrival he walked the one city block over to Chuck's Steak House. Chuck's was a quaint restaurant with a limited menu. Dinner consisted of salad, bread and steak with a baked potato if a person so desired. Steaks were selected and cooked by the customer. They served alcohol and John had a local beer while cooking his steak. Dinner lasted about one hour and as John left Chuck's he saw the Royal Hawaiian Hotel across the street. He wandered over there and went down into Davey Jones Locker. In the bar were large portholes designed to observe the swimmers in the hotel pool. John had another beer and sat at the bar. In short order, a beautiful blond woman approached him, about his age, and proceeded to hit on him. He obliged and soon they were in a serious conversation. Her name was Wyona Cameron who preferred to be called "Wawa." She was a PanAM Stewardess who had a 2-day layover on her flight to Singapore. John and Wawa hit it off and after a few more drinks she invited him to her room for the night.

In the morning John found in the bathroom a razor, shaving cream, toothbrush and toothpaste. He stepped into the shower and was soon joined by Wawa. The giggling and hugging and kissing were a sight to behold. After about thirty minutes they stepped out of the shower and began drying each other with a bath towel. This only led to more giggling and hugging and kissing. Soon they were back in bed.

They had both dozed after all the physical activity and woke once again around 11:00a.m. The hotel provided a woman's and man's swimsuits. John tried on the man's suit which fit him. He and Wawa planned to go down to the beach. Thirty-six hours had passed and John needed to check in with passenger service at Hickam. When he called he learned they were still working on the plane after which it would need a test flight. Estimated departure time was determined to be noon the next day. The two of them had lunch under the Banyan Tree on the beach and spent the afternoon sunbathing. Dinner was at Chuck's followed by drinks at Davey Jones Locker. About 9:00p.m. they drifted up to Wawa's room for more lovemaking.

Morning came early and they ordered breakfast through room service. By 9:00a.m. John had to say goodbye. It was a lingering goodbye. Both had come to enjoy each other's company and they promised to meet each other again soon. They had exchanged personal information and after a final kiss John went back to the Hilton where he checked out and boarded the staff car waiting to take him to Hickam Air Force Base.

The flight departed about noon headed for Wake Island. Flight time was ten hours. During the flight they crossed the International Dateline and the day changed from Monday to Tuesday. On landing at Wake the passengers were transported by bus to the dining hall and sat down for dinner while the aircraft was fueled and serviced. Two hours later they were airborne for Guam where the aircraft was refueled then on to Clark Air Base in the Philippines. The weather was clear and John looked out the window. He saw a beautiful green, lush countryside with high mountains on each side of a beautiful valley running through the center of the island. He espied Mt. Arayat, a volcanic cone rising in the valley to a height of 3500' about 25 miles from the air base. It was 7:00a.m. Wednesday and it had been a long flight.

John checked in with passenger service where he learned that there would be a DC-3 from Naval Air Station Cubi Point arriving around 9:00a.m and departing for Naval Station Sangley Point around 9:30a.m.

The plane finally arrived and the pilots came into the terminal to check their load for Sangley Point. John met them and introduced himself to them. They were glad to meet him and told him they were pleased to have him on board as they had been short one pilot for about two months. The plane loaded and soon was off to John's final destination. Thirty minutes later he deplaned and was met by Lieutenant Murray Wright. Murray introduced himself and they began to compare notes. They had not served together but were looking forward to working together. Murray took John down the road a short distance where John checked into Personnel after which Murray brought John to the Bachelor Officers Quarters (BOQ) which would be his home for a couple of years. Turned out Sangley was a small base and the BOQ was almost directly across the street from the base air operations. John found his assigned suite, dropped his bags and flopped into bed. He was exhausted from his long trip and tomorrow would be soon enough to get acquainted with his new assignment.

3

"BEACH LANDING"

Naval Station Sangley Point

John awoke Thursday morning having slept about eighteen hours. It was early morning and he showered, unpacked his clothes while he laid out his tropical white uniform. He dressed and went down for breakfast, which the BOQ was still serving. Murray came into the officer's mess and joined John for a late cup of coffee. They discussed what John needed to do for his check-in routine. They decided the place to start was the base Personnel Office.

When they stepped out the front door John realized he had really not seen the base when he arrived. Sangley Point was a base surrounded on three sides with water. It was attached to the land on the southwest end where it was about ½ mile wide. It was shaped like a man's bowtie with the runway on the north side of the base and running southwest to northeast. At the midway point the base narrowed to about ¼ mile wide and then widened on the eastern end once again. The aircraft control tower was on the south side of the runway at the base's narrowest point. Across the street from the tower was the BOQ and then water on the south side.

John and Murray walked the two blocks to the Administrative building and checked in at the Personnel office. Murray was the personnel officer so things went quickly and efficiently during the paperwork process. John was given his check-in sheet and Murray said he would see John later in the day. Along with the check-in sheet John was given a map of the base indicating the offices and buildings John would need to report to during this process. When he left the personnel office his first stop was with the administrative officer. He knocked at his door and was ushered in to Lieutenant Commander Chip Wozniak's office where he introduced himself. Chip was also a naval aviator so they hit it off very quickly. After a few minutes Chip invited John to join him and he escorted him up to the second deck where they entered the Executive Officer's office. John was introduced to the XO, Commander Wayne Schreiber, another naval aviator. Chip excused himself and went back to his office. John and Wayne chatted for some time with the XO inquiring as to what duties John would like to be assigned. John had no clue what he would be assigned but he had some military law courses so he let the XO know that something in the legal field would be fine. The XO arose and walked over to the door connecting to the CO's office. He knocked and opened it and the Commanding Officer (CO), Captain Gray Strumbel, looked up from his desk where he was seated. The XO told the CO that he had a new officer checking in and motioned John to step into the CO's office with him. Commander Schreiber introduced John to Captain Strumbel. The CO extended his hand and greeted John with a hearty, "Welcome aboard, Lieutenant."

John reciprocated with, "Thank you Captain. I'm glad to be here."

John and Captain Strumbel chatted for a few minutes and soon the Captain indicated the conversation was over and that he had some things to do so John and Commander Schreiber said their thank-yous and departed the CO's office. Commander Schreiber indicated that John needed to continue his check-in if he expected to compete it that day so he shook his hand and went downstairs.

He walked over to air operations. There he met Lieutenant Commander Bill McElroy the assistant operations officer. Mac as he was affectionately known, was very friendly and was quite interested in John's flight experiences. When Mac found out John had been a qualified DC3 aircraft commander his eyes lit up. He indicated that John would be checked out in the DC-3 very quickly and put on the line flying the regularly scheduled milk run to Naval Air Station Cubi Point, Clark Air Base and Sangley Point. These flights were every week, Monday, Wednesday and Friday, two flights each day. Morning flight one-way and afternoon flight in reverse. There were two DC-3s to fly these flights. John also discovered he would be standing the air operations duty. After turning in his flight logbook John continued his check-in. He had only a few stops left, one being medical where he turned in his medical and dental records, and the officer's club where he was signed up as a member of the Officer's Open Mess. This would allow him to run a tab at the club and then be billed later in the month. Of course there were dues involved for this membership.

John settled in to his new surroundings and was soon flying his check out in the DC-3. He flew a few flights as a co-pilot on the milk run and was written off as checked out on local flight procedures. Within two weeks he was ready for his aircraft commander check. Mac had been his instructor on most flights and he was a great mentor. During John's third week he qualified as Aircraft Commander and within a couple of days another DC-3 was delivered to the base. A message was received from the Bureau of Aeronautics which stated that Lieutenant John Walker was to be assigned to fly this aircraft exclusively. His co-pilot would be Lieutenant Murray Wright. Also during this two week period a plane captain and a loadmaster who were previously qualified in the DC-3 checked-in to the base and were directed to be assigned to John's aircraft. Commander John Black, the operations officer, questioned the Commanding Officer on these assignments but was told this directive came from higher authority and that's the way it would be.

This aircraft was John's intelligence aircraft. The main difference in this aircraft were the three cameras installed in the forward fuselage. On the underside were three doors covering the camera ports that were activated by a switch in the cockpit and were fitted so perfect that they were in fact invisible. The cameras were also activated by another switch in the cockpit so they were always under control of the pilots.

Meanwhile John was assigned as assistant legal officer under Commander George Bailey and was also Blackmarket Control Officer. There were four investigators, one native civilian and three Navy petty officers. They all worked in civilian clothes so they could blend into the population when working off the base. They were part of the intelligence gathering capability and John always reported their work in his weekly report to Commander Bates.

John was getting into the daily routine and this particular day was working in his office when two officers unknown to John walked into his outer office and requested to see him. They were escorted into his inner office and he invited them to sit down. After introductions all around they got right down to business. They were intelligence officers who had just arrived on the base. They indicated the discussion should be considered secret which John acknowledged and they continued. They were investigating guns being smuggled into the Philippines by Russian submarines. The guns were destined for the Hukbalahuk, the communist rebels in the Philippines. They needed John to take them to a destination on the east coast of Luzon Island to investigate a submarine spotting. A map was displayed and the spot on the coast indicated. John's first comment was that there was no airstrip to land his DC-3 in that area. The officers indicated they wanted him to land on the beach. A hot and heavy discussion ensued mostly concerning the strength of the sand on the beach to support the landing of the aircraft. They assured John that it was perfectly safe to land and takeoff there. John finally gave in and agreed to land his aircraft on the beach.

The flight was scheduled for the next day. Weather had been checked and the flight crew was briefed on the width of the beach and the landing distance available. Turned out it was 60 feet wide and 4500' long. Landing would need to be made close to the water's edge where the sand mixed with volcanic pumice had the most strength to support the DC-3.

The crew boarded the aircraft and after normal procedures rolled onto the runway for takeoff. The flight up the east coast of Luzon was about one hour to the spot the intelligence officers wanted John to land. Soon they arrived over the area and John made a low pass to reconnoiter the landing area. It sure looked narrow and short from the air. On the west side of the beach the mountains were steep sloped and dropped from over 6000' to sea level. Just south of the landing area the jungle came down almost to the waters edge. On the north end was a small inlet cutting off the beach right up to the jungle. The landing area was 4500' but visually appeared shorter due to the terrain. John observed the surface wind to be light and variable so he decided to land to the south. This would give him a good continuous look at the landing area throughout his approach. He set up a downwind leg parallel to the beach heading almost north and instructed Murray to read the landing checklist. Murray complied and reported checklist complete. John held off on extending full flaps until he turned final at about one mile. He called for full flaps and slowed the aircraft to 85 knots for landing. As he bled off the altitude he was just barely off the deck when he passed over the small inlet on the north end of the landing area. Touchdown was smooth and about ten feet from the low tide waterline. The beach was a little wet and seemed to give the aircraft more support than loose sand. John retarded the throttles and lowered the tail wheel onto the beach. Run out was about 3000'. The intelligence officers had indicated they would have to trek south from the landing site to find the mine where they were to interview the owner, so John let the aircraft slow down and taxied to the south end of the landing site. At the end he swung the aircraft around and ended up heading north where he could takeoff in that direction if the wind remained the same as when he landed. He and Murray shut-down the aircraft. The intelligence officers came up to the cockpit to check out with John. The estimated they would be gone for about two hours, which would be well before high tide. John had checked the tide table before leaving and tides in this area were only some four feet so it would not be a problem for takeoff.

The crew deplaned and wandered around the beach for some time. During this time a negrito family consisting of a father, mother and four children wandered down onto the beach. The loadmaster could speak a little of their language and he determined from speaking to the father that he had brought his family down to see the "big iron bird" that flies. Their dress was amazing to these Naval personnel. The males were clothed in loincloths while the females wore longer cotton skirts. They were all bare breasted. These negritos were from a tribe of pygmies who were isolated by the steep mountain range to the west of the beach. It was found that they had never tasted rice yet the famous rice terraces were only some 30 miles west over the mountains. The father was carrying a weapon, a long bow that was taller than himself. He was proud of his skill with the long bow and gave the crew a demonstration by shooting out the center of a sunflower at about 75 yards. Impressive indeed. The family circled the old DC-3 staring at the various parts while jabbering to each other. They were even encouraged to touch the plane but were afraid to do so. After about forty minutes of circling the aircraft in awe of what they were seeing, they headed up the beach to the small inlet where they were observed bathing.

After two hours the intelligence officers emerged from the jungle. They had been successful in finding the mine owner and interviewing him. He had told them a clandestine story of a Russian submarine surfacing about

300 yards offshore and of seeing a zodiac offload rifles and what appeared to be ammunition boxes, then bring them to shore where they were met by a group of Filipino men who took charge of the stash and disappeared into the jungle.

All-hands boarded the plane and John cranked up the engines. Checklists were complete, engines checked and brakes released. The plane accelerated slowly in the sand but soon gained takeoff speed and was airborne at about four feet over the small inlet. The negritos were observed bathing and appeared to be somewhat startled by the DC-3 flying over so close to them. John climbed out to 7000' and headed west back to Sangley Point.

John made a great landing on the end of Runway 08 then hit the turbulence as he passed the O'Club some 2500' down the runway. The club was just off the taxiway and when the wind was out of the south the burble from the interaction of the two where always noticeable. The aircraft was parked in its usual spot on the ramp and after shutdown John breathed a sigh of relief. I sure hope the missions are less tense than this one he thought. What a story he would have to tell his kids when he might have some.

4

"PROJECT HANDCLASP"

Naval Station Sangley Point

John was settling in to the normal routine. He was flying many of the milk runs to Cubi Point and Clark Air Force Base. His next intelligence flight was to be a very non-stressful flight. There were twelve small cartons and a couple of cardboard barrels delivered to the base for further transfer. They were from the Agency for International Development (AID) and designated "Project Handclasp." Their symbol, which was stamped on all boxes and barrels, was a pair of clasped hands. The cargo consisted mostly of old library books and sample drugs. These were destined for the public library and the local hospital in city of Iloilo on the island of Samar that was located some 280 miles south southeast of Sangley Point. John had been made aware that AID was actually a CIA cover but some cargos were what they were said to be while others were generally questionable.

The appropriate officials in Iloilo were notified of the expected delivery time. John and his crew departed at 8:00a.m. and headed out over Lake Taal headed for Samar. After two hours of cruising at 7000' in beautiful tropical weather John started his descent for the Mandurriao Airport. It was a grass strip with no tower or air traffic control so he was on his own as far as visual flight rules. Murray spotted the airfield first and pointed it out to John. They set up for a downwind for runway 02 which was 6000' long.

Once on deck they saw their welcoming party and taxied over to them. Greetings all around and cargo offloaded they boarded the plane and flew back to Sangley Point.

A few days passed and John was in his office. He was notified of the delivery of three large crates. These crates were once again Project

Handclasp. They were loaded and barely fit into the cargo compartment. Delivery was indicated to be the next day and the destination was Vientiane, Laos.

Flight was planned and departure was scheduled for 7:30a.m. John and Murray started up their DC-3 and departed Sangley Point for Laos. They droned over the South China Sea headed for Vietnam then on to Laos. John had never carried Project Handclasp crates so large, so he decided to see exactly what he was carrying. He stepped out of the cockpit and moved into the cargo compartment. Stopping at the first crate he peeled back the protective paper covering the cargo. To his surprise he saw High Velocity Aircraft Rocket (HVAR) pods. Each crate had nine pods and the rockets were loaded with high explosives. Great, he thought, they didn't even have the courtesy to tell me about the cargo.

The crossed Vietnam and entered Laotian airspace. After crossing a range of small mountains they broke out in a valley where Vientiane appeared dead ahead. Landing was normal and John parked on the ramp where directed. When he exited the aircraft the heat was oppressive. Temperature was 92°F and relative humidity was close to 99%. As he and Murray strolled down the ramp towards operations, two men wearing silk suits, ties, shirts and polished shoes were headed towards them. As they approached they asked John if he was the pilot of the DC-3 he was pointing towards. John indicated he was and told them their cargo was on board and to be careful offloading it.

The silk suits stopped to talk with John. They asked him if he was qualified in the loading of the rocket pods he had just delivered. He had fired hundreds of these rockets from the skyraiders he had flown and indicated that he felt he was so qualified. They asked John if he would accompany them over to the T-28 hangar and give the men required to load these pods some instruction. He said he would, so they walked over to a drab looking rundown hangar. There they met a Laotian army Major Kong Lee. John was introduced and the CIA agents relayed the info that John could help qualify his men in loading the rocket pods. Those gathered went into the hangar where there were six T-28s painted in jungle camouflage. As they did the hangar doors opened and the crates John had been carrying were brought in and deposited on the hangar deck by men in army uniforms and of various ranks. A few of Major Lee's men unpacked the pods and set them on armor carriers they had been provided for that purpose. John gathered those men who were going to load the pods and began his impromptu lecture. He spoke through an interpreter. After he discussed nomenclature he had the pod rolled under the wing of one of the T-28s. Here he covered safety issues and described the steps required to attach the pod to the aircraft. He then called forward the first loading crew and had them load the pod while he supervised. He cautioned them about plugging in the pod to the aircraft, indicating it should be done at the last minute with the aircraft pointed in a safe direction in the case of an accidental rocket launch. The crew performed the loading safely and John wrote them off as qualified.

Major Lee thanked John for his assistance and John and Murray headed for air traffic control to file their flight plan back to the Philippines. As they entered the terminal they ran into a delegation of Russian Army and Air Force personnel. It was obvious from their dress that they were there to train the Laotians. It was the Russians' way of increasing their sphere of influence in Southeast Asia. John observed the senior officer's nametag with the name Zukov. He was a Major in the Russian Air Force and was wearing both pilot's wings and a missile badge. John would report this info to Commander Bates in his weekly report.

The pilots filed their flight plan and while walking back to the airplane were approached by four men wearing jeans carrying backpacks and Model 70 Winchester highpowered rifles, chambered in .338 caliber.

One of them asked, "Sir, where are you going from here?"

"Going to the Philippines," John answered.

"How about a ride for my men and me?" he asked.

"Sure, just show me an ID and you're good to go," John said.

The four men each showed him a U.S. military ID card.

"Put your gear on the plane," John said.

"Thank you sir," he said and directed his men to board the plane.

The flight back to Sangley was uneventful. John settled into his new job and surroundings. The investigation office coupled with his four investigators was constantly acquiring new intelligence and the Chinese influence in the Philippines became more and more obvious. Weekly reports were sent to Commander Bates in Arlington, Virginia.

John had brought his pistols with him to Sangley Point. He was unauthorized to carry them off the base however because they were not registered with the National Bureau of Investigation (NBI). John needed that registration so he discussed it with his civilian investigator, Dick Suarez. Dick suggested that they take a trip over to the NBI and begin the registration process.

Arrangements and an appointment were made at NBI headquarters and Dick and John had a Special Services vehicle pick them up at Investigative Services at 9:00a.m. The morning drive through the countryside was refreshing. Once out the gate, Cavite City was teeming with people. Along city streets many barter transactions were occurring and the market place was full of food vendors doing a wonderful business. The aroma wafting though the air was captivating at times. Some pesos were being exchanged but in this small poverty stricken country little economic activity was possible.

They passed though Bacoor City and just on the outskirts of town were stopped at a Philippine Constabulary checkpoint. The Lieutenant manning it was very polite and asked for identification. Dick spoke to him in Tagalog, the native language for that area, and soon they were cleared to proceed. Makati was just as busy as Cavite City as was Passay City. The roads were crowded with people carrying goods either for sale or some, which they had just purchased and were taking back home. Feet were the favorite form of transportation.

Arrival at NBI Headquarters in downtown Manila was uneventful and the driver pulled through the gate and into the compound. He dropped Dick and John at the front entrance and found a parking spot in the shade of a monkey pod tree.

Dick led the way to the registration section. Here he introduced John to Edgar Bond who was the section chief. Edgar was a forensic scientist who also headed the NBI evidence laboratory. Turned out he was an Olympic Free-pistol shooter and had just returned from Melbourne, Australia, where he had competed in the Olympic shooting events. He gave John a long form to fill out, took his pistol and fired a bullet from it into a bullet trap then retrieved it in mint condition. The bullet was tagged and bagged, as they say, and then filed in the myriad of file drawers. John finished the form and Edgar took it and also filed it in his records section. John's gun was now registered and he could carry it anywhere in the Philippines.

While in Edgar's office a message was received from the Director's office that Dick and John should stop by after they were finished there. They thanked Edgar, departed, and climbed the stairs to the second floor where Colonel Turkban's office was located. It was a sparsely furnished space with an old desk and chairs and a few filing cabinets. The Colonel was obviously operating his bureau on a shoestring.

As they entered Colonel Turkban welcomed them.

"I heard you were in the building, Dick. Just wanted to meet your new boss," the Colonel said, as he extended his hand towards John.

Dick turned and gestured towards John, "Colonel, let me introduce Lieutenant John Walker."

As they shook hands John said, "A pleasure to meet you sir."

"My pleasure, John. Listen I wanted to run something by you and Dick. It concerns a mutual problem and seems to be getting worse by the week."

"What might that be, sir?" John asked.

"Well, it seems that your Special Services drivers are dabbling in smuggled cigarettes. What is happening is they are taking military personnel and dependents to their destination in and around Manila. The people renting the vehicle then turn them loose to return to pick them up at their designated time. It can be for a period as much as eight hours, sometimes less. What the drivers are doing is driving out to Batangas province on the west coast and picking up recently landed cases of cigarettes and bringing them into the city and dropping them off at the crime syndicates designated warehouse. Of course they are being paid a bonus in pesos for every case they deliver. It is getting rampant and must be stopped," the Colonel reiterated.

"That sounds pretty serious, Colonel," Dick responded. "What are the options to put a stop to it?"

The Colonel continued, "First of all I asked the Constabulary to establish a couple of check points on the road from Batangas to Manila and to confiscate any cases of cigarettes they discover in their search of Special Services vehicles. The drivers cannot be arrested at that point unless we have proof positive the cigarettes are smuggled so we must let them go but we know cases of cigarettes in Special Services vehicle are in fact smuggled because the base does not allow cases of cigarettes in those vehicles to be driven off the base. That's where you guys come in. We will pass our reports of confiscated cigarettes to your office with time, place, vehicle number and driver's name. If you can see to it that the driver's employment is terminated that will send a message to the driver pool it isn't profitable to smuggle cigarettes."

John spoke up, "Sounds like a workable plan, Colonel. I will need to get the Special Services Officer to buy into our program but I think that is possible. Is there anything else we can do on our end?"

"Yes, I think monitoring the vehicle mileage on all trips. The passenger should make note of the arrival mileage at their destination and report any excessive mileage to the Sangley Point dispatcher on return to the base. That will also keep the drivers from engaging in nefarious activities," the Colonel said.

"I hadn't thought of that Colonel," Dick said. "I believe it's doable if we get the passengers onboard."

"Good. I'm glad we got that settled," Colonel Turkban said. "John, I hear you like to shoot pistols. How'd you like to go through our firearms training?"

That got John's attention. "Wow Colonel. That would be an exhilarating experience. When do we start?"

"I am going to start training new agents next Tuesday at 8:00a.m. on the range. It is located across the street from headquarters past the parking lot. Do you have a revolver?" he asked.

"Yes sir, I have a Navy Smith & Wesson K-38 with the barrel trimmed down to 4". I carry it while I'm flying all the time," John said.

"Okay that'll do for the training, bring it next Tuesday and by the way we shoot only wax bullets in Hogan's alley," Colonel said.

John was on cloud nine as he and Dick exited the building and searched for their driver. They spied him in the shade of the monkey pod tree and hustled over to the car. The drive back to the base seemed quick as the discussion of the morning's events was exciting and John was pumped up on knowing of the training he was about to receive.

When they returned to the office John placed a call to the Special Services officer. Jack Fisher came on the line and John outlined the problem and explained what they needed to do to solve it. Jack agreed in full and said he would implement the program as soon as he could put pen to paper. Jack further offered one of the other problems he had observed with the driver's pool. His drivers of Chinese birth were being pressured by the Mainland Chinese government to publicly declare their duel citizenship and begin to talk with Chinese agents about the base and their work. An example of how the Chinese communists were trying to expand their sphere of influence in the Philippines. John included this information in his weekly report.

5

"THE MOUNTAINS"

Naval Station Sangley Point

Combat pistol training began at the NBI the very next week and John looked forward to it each Tuesday. He enjoyed meeting other NBI agents and the training, which was personally supervised by Colonel Turkban. There was much graft and kickbacks offered in trying to lure the agents to look the other way. Colonel Turkban was fully aware of this and had established a special squad of his most dependable men. They were known as "the untouchables", patterned after the United States FBI's 1920s squad of the same name.

They accepted John into the inner circle of agents as he trained with them every Tuesday. He was also introduced to Jose Feliciano, a local disk jockey. Jose was an undercover NBI agent in addition to being the Philippines Olympic Free Rifle Champion. In the course of hobnobbing with these professionals they appeared on Jose's TV show, which involved a quick draw pistol contest.

The Constabulary was doing their job at the road checkpoints and smuggling was in slight decline. A few special services drivers had been fired and John hoped they had a handle on things. To his dismay, one morning Dick Suarez entered John's office accompanied by the Constabulary Lieutenant who had been on the checkpoint when they had gone to Manila. He was asking John's help. In executing his duties he had stopped a special services car and had discovered eight cases of cigarettes. He confiscated them and in dong so was threatened by the driver who said, "I have connections and I'll see to it that you are put on suspension for this."

Sure enough the next day the Lieutenant was suspended from duty for a month without pay. He pleaded with John to help him get reinstated because he couldn't feed his family and all he was doing was his job.

John assured him he would look into it and do his best to get him reinstated with back pay. The Lieutenant and Dick left his office and he called Colonel Turkban. The Colonel was successful and within days the Lieutenant was reinstated with back pay. John felt a lot of satisfaction.

During the course of his NBI training he found out that all NBI agents had to report to Manila once a month and qualify with their pistols. If they did not qualify they did not get paid for the month. To test his training John began competing in the rifle and pistol matches, which were being held monthly at Naval Station Subic Bay. He also kept in touch with Edgar Bond and Jose Feleciano. When the Philippine National Rifle and Pistol championships were scheduled he was invited by them to participate. The pistol and smallbore matches were held at Fort McKinley and John assembled a team to compete. He arranged to have a ten-passenger Mercedes bus available to take them everyday to the range from Sangley Point.

The first gun competed in was the service pistol. At the end of the day one of his shooters won the individual championship and the team was victorious winning the gold medal. In the smallbore competition John's team was ill equipped and their older rifles were no challenge to the newer ones being fired by other competitors. Jose easily won the three-position championship but one of John's shooters borrowed a rifle from one of Jose's teammates and won the prone championship. In the police pistol championships John's shooters were at a great disadvantage in that they had never fired this type of competition. They showed their mettle however and still beat the Manila police, who ended up in last place. Colonel Turkban's team won handily. The last day the awards ceremony was conducted and after the medals were handed out the teams moved to the northern town of Baguio, high in the mountains, where the high power rifle championships would be contested on the rifle range of the Philippine Military Academy.

The first day the teams assembled at 8:00a.m. in the assembly area behind the range. Targets were assigned and they took their positions firing a couple of stages of the match. Approaching noon a ceasefire was called and all assembled took a break for lunch. John and his team found a spot up the mountain about 100 yards behind the range and sat down under a huge mahogany tree. A Philippine Constabulary Captain joined them. He introduced himself as Bonnie Murrano. Everyone greeted him and John walked over and talked with him. John knew exactly who this man was. He was a national hero of the Constabulary who was the most decorated combat soldier who ever served. They immediately became good friends.

Suddenly and without warning Bonnie jumped up, drew his .45 caliber pistol from his holster, and charged down the mountain shouting loudly in Tagalog at the young children who had gathered on the firing line where they were picking up the fired rifle brass. The kids froze in their tracks and were terrorized by the huge pistol pointed at them. With their arms outstretched, opened their hands and let the brass fall to the ground. With Bonnie still shouting at them they all suddenly turned and ran as fast as possible off the range and disappeared.

John sat through all this in amazed silence. He could not understand what was happening and wondered what set Bonnie off in such a tirade. Bonnie holstered his pistol and walked slowly back up the mountain and sat down to finish his lunch. John continued his conversation with Bonnie but kept it light until Bonnie had a chance to calm down. After sometime he finally put the question to Bonnie.

"What the Hell was that all about, Bonnie?" he asked.

Bonnie showed some disgust, "John, if I let them take that brass, they will give it to the Hukbalahup who will reload it and next week they will be shooting back at us with the brass we provided them. I was not going to let that happen."

"Gosh Bonnie, that makes complete sense now that you explained it. Those kids were really scared and I guess that was the intent, right?"

"You better believe it. That was meant to scare them enough that they won't ever come back to the range, let alone try to pick up the spent brass," Bonnie said.

They all finished their lunch and after a short nap were called back to the line to finish the match. John was victorious as was his team. What an experience, John thought.

John returned to his daily routine at Sangley Point flying the weekly milk runs to Naval Air Station Cubi Point and Clark Air Force Base. The next test of his flying skills came about two weeks later. He was directed to fly over to Fort McKinley, pick up about twenty foreign military officers and deliver them to Baguio for a conference at the Philippine Military Academy. This flight would be a challenge. The runway was only 4200' long, ran uphill to the east and was located at the end of a steep narrow canyon. The big problem was the canyon started out going east for about one-half mile then turned ninety degrees left and ended another one-half mile with the field running east requiring a sharp banked turn to reach the threshold of the runway. A controlled speed of only 90 knots was required to negotiate the turns and not run into the canyon walls, which towered another 1500' above the field elevation of 6000'. That was the only safe approach. John slowed his airplane to 90 knots and entered the canyon at 6300' as he approached the first turn he banked sharply and rolled out heading north. He proceeded up the canyon and approaching the end slowed while Murray lowered the landing gear and flaps to the full down setting. Just before crashing into the rock wall in front of him he banked sharply to the right, then rolled the wings level and set the aircraft down as sweet as you please on the end of the runway. Even Murray commented, "What a beautiful landing". The landing roll out was very short on the steep uphill runway. John taxied back to the operations terminal, shutdown and discharged his passengers. John smiled at Murray as he got up out of the pilots seat.

"There's your seat going home," he said as he pointed to his just vacated seat.

Murray scowled, "Thanks a bunch, old friend. You sure know how to put a guy on the spot."

"Hey Murray, you need the training, besides one day this plane will be yours and you will need to be ready for it."

Murray climbed over into the pilot's seat while John went aft and exited the airplane to check with the operations duty officer to see if there were any people or cargo to go elsewhere. There was only a Navy Lieutenant Commander and his wife waiting who needed to go to Cubi Point. John told them to hop aboard and he would be with them in a minute or two. They duty officer indicated there was no cargo so John hopped aboard and climbed into the copilot's seat. After startup and completing the checklists Murray taxied uphill to the takeoff end of the runway. At the end he did a

180º turn and pointed the aircraft downhill and directly at the rock face of the canyon just off the end of the runway. John instructed him that he would need to make a sharp-banked turn just as they passed over the end of the runway in order not to hit the rock face of the canyon. Murray added full power on the engines, released the brakes and they were airborne just 3200' down the runway. He immediately called for gear and flaps "up" and accelerated to 90 knots. At the designated spot he commenced his left turn and cleared the rock face by at least 150'. Clouds had descended and were hanging over the mountains so they were unable to climb and had to transverse the canyon the reverse route that they had entered. At the end of the canyon they broke out and Murray was able to descend to 5000' and proceed down the valley towards Clark Air Base. Soon they approached the route into Cubi. Murray descended to 1500' and passed Mount Santa Rita, which was three miles from touchdown at Cubi Point. John contacted the tower and they were cleared for landing. They dirtied up the aircraft and landed normally on the 8000' Cubi runway.

They dropped off their passengers and headed for home. Murray had handled the aircraft in an outstanding manner and John let him know it.

One week later they repeated the drill. The foreign officers were picked up in Baguio and brought back to Manila. This time they were veterans and the trip was a piece of cake. John made notes for his weekly report.

There was some fallout from the incident at the Constabulary checkpoint in Makati. Two weeks later, the fired special services driver was found murdered in the city of San Pedro. The NBI was called in to investigate. The investigation led them to a couple of legislators in the National Senate. At this time in the Philippines the Senators were granted immunity from prosecution but they were tied to the smuggling ring although not enough evidence was developed on the murder to charge them with that crime.

A short time later the Untouchables conducted a raid on a gambling casino in Pasay City. Two agents knocked on the outer door to the casino. The casino's procedure was to lock the outer door before opening the inner door. One of the agents had a small piece of bamboo which he jammed in the outer door, which failed to close completely just as the inner door was opened. This allowed the rest of the squad to breach the outer door and enter the casino. As the lead agent announced their presence people started screaming and trying to run for the exits. They all were stopped and finally brought under control of the squad. After herding the patrons against one wall a gentleman stepped out of line and spoke to the senior agent. He indicated he was a senator and invoked immunity. He asked to be released immediately and the senior agent told him he was free to go. The senator called his wife out of line to leave but she was stopped and told to get back in line. A long fever-pitched discussion ensued between the senator and the agent. The agent won the discussion and the senator's wife was booked and fingerprinted. This incident created a crisis within law enforcement. The senator went back to the chamber and drafted a law to defund the National Bureau of Investigation. The legislation passed and NBI agents went without pay for a month. Besides law enforcement the bureau was charged with intelligence gathering. Both areas were affected by the loss of pay. After a month of wrangling the national legislature saw the light and back pay for all was forthcoming.

John was certainly relieved as his stream of intelligence once again started flowing.

There was always a hot spot developing in Southeast Asia. Indonesia began to flare up and a way was needed to gather some intelligence. At air operations terminal a DC3 had just landed from Clark Air Base and a group of Navy men deplaned. John just happened to have the operations duty that day and he met them as they entered the terminal building. Commander Ralph Touch approached John and introduced himself. He had noticed John's nametag over his right pocket and indicated he needed to confer with him in the next day or so. John made arrangements for the next day and gave the commander direction to his office.

Ralph entered John's office and closed the door behind him. They exchanged pleasantries and sat down. Ralph indicated his official mission was to take his team of five members to Indonesia and repair a Grumman UF-2 "Albatross" which we had given their air force but was now in disrepair and currently unflyable. His covert mission was intelligence gathering. General Sukarno was president but was being challenged for leadership of the country by General Suharto. Once again the underlying source of trouble was the conflict between the Russians and the Communist Chinese. It was going to be a repeat of what we had just experienced in Laos, John mused.

John and Ralph exchanged any intelligence they currently had and Ralph said he would be leaving by commercial air for Jakarta, Indonesia, the next morning. John wished Ralph a safe journey and success as he departed.

A few weeks passed without word from Ralph and his team. A message was received by John that the team was okay but was experiencing difficulty in repairing the Albatross. They sent along a list of parts required to Naval Aviation Supply Depot in Oakland, California. Commander Bates working through back channels directed Oakland Supply Depot to ship them to Sangley Point and for the station, meaning John, to transport them to Commander Touch In Yokyakarta, Indonesia.

A week later the parts arrived at Sangley Point via military aircraft. John scheduled his departure for the next day. He and Murray would transit via Singapore and Jakarta to get to Yokyakarta. Commander Bates directed John to get pictures of as many military installations as possible along the way.

The flight to Singapore was uneventful and after landing they made their way downtown to the Singapore Hilton for an overnight stay. They checked in with the embassy by phone and the embassy pilot advised them to exchange their money on the black-market as the Indonesian Rupiah was becoming very inflated and the official rate would kill them as far as costs were concerned.

John and Murray found a wonderful Chinese restaurant in Chinatown on Pagota Street. They took a cab and exited right in front of the Chu Shun Restaurant. It looked newly furnished with a Chinese arch for an entrance finished in a reddish color with Chinese symbols on the columns. They entered and were quickly seated. The restaurant was sparsely populated with customers but with plenty of service personnel.

After a superb dinner they were relaxing waiting for dessert. Murray ordered Goa for both of them, Goa being rice based snacks that are typically steamed and may be made from glutinous or normal rice. John asked the waiter to have the manager come over to their table. He knew from experience that the manager could direct them to a Chinese moneychanger who would give a good rate of exchange for their American dollars. Yung Ching Sou approached the table and John asked him for directions to a moneychanger. Yung smiled and said his cousin was in that business and he would call him.

Yung came back in a few minutes and said his cousin would be there shortly and would change American dollars for Rupiahs. John had checked the official exchange rate and found it to be 3 to 1. When Yung's cousin showed up he was introduced as Chi Kung Fie. Chi took them back to an unoccupied booth in the rear of the restaurant. He quoted the current black-market price as 2900 Rupiah to one dollar. His fee was one percent of the transaction. John changed $300 American and received R-870,000. Murray also exchanged some dollars but nowhere near what John had. John gave Chi $303 and thanked him for his business. Chi arose and bowed and departed the restaurant. John and Murray headed to the hotel for a good night's sleep.

6

"OUT OF GAS"

Singapore, Malaysia

The DC-3s crew was off into the wild blue yonder by 8:00a.m. They had filed a flight plan to take them over North Sumatra enroute to Jakarta, Indonesia. There were two Indonesian military bases on their route of flight and John wanted to photograph them. The weather was cooperating; scattered clouds with visibility over ten miles.

As they approached the first base John opened the camera doors and within three miles began filming. After passing the base he closed the doors and turned the cameras off. He repeated the procedure over the second base. Approaching Jakarta they were directed to switch to Jakarta approach control. Murray selected the appropriate frequency and called. Approach cleared them to descend to 3000' and gave them an altimeter setting. As John leveled the aircraft at 3000' another aircraft appeared about ¼ mile off their right wing. Murray identified it as a Mig 21 with Indonesian Air Force markings. The Mig-21 wiggled his wings, slowed, and dropped his landing gear and flaps. This was the international signal to follow me and that's when John knew they were possibly in trouble.

"Oh shit," he mumbled to Murray. "Now we're in for trouble."

"I think we will be okay though," Murray replied.

"Have you guys got your diplomatic passport?" John asked.

"That's the red one, just as a reminder. Keep your eyes on me and follow my lead. If I pull out my red one you guys do the same."

Murray wondered out loud, "I wonder where he's taking us?"

"From the direction, I would say he's headed for the joint Commercial/ Military airport just west of Jakarta. Switch to the tower frequency for the airport, Murray."

They next heard the tower, "Dakota 83 do you read us, over."

Murray keyed his mike, "Jakarta read you loud and clear."

"Roger Dakota 83 we are advised you are being directed to land at our field. Call entering downwind for landing Runway 33, over."

"Roger tower. Dakota 83 has field in sight. Entering downwind for landing Runway 33."

John continued downwind and called for the landing checklist. Passing abeam the end of the runway, Murray once again keyed his mike, "Dakota 83 turning base. Gear is down and locked."

The tower responded, "Dakota 83 cleared to land."

After rollout on landing John turned off the runway and a vehicle with a "Follow Me" sign mounted on its tailgate turned in front of him. It was flanked by two other pickups containing men armed with rifles in military uniforms. John followed the truck to the parking area. As he approached he saw, on the edge of the airfield, what appeared to be an angry mob with protest signs and probably numbering in the 6000 range being restrained by many military personnel. On the ramp were many military trucks and personnel with a few staff cars. "This was going to be ugly," John thought.

He brought the aircraft to a stop and shutdown the aircraft. As he stepped off the aircraft an Indonesian Army Colonel and his staff met him. The Colonel got right to the point. He was being charged with violating Indonesian security protocols and was accused of photographing military bases. He denied all the charges and stood his ground as the Colonel ranted and raved about Americans spying on them. After much discussion the Colonel stated that his officers were going to go aboard the aircraft and inspect it. That's when John sprung into his counteroffensive. He had his briefcase in his hand, opened it and withdrew his red passport. He stuck it in the Colonel's face and told him in no uncertain terms that the aircraft was covered under diplomatic immunity and it was in fact U.S. soil. If the Colonel breached diplomatic protocol John promised him that within eight hours the sky would be filled with F-14s and FA-18s and there would be ordnance falling from the sky.

The Colonel withdrew to his assembled staff and went into a long discussion. In the meantime John had been given permission for Murray to call the American Embassy. He was escorted off to the operations building.

The assembled protest crowd was still shouting and was very noisy but the military had done a good job of keeping them under control so the Americans were not at risk. The crew had spent some four hours on the ramp during these discussions and daylight was running out. They had been scheduled to fly on to Yokyakarta but it didn't look like the Colonel was going to allow that to happen. John was still negotiating when Murray returned from operations. He took John out of earshot of the Colonel and told him the Ambassador was on his way with a squad of Marines. John went back and continued his negotiations with the Colonel but was now stalling for time.

Within thirty minutes the Ambassador arrived with the armed Marines who deployed around the aircraft. John greeted the Ambassador and climbed into his SUV to discuss the situation with him. He told him what he had told the Colonel and where the negotiations had progressed.

The Ambassador exited his SUV and walked over to the Colonel. Within minutes the Ambassador returned to where John and Murray were standing and relayed to them what agreement they had come to. John and his crew would be required to spend the night in Jakarta but would be allowed to continue their flight the next morning.

The Ambassador instructed his senior Marine Sergeant that his men would guard the aircraft over night and that no one except John Walker was allowed to board it. The Sergeant acknowledged and assured everyone that his orders would be followed to the letter.

John's flight engineer locked the aircraft after everyone obtained his travel kit. They boarded the Ambassador's SUV and departed for town. Four Indonesian military vehicles, to ensure their safety from the gathered crowd, accompanied them.

They arrived at the Sleep Inn after a long drive though the crowded streets of Jakarta. They had encountered the usual busses, cars, taxis and water buffalo drawn carts. Jakarta was your typical equatorial city, hot and muggy, which contributed to the smells and odors encountered.

The crew were assigned rooms on the third floor of the hotel, which gave them a scenic view of the city. The hotel was situated on a roundabout with the British Embassy on the opposite side. After a hot shower they settled in for a little libation and relaxation. Murray and John were in one room while his flight engineer and loadmaster were in the room next door. Murray and John were still keyed up from the afternoon happenings. Indonesian Military personnel were deployed around the hotel and restricted John's crew from leaving so they had to have dinner in the hotel's dining room.

They wandered down to the dining room around 6:00p.m. and had a leisurely dinner. About the time they finished, a crowd began to gather outside the hotel to protest the Americans once again. The crew went back up to their rooms and had a front row seat to what was happening outside.

The unruly crowd began shoving at the police while yelling anti-American slogans. The signs they carried likewise were very anti-American. After this continued for some thirty minutes it turned even uglier. People began throwing stones, which was answered with tear gas. Molotov cocktails soon were evident although none reached the hotel proper. The crowd tired of these tactics without success and as if swept up by the wind turned toward the unguarded British Embassy. There was a sudden rush and Molotov cocktails were hurled at the building, which quickly caught fire. Now it was like a zoo outside. The military waded into the crowd with police batons. Snipers began shooting the protesters while others rescued the people who could have been trapped in the embassy. Police and fire trucks responded to the alarm and were soon spraying water on the burning building but to no avail. The embassy was a complete ruin.

Up in their rooms John had turned out the lights. He and his crew were watching all the drama unfold. The flight engineer and loadmaster indicated they were in fear for their safety and asked John what they should do. John in all his wisdom told them they had three options. One they could go up to the top floor to try to avoid being captured by the mob. If they did that however, and the hotel caught fire they might be trapped. Two, they could go down to the main floor and be captured and possibly beaten to death or three, stay where they were and hope for the best. Everyone agreed they would stay put and hope for the best.

The drama outside the hotel was subsiding. The embassy fire was almost out but the building a complete loss. The crowd had been dispersed with police riot tactics and the police were withdrawing. The military were still guarding the hotel. John and Murray remained dressed but dozed in and out for the rest of the night.

Morning dawned and the crew ordered room service for breakfast. They didn't want to expose themselves in the public area of the hotel until the last possible moment. The American Ambassador had promised an SUV to arrive at the hotel by 8:00a.m. At 7:55a.m. and as promised his personal SUV pulled into the offloading driveway of the hotel. Murray spotted it arriving and alerted the crew that they were moving to board the SUV as quickly as possible.

Once aboard, the SUV proceeded down the driveway for the airport. Again the four military trucks escorted them with ten armed soldiers on board each truck. The city was bustling and people were going about their daily business. The smells of cooking permeated the air as well as the poverty that was present along their route to the airport.

Upon arrival the Colonel and his staff were again present. John was engaged in discussions while Murray made contact with the fuel farm to get some fuel for the aircraft. The base-fueling officer told Murray that he had orders not to sell them any fuel. Murray reported back to John interrupting his discussion with the Colonel. When John found out he turned angry but knew he had to maintain a cordial position or things would really get ugly. John finally convinced the Colonel to allow them to deliver the aircraft parts they were carrying. He advised him that it was a benefit to the Indonesian Air Force because the plane was needed for search and rescue. The Colonel also promised John that fuel would be available at Yokyakarta.

A flight plan was filed and the crew manned the aircraft. Taxi and takeoff were normal and finally they were on their way. The crew could feel an air of relief. They were glad to be out of the dangerous situation they had found themselves thrust into. After three hours air traffic control switched them over to Yokyakarta Tower for landing. Murray was pilot in command for this leg of the journey and after a perfect landing taxied to the ramp. They shutdown and upon exiting the aircraft were met by Commander Touch and his team. He was happy to see them, and they were glad to be on a friendlier base with a lot less tension in the air. The loadmaster brought out the aircraft parts they were carrying and gave them to Commander Touch's team. They were profusely grateful for the effort. John and Ralph discussed the situation on the base and Ralph gave John his written intelligence report to be forwarded to McLean when he returned to Sangley Point. Ralph was stunned at the story John relayed to him concerning the escapade they had just endured in Jakarta.

Murray entered base operations while John and Ralph were talking and approached the base-fueling officer. He also had been instructed not to sell them any fuel even though the Colonel in Jakarta had promised them fuel would be available at this base.

Murray brought his bad tidings to John and Ralph. Ralph was appalled because relations between he, his team and the Indonesians were very good. Ralph told John he would talk with the base commander and see what he could do. He asked John to accompany him. They walked over to the base commanders office and asked his clerk to notify Colonel Desharto that Commander Touch was there to see him.

They were advised to enter and Colonel Desharto greeted them.

"Good morning, Ralph. What's on your mind this morning?"

"Good morning, sir. This is Lieutenant John Walker. He is the pilot who brought me parts to fix your UH-2. Your fuel officer is denying him fuel. Is there some problem?" Ralph asked.

"I'm sorry, my friend. Colonel Bronshian, deputy chief of staff of the Army, passed the word this morning not to sell him any fuel." Turning to John he said, "He is the one who gave you all the trouble in Jakarta, John."

John smiled broadly, "Yes sir I will never forget him."

"I have called a friend in Bali who manages the airport there. He assures me he will sell you fuel should you wish to go there. What is your choice?" Colonel Desharto asked.

"Well sir, I have about one hour and fifty minutes of fuel remaining and Bali is about one hour and a half flight time from here. If the weather is VFR the whole way I guess I will chance it," John responded.

"Okay then, I will confirm that you will arrive sometime this afternoon in Bali for fuel," he said.

Ralph arose. "Thank you sir for all the help. We better get John back to the flight line and on his way. I will talk with you later."

John and Ralph departed the Colonel's office and headed for the flight line. On arrival at operations he and Murray filed a VFR flight plan for Bali, said goodbye to Ralph and his team and manned the aircraft. John climbed only to 1500' in order to save fuel and after level off directed Murray to lean the fuel mixtures as much as possible without damaging the engines. This flight was going to be a squeaker. They should land with about twenty minutes of fuel. Murray tuned in the VOR radio to Bali and it indicated directly ahead. After one hour and five minutes they had the island of Bali dead ahead and Murray switched to Bali tower.

He keyed his mike, "Bali Tower, Dakota 83 fifteen minutes out for landing, over,"

The tower answered, "Dakota 83, roger cleared for a straight-in approach to runway 09. Winds are east at 5 mph, altimeter is 29.98, over."

"Bali tower, Dakota 83 copied, we are approaching ten miles have runway in sight," Murray reported.

John called for the landing checklist, lowered the gear and flaps and began his descent for landing. They landed with seventeen minutes of fuel remaining.

John's comment, "Does every leg of this flight have to be a cliffhanger?"

"Seems like we're destined to be on edge this whole trip," Murray said.

"I think we deserve a break, Murray. What do you think? Australia sounds like a good place to R&R?" John asked.

Murray immediately cheered up, "Hey buddy, I can take that any day of the week. Are you serious?"

"I'm serious," John answered. "Get out the charts and start planning."

After refueling John went into the terminal to pay the bill. He asked the manager how much he owed him. After the manager told him he reached in his pocket and pulled out his rupiahs. He had more than enough to pay for the fuel. The manager held out his hand, palm facing John.

"No, no," he said. "American money."

John thought, "Oh shit. All these rupiahs and he wants American."

John went back to the airplane and returned with a government voucher. He was a little dismayed. Rupiahs at 2900 to 1 and dollars 3 to 1. "The airport manager sure made a pile of money on this transaction," he thought.

All their business complete in Bali the weary travelers took off for a couple of days R&R in Perth, Australia.

7

"CAMBODIA"

Perth, Australia

John and crew spent a couple of days resting and relaxing in the winter sun of Perth. A chance meeting, in the pub at their hotel, of a steward of the local racetrack, got them an invitation to the races as his guests. They were treated as royalty as a car was sent to their hotel, to take them to the track where they were met by their acquaintance and a steward assigned to each of them as a host.

During the races, dinner was served with each course being served after each race. The hosts made all the bets on the races for these young Americans and by the end of the day they were all richer by a large amount. It was a tremendous experience for them.

With R&R over the crew manned their aircraft and took off for Singapore. Not wanting to repeat being intercepted by a MIG-21, after passing Christmas Island, John headed for the Sumatra Straights. After passing between the islands of Sumatra and Java he navigated his aircraft to pass between the Banka-Belitung Islands then direct to Singapore. After flying most of the day they finally touched down at Changi International Airport. The taxi took them to their favorite hotel, the Singapore Hilton where the staff welcomed them back and the manager made sure they were well taken care of. They dined at their favorite Chinese restaurant and returned to the hotel for a good night's sleep.

The next morning they were up early and were off to Sangley Point. Murray made a great landing despite the burble off the O'Club and taxied to their usual parking spot. Their work wasn't finished until the camera film was offloaded and placed in the express container for shipping via military airlift to McLean, Virginia. John's weekly report would have to wait for tomorrow as he was extremely tired from the long flight.

The next morning John entered his office, closed the door, and sat down to write his report. It was a complete and detailed report of the happenings and observations of the past week. He described being intercepted by the MIG21 and his encounter with the Indonesian Colonel. He reported his observations of the airfields they photographed and the scene at the Jakarta Airport. There might have been many Russian Aircraft but the most interesting was the Chinese cargo plane, which he observed offloading military supplies at the airfield in Jakarta. He explained necessary use of their diplomatic passports and the demonstrations against them including the burning of the British Embassy. When he finished he sealed it in an envelope and mailed it off to Commander Bates.

During the next week the rainy season began. The rain started and never stopped each and every day. One result was the flooding of the first 2000' of the runway leaving 6000' useable. Night landings were avoided if possible because of the indeterminate runway ending.

Word was passed to all base officers that there would be an intelligence briefing on the situation in Cambodia. A civilian checked into the BOQ. John bumped into him in the lobby and after introductions he stated he was with the Agency for International Development (AID) and stationed in Cambodia. John put two and two together and calculated that this person was going to brief the base officers.

The next day everyone gathered in the Commander Naval Forces Philippines conference room and awaited the beginning of the briefing. The entrance of Admiral Welsh brought everyone to attention. Accompanying him was the civilian John had met the day before except now he was a Lieutenant Commander in his naval uniform. His briefing was complete with the gist of it centered on the push by the Chinese communists to influence all aspects of Cambodian government. He indicated the people were still suffering from the long-term effects of former leader Pol Pot and his ruthless administration. When he finished the Admiral rose and thanked him for his briefing. A Q. and A. session followed for about 45 minutes. When it was over all officers were filing out and the Lieutenant Commander stopped John and asked him if he could stop by his office. John responded in the affirmative.

Fifteen minutes later the man from AID knocked on John's door and entered. He closed the door after entering and after being seated spoke to John concerning a discussion he had with Commander Bates. John already knew he was CIA but his conversation confirmed it. He told John that Commander Bates would be in contact with him concerning a possible flight over Cambodia. He explained to John the Chinese were suspected of building a new base in an area of Cambodia which was inaccessible and that was the reason for the flight. They looked at a map and he pointed out its location to John explaining some of the physical features to look for when trying to find it. They both agreed that an early morning flight going west and a late afternoon flight headed east would result in the best pictures. John expressed his thanks and the AID worker departed for the BOQ.

Within a few days John received an encoded classified message from Commander Bates directing him to photograph a site near the town of Ban lung, Cambodia. John and Murray planned the flight and the next morning they departed before 6:00a.m. from Sangley Point bound for Bangkok, Thailand. This route of flight would take them over Pleiku, Vietnam, and the site to be photographed. After passing Pleiku they descended to 6500' for their pass over the site. This was the optimum altitude for their cameras and the light conditions. The weather was cooperating and the sky was scattered clouds, visibility more than fifty miles. As the approached Ban lung, Murray was the first to spot the target site and John banked slightly right leveling the aircraft just before he was required to turn on the cameras. He opened the camera ports and turned them on. They photographed until they were forty miles past the target, closed the doors and turned off the cameras, then climbed back to their assigned altitude of 8000'. The remainder of the flight was normal and they entered Thai airspace over the town of Aranyaprathet headed directly for Bangkok.

After landing the crew was directed over to the General Aviation Terminal, parked the aircraft, locked it and caught a hotel shuttle to the Grand Sukhumvit Hotel. The trip took them across the many canals in the Bangkok area where there was a lot of commercial activity. Many of the goods from inland were transported on these canals. The poverty and slums were everywhere. Finally the shuttle turned onto Sukhumvit Street and into another world. Middle and upper class homes were the norm and the shoppes and commercial areas were clean and well manicured. It was still early afternoon when the crew checked into the hotel. They were assigned adjacent rooms on the fourth floor, which they easily reached by elevator. John told Murray he was going down to Johnny Gems mineral shoppe in the hotel lobby and spend a little time. He had visited Bangkok before when the USS John F. Kennedy had made a port call during his assignment with Air Wing 6. He had warned the crew against buying anything for the offered price. The shopkeepers preferred to haggle on the price, which was their tradition. If you offered to buy on the first price quoted they would not sell it as they would be insulted that you did not want to haggle.

John entered Johnny Gems and was greeted like he was a long lost friend. He was offered a chair, a cigar and a drink of his choice, even before he was asked what kind of gems he was interested in. He asked Johnny if he could look at some star sapphires. A tray was brought and set on a small table next to his chair where he could peruse them. He selected a five carat stone and that's when the haggling began. Johnny quoted the first price and John countered. This went on for some thirty minutes or so and finally John said that was his final offer. Johnny smiled and walked away to consider the offer. They poured John another drink while John perused some emeralds they had brought and placed on the tray.

Finally Johnny came back and agreed to John's final offer. He appeared happy that John had respected their tradition and offered John a free dinner in the hotel's dining room. John made the purchase on his Visa card and the gem was packaged and wrapped for him to take. Johnny bowed then shook John's hand and thanked him for his purchase. John in turn thanked Johnny for his hospitality and left the shoppe.

He returned to the room to find Murray stretched out on his bed relaxing. John told Murray he was going to shower and then he would be ready for dinner. Murray contacted the crew and asked if they were ready for dinner. They answered in the affirmative and soon knocked on the door indicating they were set to go down to the dining room. John finished dressing and they were all on their way.

The crew entered the dining room and was seated at a table for four near the front windows of the hotel overlooking the main street. The walls of the dining room were adorned with what appeared to be ancient silk tapestries of rural scenes from old Siam. It was a plush facility with deep carpet and matching silk draperies on the windows. The crew mused that they were dining in high cotton tonight. The wait staff matched the décor of the room and soon the crew was munching on all kinds of exotic seafood. When they finished their dinner a round of after-dinner drinks was ordered and they sat for another hour chatting about the day's activities and their jobs in general.

After leaving the dining room they made their way back to the fourth floor and John told them they should depart the hotel around 11:00a.m. A midafternoon photo run over Cambodia would give them the right lighting on the target area.

After a leisurely breakfast the crew gathered for a shuttle ride back to the airport. It was a beautiful sunny tropical day but with expected thundershowers later in the afternoon. John hoped to avoid most of them over the target area. On arrival at the airport they stopped at the commercial terminal and found a restaurant and had a light lunch. After lunch John and Murray filed a flight plan while the remainder of the crew went to the aircraft and readied it for flight. Within thirty minutes John and Murray arrived and they were off on their return trip to Sangley Point. As they crossed the border into Cambodia the thunderstorms had begun building and dodging them became an ever-increasing impossibility. Within fifty miles of the target area the thunderstorms turned scattered and John was able to stabilize the aircraft, which would take them between storms and over an unobstructed target area. John opened the camera doors and activated the cameras at thirty miles from the target and turned them off about thirty miles past. Murray and John visually observed the target area and made some mental notes for their weekly written report to Commander Bates. They never discussed their conclusions on what they had observed so Commander Bates could get two perspectives instead of a common one from each report.

After passing Plieku, Vietnam, they crossed the coast and continued over the South China Sea towards home. The rainy season in the Philippines was still raging and soon they entered the clouds hanging over the whole area and producing the rainfall. After contacting Manila Approach Control they were directed to switch to Sangley Point Ground Control Approach (GCA) radar facility for a precision approach to the runway. Murray was flying the aircraft and at six miles and fifteen hundred feet he was on heading for the duty runway. The controller told them they were approaching glide slope and to begin a normal rate of descent, about 600' per minute. Murray called for the landing checklist and John lowered the landing gear and partial flaps while Murray slowed the aircraft to landing speed. The rain on the windscreen was solid and hard to see through. Minimum approach altitude would be 100' and ¼ mile. Passing through 300' Murray called for the windshield wipers to be turned on. As they approached 100' and ¼ mile John who had been looking out the windshield called "runway in sight." Murray transitioned from instruments to visual flight and called out "runway visual" and made one of the most beautiful, smooth landings anyone would ever want to experience.

It had been a good flight and the crew off-loaded the film from the cameras and packaged it for shipping to Langley.

From the intelligence gathered by his investigators, John's weekly reports to Commander Bates contained more and more evidence that the Communist Chinese were imposing more influence in the Philippines than first suspected. Many base employees of Chinese ancestry were reporting Chinese agents attempting to recruit them to spy on what was happening on the base. Also there was more Chinese naval presence in the seas surrounding the islands.

A couple of days passed and John had been working steadily. His investigators had uncovered a concerted effort by Chinese agents to get base employees; they had already recruited, to photograph the buildings on the base as well as key officer personnel. It appeared as though the Chinese were building a dossier on Naval officers once again as they had during the Vietnam War.

John was engrossed in his work and was startled by a knock on his door. He called out for them to enter and in walked Captain Touch. They greeted each other and a cup of coffee was ordered. "Congratulations on the promotion," John said.

"Well thanks, John," Ralph responded.

They sat and discussed what was happening in Indonesia and John asked Ralph what he was doing in Sangley Point. He reported that he and his team had completed their work in Indonesia and had flown the UH-16 (UH-2) Albatross into Singapore for a complete overhaul. It had taken them three months to get the aircraft flyable enough to get it to Singapore flying visual flight rules (VFR).

Ralph indicated that his work was done on this assignment and Commander Bates had reassigned him back to Santiago, Chile, for a second time. They finished their coffee and Ralph departed for the BOQ. He indicated his plane departed Manila in the morning and John wished him well in his next assignment.

In the next three months reports trickled in about the status of the HU-16 Albatross. It had been ready to return to Indonesia three times but each time someone tried to fly it back it turned up sabotaged. Finally the base received a message and it stated that Sangley Point should send a couple of pilots to retrieve it for the U.S. Navy. All pilots were surveyed to find out if anyone had Albatross experience. Turned out no one had flown the UH-16. Volunteers were asked for and John convinced Murray they should volunteer. Arrangements were made for them to get to Singapore and soon they were on their way by commercial air. First stop was in Ho Chi Minh City. All passengers were asked to deplane and to clear customs and immigration. John and Murray were traveling in civilian clothes so the chose to show their blue nondescript passport. All it indicated was that they were U.S. citizens and nothing else. They were individually photographed and then put back on the 737 and headed for Singapore. The two of them agreed it was probably the Chinese behind that little episode and was a way of tracking them. Pictures secretly taken of them back at Sangley Point by base employees were probably being compared even now and added to their dossier.

They arrived in Singapore, checked in by phone with the U.S. Embassy then spent the night. The next morning they traveled to the International airport and showed up at a company called Royal Aircraft Overhaul and Repair Service. The Albatross was fully restored and ready for flight. John showed the service manager his letter of authorization and he released the plane to them. It was fueled and ready for flight. John and Murray climbed into the cockpit and with the help of the aircraft handbook, located all the necessary switches needed to fly the aircraft. The pilots checked a few of the airspeed restrictions and cruising speeds and power settings, then cranked it up and departed for Sangley Point. It sure beat a NATOPS familiarization syllabus.

Once at altitude they set it on cruise, leaned the mixtures and headed for Sangley Point. John checked the approach and landing speeds and made a perfect approach and landing on the runway. The whole flight had been uneventful and they parked it on the ramp. Within a couple of days two pilots showed up from Ferry Squadron 32, and took the plane and headed for the states. John chalked that one up to a great learning experience.

8

"NIGHT ACTION"

Admiral Welsh was aware of John's mission and virtually scheduled his inspections so the aircraft and John could be utilized to the maximum. His aide contacted John and indicated the Admiral was planning to attend the World War II celebration of the Leyte invasion of the Philippines. It was located on the island of Leyte, in the city of Tacloban, that was about one and a half hours southeast of Manila.

There were reports of gunrunning in that area and John was charged with finding out whether the Russians or Chinese were responsible. John found his favorite Constabulary officer, Captain Murrano, had been temporarily assigned there and was heading up the investigating team.

The dates were set for the visit and the Admiral was planning on remaining over night. The mayor was hosting the Admiral and his aide so John and his crew were free to stay where they wanted. John sent a message through the Constabulary's Manila communications office to Bonnie and asked him to make accommodations available for them.

The day came and the crew was off with the Admiral to Tacloban. On landing they were met by the Mayor and his entourage who whisked the Admiral and party off to town for the visit and celebration. When the hubbub had cleared a couple of Constabulary jeeps pulled up with Bonnie in the lead vehicle. He greeted John and the crew who all boarded the jeeps for the ride to the detachment headquarters. Quarters were assigned to the crew while John met separately with Bonnie.

They discussed the gunrunning and Bonnie said he had been investigating that and cigarette smuggling for a month and a half. He had a lead on a possible delivery that night and asked John if he would like to go along. John said that would be a hoot so they planned on it. Bonnie wasn't sure how the contraband was being brought to the island nor who was responsible but he knew where it was being brought ashore. He and John went into his storage room where he fitted John with some scuba gear and issued him an M-16 rifle and four twenty rounds clips of ammunition.

"Do you know how to use one of these?" Bonnie asked.

"Yeah, Bonnie. I have had some time on the range with one of those. What distance are they sighted in for?" he asked.

"These are sighted-in for 300 meters that will put you an inch and a half high at 100 meters," Bonnie responded.

John looked through the Advanced Combat Optical Gunsight (ACOG).

"And if we're going in the water with them how about the ACOG. Is it waterproof?"

"Yeah, John. they're good down to about 100 feet. After that they might develop a leak but don't worry about it. We're going to use the darkness to stay on the surface. That's why only a snorkel and not tanks. I figure about 1:00a.m. we can swim out about one-half mile off shore and wait for whatever is bringing the guns and cigarettes and intercept them there. I figure it's either a submarine, which would be Russian, or a Junk, which would be Chinese. If it's a sub we'll make contact after they hit the beach but if it's a Junk we can board it and take them prisoners if possible. The Junks usually have rope lattices on each side and if they are true to form, I can board one side and you the other. Then if they try to resist we will have them in a crossfire. Check out all your gear and make sure the batteries in your flashlight are working. We might need that tonight."

John and Bonnie set out to check out their rifles and gear. John tried on his wet suit to see if it fit properly. Everything appeared to be in good working order. They put the gear in Bonnie's jeep and John went back to his room and stretched out to relax. He and Bonnie decided to meet later and go to a local restaurant for a late dinner.

Bonnie came by about 7:00p.m. and picked up John. They went to a quiet little place on a back alley. Bonnie recommended the crab cakes so that's what John ordered. He started out with an appetizer of shrimp lumpia. The waitress brought them a San Miguel beer. It was a quiet long drawn out dinner and plenty of conversation about the mission and shooting in general.

About 10:00p.m. they departed the restaurant and Bonnie drove down the beach road south of the city. About fifteen miles out he was passing a particularly deserted stretch of road with beach access.

"That's probably where they will try to land the contraband tonight, John. They'll pull their vehicles into the coconut grove over there to try to avoid being detected while they wait for the zodiacs to bring the stuff ashore. Once they unload the contraband they'll load the zodiacs on their trucks and cover them with a tarp and they'll be off to their headquarters. It'll only take them about fifteen minutes to clear the beach once the zodiacs hit shore. If a sub is offloading the guns we need to swim like Hell to catch them on the beach. If it's a Junk we'll take them at sea. I haven't yet determined where their headquarters are and where they are taking the guns, so we need to take a couple of local prisoners if possible. By the way, the mayor is in the middle of smuggling the cigarettes but not the guns. We're not ready to arrest him yet so we won't embarrass your Admiral while he's staying at his house."

"I'm going down the beach another half mile. There are a couple of old shacks there where we can hide the jeep from view and relax inside in the dark for an hour or so. I have one stocked with a couple of cots so we can stretch out and get a little rest."

Time was approaching the H-hour and Bonnie told John to get dressed. They both donned their wet suits, checked each other's gear and about 1:00a.m. slipped into the water and began swimming out to sea while heading for a spot one half mile off the beach they had reconnoitered. They had been swimming for only about fifteen minutes when a Chinese Junk appeared on the horizon. They could hear the chugging of the engine when suddenly it quit. Bonnie and John observed them take down their sails and the junk coasted to a dead stop in the water about 500 yards from them. About the same time they heard the sound of two zodiacs coming toward the junk from the beach. Bonnie gave John hand signals to take a position just ahead of the junk. He also signaled that he would take the seaward side while John should take the landward side on the junk.

The zodiacs arrived alongside the junk, tied up to it and the men climbed aboard. Bonnie signaled to John to proceed. It was now or never.

John came around the starboard side and found a rope lattice near the bow. He stowed his facemask, swim fins and snorkel then proceeded to climb the lattice as quietly as possible. Bonnie did the same thing of the port side of the junk. As John reached the gunnel he peeked over it to see what was going on. The crew and the men off the zodiacs were busy moving contraband up from below decks. They had already brought up about 20 cases of rifles and a pallet of ammunition. It was a half moonlit night, which gave the junk a sinister glow. John spotted Bonnie and waited for his move. Suddenly Bonnie half exposed himself and yelled in Visayan for all hands to hit the deck that they were under arrest. Bonnie yelled a second time directing them to surrender and hit the deck. The zodiac crew complied while only half of the Chinese crew did so. Two Chinese crewmembers reached for their AK-47s and aimed them at where the voice was coming from. Bonnie fired a three round burst simultaneously John did likewise. The two crewmembers crumpled to the deck in a heap and the AK-47s slid across the deck. No more resistance was encountered and Bonnie climbed over the gunnel of the junk. John followed over the starboard side. He kept his M-16 trained on the captives while Bonnie cuffed them. He searched the prisoners for guns and disarmed a few who were carrying pistols. Fortunately for them only a couple of AK-47s were found in the Chinese' possession. There were six smugglers off the zodiacs and three Chinese crewmembers. Once the prisoners were cuffed John moved closer while Bonnie tied them together with a line he cut from the junk's rigging. Bonnie told John to guard the prisoners while he did a quick search of the junk. He found a waterproof container in which he stuffed the many papers he found in the cabin. He also made a few mental notes of other things he saw strewn around the cabin.

Bonnie came back up on deck. He again yelled at the prisoners and directed them to board the zodiacs. John sat on the rail of the junk and kept his M-16 trained on them while they struggled down the lattices into the zodiacs. Bonnie boarded one zodiac while John took the other. Bonnie had five prisoners and John ended up with the other four. Bonnie told John they would head back to where his car was hidden on the beach. He had a walkie-talkie in his gear, which he broke out. He had two men in vehicles he directed to follow the trucks hidden in the coconut grove awaiting the zodiacs to return. Bonnie knew if the zodiacs didn't arrive shortly they would flee back to their headquarters and Bonnie wanted to find out where. He also instructed his men to return once the trucks got to their destination and help return the prisoners to Constabulary headquarters. John and Bonnie started the engines on the zodiacs and headed for the beach. Before leaving the junk Bonnie had rigged a couple of C4 explosive devices and set the timers for twenty minutes. John and Bonnie were a half-mile away from the junk when the C4 went off and the junk went up in a ball of fire. Secondary explosions lit the night sky like fireworks. Within a few seconds it was on its way to the bottom.

Once back on the beach Bonnie and John herded the captives into one of the shacks. After they got them settled Bonnie broke out the treasure trove of papers and other items from the waterproof container he had filled on the junk. All the papers were written in Chinese and Bonnie had also found Chinese cigarettes. There was no question the origin of the guns were Chinese. Neither Bonnie nor John was fluent in Chinese so the content of the papers would have to wait for a translator. Bonnie thought about interrogating the Filipino prisoners but decided to wait until he had them all back at headquarters.

Two Constabulary officers showed up and the prisoners were loaded in their pickups, driven to the stockade and placed in cells. John and Bonnie drove back to headquarters where they cleaned their rifles and stowed their scuba gear. They finished, turned and smiled at each other then shook hands for a job well done. Bonnie told John he could be on his team anytime.

John went back to his quarters and crashed for the night. It had been a tense and stressful night but he enjoyed helping Bonnie with the mission.

The next day the Admiral and the Mayor helped the city of Tacloban celebrate its liberation from the Japanese in World War II. The school band marched in the parade as well as a few remaining veterans from the war as well as the local American Legion Post. Afterwards the Mayor hosted a lunch for all the dignitaries at the Hilton Hotel. John and Murray had been invited but since the Admiral wanted to depart for Sangley Point immediately afterward they went straight to the airport and readied the aircraft for departure.

Murray had filed a flight plan and at 1:30p.m. a limo drove onto the ramp with the Admiral, his aide, and the Mayor and his assistant aboard.

Murray was already in the cockpit while John remained on the ramp to greet the Admiral. The crew quickly put the luggage aboard. The Admiral boarded and John went up to the cockpit to start the engines. Within minutes they were winging their way back to Sangley Point in the beautiful tropical weather spread before them.

They leveled the plane at 7000' and accelerated to cruising speed. John put the aircraft on autopilot and told Murray he was going back to the cabin to talk with the Admiral. The Admiral was in the front row of seats and reading the morning Manila Times newspaper. John asked the Admiral if he could talk with him for a few minutes. The Admiral nodded in agreement so John took a seat opposite the Admiral and began the conversation.

"Sir, a few things occurred last evening which I thought you should be made aware of. I participated in a raid on a Chinese Junk where the Philippine Constabulary captured three Chinese and six Filipinos. Two other Chinese were killed in the action when they resisted. They had approximately 200 guns and plenty of ammunition, which they were smuggling to the Abu Sayyaf. When we left the junk we blew it up and sunk it. During the course of operations with the Constabulary I was told on good intelligence that the Mayor was tied to just cigarette smuggling and not the gunrunning. The Constabulary delayed arresting the Mayor so as not to embarrass you but tomorrow I believe they will take him into custody."

"Thank you, Lieutenant, for bringing me up to speed on things in Tacloban. I don't know how you get yourself into these situations but damn, be careful," the Admiral advised.

"Yes sir, I will be careful. Most times we have things under control. Last night was quite exciting and I must admit I enjoyed it. I will make my usual report to my seniors when we get to Sangley Point. Thanks, sir, for your concerns," John replied.

John retuned to the cockpit and the flight continued. He and Murray discussed the events of the past few nights and in a sense Murray wished he could sometimes participate but John had warned him that one of them needed to be in an uncompromising position at all times for the safety of the aircraft, which usually left Murray on the sidelines.

Things at the base were normal for the next week or so. Routine flights to Cubi Point and Clark Air Base were conducted three times a week and

John continued to gather intelligence through his investigators and agents from his office. The Communist Chinese effort to increase their influence over the Philippines was becoming more and more obvious.

The next week rolled around and John and crew were off to Taiwan, taking the Admiral on one of his inspection tours. The first stop was the Kaohsiung International Airport located near Kaohsiung City on the southwest coast.

John came back in the cabin to wish the Admiral well on his departure.

"I see you have your paregoric Admiral," John said. As he held up three bottles, "I sure do."

"Sir, I understand you will be four days on the road working your way up to Taipei," John said.

"That's correct, Lieutenant. You have four days in Taipei to relax and wait for me," the Admiral said.

John smiled, "We'll be there for you, sir. Have a good tour."

The Admiral and his aide departed the aircraft and John flew off to Taipei.

John's crew was staying at the Green Garden Hotel. It was such a small hotel they didn't even serve dinner. Breakfast and lunch were available so John and Murray went to the kitchen for breakfast. John had been studying Mandarin Chinese so he tried a few phrases on the kitchen help, which only brought about a few giggles. He did manage to order a couple of soft-boiled eggs and some Chinese corn bread. He and Murray settled for some hot tea to wash it down.

After breakfast Murray decided to do a little shopping while John said he needed to get his passport from the aircraft. They agreed to meet at the Military Assistance Advisory Group headquarters, which was just down the street from the hotel, and have lunch in their dining room. John stepped out into the street and flagged down a taxi. He arrived at the Taipei airport and went to the military liaison office. They would issue him a pass to proceed to his aircraft since they were charged with airport security.

John stepped out onto the tarmac just as all Hell broke loose on the airfield. Emergency vehicles as well as military vehicles were rushing out towards the duty runway. In the haze and bright sunlight he squinted and off to the west on short final for runway 09 was what appeared to be a Mig 25. The Mig was not being escorted so it was not clear how he proceeded this far without detection. Within a minute he was touching down on the runway followed by all the vehicles. There were sirens going off and flashing red lights everywhere. When the pilot slowed the aircraft sufficiently he turned off at an adjoining taxiway and shutdown the aircraft. He opened his canopy and just sat and waited for instructions from his would be captors.

A nationalist Chinese military officer climbed up on the side of the fuselage using the handholds and the defecting Chinese Communist pilot handed him his sidearm. From the animated discussion, which took place it was clear he had been told to deplane. A couple of soldiers were holding their rifles trained on him as he climbed down from the Mig. As soon as he touched the ground he was searched and then placed in a limo, which had arrived on the scene. As quickly as he boarded the limo it sped off the airport. A tug arrived and hooked up to the aircraft and it was towed to the hangar that was directly next to where John was standing. The hangar doors remained open and after being chocked the aircraft abandoned. Not a soul remained in the hangar to guard the aircraft. It appeared that the Nationalist Chinese were more interested in the pilot than the aircraft.

Since no one was around John decided to climb up into the aircraft to have a look around. He had a small camera with 8mm film in it so he took a complete set of pictures of the cockpit. In a pocket next to the pilot's seat he found a pilot's handbook written in Russian, which he also photographed in minute detail. He made some written notes in his little green book, which he always carried for such purposes. He extricated himself from the cockpit and walked around the aircraft photographing the control surfaces and the flaps. These would be of particular value to our engineers who would be studying the pictures. He spent over an hour studying and photographing the aircraft. Now if the Chinese didn't turn over the aircraft for study to the U.S at least they would have some close up pictures.

John finally made it out to his aircraft and after retrieving his passport, locked the aircraft and walked down the ramp to the commercial terminal. As he entered he ran into an interesting Chinese man.

"I see you like that Mig 25," the man said.

John was taken aback as he hadn't realized that he was being observed.

"Being a pilot myself I'm always intrigued by any high performance aircraft,' John said. "Besides the people out there didn't seem interested in the least so I thought I would see how it was made. I'm John Walker," he said as he bowed slightly. Extending one's hand to an oriental was not good manners.

"I am Chi Tran," he said and returned the bow. "Well, Chi Tran, you speak very good English. What do you do here in Taiwan?" John asked.

"I am learning to be a travel agent," Chi offered. "I like to travel myself and the job offers me that advantage. And what do you do, John?

"See that DC-3 out there on the ramp. I fly that wherever my boss wants to go or directs me to go," John said. He did not want to offer more information than necessary to this stranger.

"Just for your information the engines in the Mig 25 are designed only for 250 hours of operation. After that they are supposed to be junked and new engines installed. They also have an air bottle, which they use for air starts in the case of a flameout at high altitude. It is usually good for three tries," Chi said.

"How do you know so much about Mig 25s?" John asked.

Chi fidgeted a little, "I am a student of Chinese Communist history and like to keep up with the latest developments in the Chinese military and what their current capabilities are."

"I'm trying to learn to speak Mandarin and like you I am interested in Chinese Communist history and current events," John said. "Why don't we meet for dinner tomorrow night?"

"Okay, that sounds great. Here's my business card. Call me tomorrow and we can set the time and place," Chi offered.

John took the card and promised Chi he would call tomorrow. They exchanged bows and went their separate ways.

When John returned to the hotel he ran into Murray. They went into the kitchen, sat down and asked the staff to bring them a beer. Murray went on about all the bargains he ran into while in town shopping while John told Murray about the neat guy he ran into at the airport. They both decided there was something more to this guy than being just a travel agent. They looked forward to meeting him for dinner the next day.

9

"A NEW FRIEND"

Taipei, Taiwan

The next morning John and Murray slept in late and had a late breakfast in the hotel kitchen. After breakfast they walked out into the street and flagged down a taxi, to take them to the embassy. They checked in with the receptionist who directed them to the station chief's office. John knocked on the door and entered and there stood his old buddy Navy Lieutenant Walt Peterson. He and Walt had served together in VA-45 where they flew Skyraiders and were in the same class at the Postgraduate School in Monterey, California.

"Walt," John shouted. "I didn't know you were stationed here? What have you been up to?"

"Hey, John. Good to see you again. I've been flying the embassy DC-3 and filling in as the station chief. What have you been up to?"

"I have this DC-3 out of Sangley Point. Been there for two years. I work for Commander Bates," John said.

I'm on Bates' payroll also," Walt said. "Is there anything I can do for you?"

"Walt, I met this Chinese national at the airport yesterday and he wants to have dinner this evening. His name is Chi Tran and I was interested in whether you had a dossier on him?"

Walt smiled, "Name rings a bell but let me look him up in our files and see what we have."

Walt went into his gray filing cabinet and when he got to the "Ts" found what he was looking for. He pulled it and he and John sat down and perused what was inside. Chi Tran had infiltrated the Communist

Chinese spy agency. He was a natural born mainlander but was recruited early in his life and was actually a Mossad agent.

"What do you think, Walt?" John asked.

"I think you are okay having dinner with him, but just be careful what you say to him. He will report only good things about you to the communists but is trying to find out if you are with the company. That fact he would relay to the Mossad. You can probably get him to buy you a good dinner though," Walt said.

"Okay I'm glad I found that out before we had dinner." John looked at his watch. "It's about lunch time. How 'bout I spring for lunch?"

"You can do that," Walt offered. "Let's go down to the embassy cafeteria. They usually have a great special I think you will enjoy."

Walking out of the office, John stopped. "This is my copilot Murray Wright. Murray meet Walt Peterson. He and I go back a long way in the Navy. We flew Skyraiders together and attended Post Graduate School in the same class."

Murray extended his hand, "Pleased to me you, Walt. Nice to meet John's old friends."

The three of them proceeded to the cafeteria and enjoyed a long lunch with lots of sea stories laced with flying. After lunch John and Murray took leave and Walt offered to help with anything he could while they were in Taipei.

When they returned to the hotel John located a phone and pulled out the business card Chi Tran had given him. He dialed the number and after two rings it was answered by a young sounding woman. She answered in Chinese. John then spoke to her in English asking if she could speak English. She answered him in almost perfect English and asked him how she could help. He asked to speak to Chi Tran. Within a few seconds Chi Tran came on the phone and asked to whom he was speaking. John identified himself and Chi indicated he was glad to hear from him. They made plans to go out for dinner about 7:00p.m. that evening. Chi told John he would pick up the two of them at the hotel about that time. John thanked him and said they would be ready at 7:00p.m. and meet him in the lobby.

John hung up and went into the kitchen where Murray was already consuming his first beer. He told Murray what time they were going to dinner and ordered a beer from the kitchen staff.

At 7:00p.m. John and Murray were dressed and went to the lobby waiting for Chi to arrive. Five minutes later Chi stepped into the lobby, smiling and greeted both of them. He apologized for being a little late but indicated traffic was a little heavy on the main street, which slowed his arrival. They all stepped out onto the street where Chi's car was parked. John got into the front passenger seat while Murray took a seat in the back. It was a small Nissan Pathfinder SUV in immaculate condition. Chi drove out the main street south of town and after a couple of miles pulled into a driveway with a small parking area set in a persimmon grove. There was a small building, which Chi told them held the restaurant. There were no signs outside indicating this was a restaurant but Chi assured them they would enjoy the food. As they entered an elderly lady who appeared to be either family or owner greeted them. She escorted them into one of the private dining rooms. They took off their shoes as they entered and were seated on straw mats at low tables requiring them to sit cross-legged. A young lady appeared in traditional Han peasant Chinese dress going back to the Qing dynasty. She was the hostess and server for the evening. Chi chatted with her and ordered dinner. She first served a sweet red wine in baijiu glasses. Baijiu glasses were very small and many times were refilled before the egg drop soup was brought to the table. The serving bowl resembled a tureen and the group had at least two bowls of soup each. Next came an order of sweet and sour pork served on wild rice along with a platter of teriyaki chicken. Vegetables were sprouts, bamboo shoots along with Chinese cabbage sprinkled with bacon bits. Hot tea was served with the meal. After consuming all they could, the table was cleared and Bing or Moon cakes along with Nian Gao were placed carefully on the tables for dessert.

The conversation during dinner centered on the Mig 25, which John and Chi had seen the day before at the airport. John and Murray were fascinated by Chi's knowledge of the airplane. John changed the conversation to Mainland China and asked Chi if he had ever traveled there. Chi said he had. He said he had a travel office in Hong Kong he worked with and sometimes went into mainland China from there.

John was interested in how the Chinese peasants were faring under Mao and his successors and that sparked further discussion on the increase in technology and manufacturing away from the large cities of China. It appeared as though pollution still needed to be brought under control but the peasants were benefiting from all the industrial development. Unemployment was still extensive but slowly decreasing.

After the long dinner they arose and Chi took care of paying the bill and soon they were off to Taipei and their hotel. On arrival Chi let them out in front of the hotel but not before giving John his business card with the Hong Kong information telling him if he ever gets there to look him up and they could once again have dinner.

John and Murray thanked him for a great evening and stepped into the lobby of the hotel. The clerk behind the desk called out to John and handed him a message. It was from the embassy. The Admiral indicated he was running late by one day so they would have another day in Taipei before going back to the Philippines. Before they bedded down for the night John told Murray of the delay and said they could decide what to do when they arose in the morning.

They awoke late and had a leisurely breakfast in the hotel kitchen. During breakfast they discussed what they should do today. They hadn't been to the Military Assistance Advisory Group (MAAG) compound as yet so they decided to check out the Post Exchange (PX) and have dinner at the officer's club. The cadre was mostly U.S. Army but other services were represented. It was only about six blocks away from the hotel so they decided to walk. They had skipped lunch after such a late breakfast and arrived at the MAAG compound around 2:00p.m.

They were not shopping for anything in particular but in the sports department John came across an Anschutz Model 1410 smallbore rifle. It was used mainly for competitive shooting and John thought he would like to have it should he ever have a chance to go back to that shooting discipline. It was on sale for $300"U.S. and came with a complete set of iron sights. He thought it to be a great deal so he pulled out the cash and paid for it on the spot. He also came across a spotting scope. A Prominar Model 412 with a 20-power magnifier and a 40mm objective lens. It would be a compliment to his new rifle so he purchased it also. After wandering in the PX for most of the afternoon the two naval officers made their way over to the officer's club for an early dinner. They were ushered into the dining room and agreed they were famished, having skipped lunch.

John ordered the full lobster dinner while Murray settled for the seafood platter. Of course the warm waters of the South Pacific yielded only langouste, which were the tropical lobster minus the claws. Since only the tail was edible John ordered two. They lavished in the luxury of this extravagant dinner and spent some two hours devouring it plus their drinks.

After dinner they made their way back to the hotel and settled in for an early wakeup. The Admiral would be at the plane by 9 o'clock and they wanted to have everything in order for the trip back to Sangley Point.

The Admiral arrived at the plane five minutes early. John greeted him. He had his normal luggage and a few gifts, which the Chinese military had given him during his tour of the bases. After everything was loaded aboard John took the copilot's seat in the cockpit and Murray cranked the starboard engine.

They were quickly airborne and on their way back to the Philippines. The flight was routine and Murray made a beautiful landing at Sangley despite the wind burble coming over the O'Club.

Sangley Point, Philippines

John and Murray settled in to the normal routine for a couple of weeks and then were directed to fly to Hong Kong. They were advised to perform a photographic reconnaissance of the harbor. CIA was interested in what ships were in port and what countries had visiting navies there. Their cover was to pick up a baby grand piano destined for the states but to be loaded on a navy transport in the Philippines. This would be a tricky flight, as they would have to feign an emergency so they could circle the harbor taking pictures.

By the next Tuesday the weather was clearing in the Hong Kong area making it suitable for their mission. John climbed into the pilot's seat and they were off for Hong Kong. As they approached Hong Kong approach control had them in radar contact and vectored them between Hong Kong Island and Tung Lung Island. It put them on the Instrument Landing System for a straight-in approach to Kai Tak Airport. As they crossed abeam Hong Kong Island Murray keyed his mike and advised approach control that they had an unsafe indication of their landing gear and would need to circle to check it out. John had already activated the cameras and was taking pictures even as they leveled off to circle.

Approach control advised them to remain over water as much as possible. This fit perfectly into their plans and John climbed to 3000' and proceeded west over the harbor. He stayed just off the shoreline, which put him over all the wharves where the ships were moored. About ten miles west he turned port and proceeded back towards the airport filming the harbor. As he crossed the extended centerline of the airport, Murray reported the landing gear was down and locked. Approach control rogered and switched them over to Kai Tak tower. John secured the cameras and closed the outer doors, then began a shallow right turn to intercept the centerline of the runway. He was about six miles from the end of the runway when Kai Tak Tower cleared them to land Runway 31.

The wind was out of the west and burbling over the mountains leading down to the runway. There were gusts to about 27mph but the o'club at Sangley had trained these two navy pilots to deal with this type of crosswind landing. John compensated for the crosswind and adjusted for the burble. He made a beautiful landing, lowered the tail on the tail wheel and rolled out straight ahead on the runway. They switched to ground control and were directed to the parking area for transient aircraft.

After securing the aircraft the crew took a taxi to the Blue Moon hotel in Kowloon City. After checking into their room John picked up the phone and placed a call to the offices of Chi Tran. He had been encouraged by Commander Bates to foster that relationship. As luck would have it Chi Tran was there in Hong Kong. Chi was glad to hear from John and after some discussion they made plans to have dinner that evening in Hong Kong. They agreed to meet and have dinner at the Golden Pheasant. John hung up and told Murray he was also invited. John had been to Hong Kong when his carrier U.S.S. Intrepid had made a port call back a few years and he had previously eaten dinner at the Golden Pheasant. He told Murray it was just around the corner from Mai Lings, which had the best French Onion soup in Hong Kong.

Dinner with Chi was to be 7:00p.m so the two of them hailed a taxi at 6:00p.m. They headed for the harbor and the pier for the Star Ferry. The taxi dropped them at the tollbooth for the ferry and after depositing a 10-cent coin in the slot they proceeded to board the ferry for the eight minute ride across Victoria Harbor for Hong Kong Island. The whole settlement and surrounding area of the British Colony was known as Hong Kong but the main island was Hong Kong from where the colony derived its name.

Upon reaching the Hong Kong side Murray and John caught another taxi and proceeded to Mai Lings. They would start their dinner with a tasty bowl of Mai Lings' French Onion soup then go around the corner to meet Chi at the Golden Pheasant for dinner.

They entered the Golden Pheasant and spoke to the Maitre d'. They mentioned Chi's name and were escorted back to one of the private dining rooms. When they entered they were impressed with the lavishness of the place. A white tablecloth adorned the large oak Old English table and was surrounded by six huge matching oak chairs. The places at the table were set with the finest English silverware while the table had two vases with fresh flowers. There were also two wine glasses at each setting along with a large tumbler for water. It looked as though they were in for a formal dinner. As they were about to be seated Chi entered the dining room and greeted the two of them like they were long lost friends. Chi's English was excellent and he invited them to be seated. He took the seat at the head of the table while John occupied a seat on his right and Murray a seat on his left.

Two waiters quickly appeared dressed in high neck white serving jackets, highly creased black trousers and well polished black shoes. They ordered cocktails and engaged in conversation. Chi offered that he was engaged in the data processing business as well as the travel business, which was in its infancy and growing at a rapid rate throughout the Far East. John was fairly fluent in the computer language surrounding business because of his correspondence courses and his exposure to the technical side of computers at the Naval Post Graduate School. He and Chi had hit it off from their very first meeting and it was a relaxing situation for all concerned.

After they finished their drinks the first course was served. It was a fish dish of smoked Bluefin tuna and was quite tasty. Chi had taken the liberty of ordering Chateaubriand. It was brought out from the kitchen on a carving cart. The cart was placed alongside Chi and the meat carved for all to observe. The dinner was superb and appreciated.

Sherry wine was served after dinner and the three men sat back and relaxed while they digested their dinner and sipped their wine.

Dinner had lasted almost three hours and John told Chi they needed to get back to the hotel as it had been a long day. Chi said he understood and insisted his personal car would take them to the pier to catch the ferry back to Kowloon.

They shook hands. John and Murray thanked Chi for his hospitality then departed for the ferry. Chi's car dropped them at the pier and they caught the Star Ferry back to Kowloon. On the Kowloon side they flagged down a taxi and proceeded to the Blue Moon and a good nights sleep.

The next morning, after breakfast, they went to the waterfront and boarded a water-taxi to the China Fleet Club. The China Fleet Club was a favorite meeting place for navies and military personnel from all countries. This would help identify what countries ships were in port. It was also a series of exotic shops and a place where most any product made in the world was on sale. Here is where the baby grand piano they were supposed to pickup was located. They found the shop and made arrangements for the piano to be delivered to the plane at 8:00a.m. on Thursday morning. It was soon lunchtime and they made their way to the China Fleet Club's most popular restaurant. During lunch John and Murray made mental notes of what and whom they observed. They would include this in their mission report to Commander Bates. One thing of great importance, John observed what he perceived to be Chinese communist agents trying to barter counterfeit $20 bills in U.S. currency. During this period green money was very valuable on the black market as the U.S. military was still on script in Japan and the Philippines. Script is military money used on U.S. military bases to prevent green money from infiltrating into the local economies. John knew the bills were counterfeit as he had seen two $20s with the same serial number.

Sailors were observed from twelve different countries with other military personnel from another two. All this would go into his mission report.

After lunch John told Murray they needed to stop to see Peter Chang. Peter ran a tailor shop and specialized in men's clothing but he dealt in many other items. He was located on Salisbury Road in Kowloon so they took a water taxi back to the Kowloon side of Victoria Harbor.

When they entered his shop Peter greeted them like long lost friends. He had served the U.S. Navy and military since the end of World War II and his walls were covered with the pictures of many U.S. military leaders for whom Peter had made tailored suits and accessories.

John asked Peter if he could get a couple of monogrammed short-sleeved dress white shirts. He told Peter they were leaving in the morning. Peter said that would be okay and that he would have them delivered to their hotel that evening.

John also asked Peter if he could still get an appraisal on gemstones. Peter indicated he still had those connections and John told him he would bring some on the next trip to Hong Kong. John had bought the stones in Bangkok, Thailand, at Johnny Gems and just wanted a fair appraisal. He thanked Peter, paid him for his shirts, and the two naval officers departed for their hotel.

The shirts from Peter Chang were delivered that evening. Next morning they checked out of the hotel and proceeded to the airport where the piano was delivered to the aircraft. Soon they were winging their way back to Sangley Point.

10

"JUNGLE WARFARE"

Sangley Point, Philippines

Admiral Welsh was planning a trip to Cagayan de Oro on the island of Mindanao to speak to the local American Legion chapter. Commander Bates made contact with John and directed him to pilot that flight and visit the "U.S. weather station" just south and west of the city. That's what it was known as, but in reality it was a NSA listening station for all communications transmissions in Southeast Asia and Australia. Apparently there had been many temporary electrical blackouts during the past month and Langley wanted an update on what was happening there.

The Admiral was also planning on staying a couple of days at the DelMonte plantation to play a few rounds of golf, which would give John more time to visit the listening station.

John dropped the Admiral at the main airport serving Cagayan De Oro then flew over to the DelMonte plantation. It was a grass strip in the middle of a pineapple field. The crew were met by a station wagon and driven over to the cabins located on the golf course where they would stay for the duration of their visit. Once there, a vehicle from the NSA station picked up John and transported him to their location.

When the vehicle arrived Marvin Johnson, station manager, met John. He escorted John into the main building, which contained most of the listening equipment and personnel. Outside on the nearest mountain was an antenna array, which gave them the capability of listening to radio communications from as far north as Pyongyang, North Korea, to Perth, Australia, in the south. Marvin and John discussed the power grid situation. The station was equipped with a backup generator but Marvin indicated there had been some sabotage and keeping the station up and on line was at times difficult. Message traffic back and forth to NSA and Langley had been interrupted and sometimes even blocked by groups unknown. That was the main reason for John's visit was to make a separate report away from the station so as to prevent interference from outside sources. John made some notes while Marvin gave him a tour of the base. From all indications contaminated fuel for the emergency generator was another one of the main sources of sabotage and severing the power line supplying the base was the other. After lunch Marvin told John he would drive him back to DelMonte.

They piled into the station Jeep and started down the winding jungle road. It was about twelve miles back to the main highway and only a one-lane dirt road, which caused Marvin to drive slowly and carefully. As he rounded a turn in the dense jungle, men suddenly appeared in the middle of the road, armed with pistols and AK-47s.

Marvin turned to John. "They appear to be Abu Sayyaf rebels, John. Do you have a weapon?"

As he reached into his briefcase and pulled out his 1911 .45 caliber pistol he replied, "Yeah, but I have only two extra mags."

"I have mine also, John. Keep it out of sight until we get the lay of the land and find out what they want," Marvin said as he slowed the vehicle.

The one who seemed to be the leader waved his hand for them to stop, all the while maintaining his other hand on his AK-47. There were two of them on the road and two on Marvin's side while John saw four on his side of the road. He also spotted another man standing off the road in the edge of the jungle acting more as an observer than as a member of this group.

Marvin brought the vehicle to a stop and the leader came around to his side of the Jeep. He leaned in and while avoiding pointing his rifle at them he advised Marvin that his group was tired of the Americans spying on his comrades and that they should get out of the Jeep and come with them. Marvin and John knew that would mean a death sentence and wasn't going to happen. When Marvin stopped he had put the Jeep into first gear and left the engine idling. As the leader turned away from Marvin to talk with one of his comrades Marvin shouted one word to John, "Now."

That was the signal they had agreed to as a signal to open fire. John had sized up the group on his right and as he raised his pistol he spied two of the rebels who had their rifles at the ready. He fired three shots and killed the first with a dead center shot to the head and the second with two shots to the chest. They both went down like rag dolls in a clump of dirt. Marvin released the clutch and the Jeep jumped into motion just as he fired his pistol at the leader. The first shot spun him on his heels and the second took him down in a pool of blood. The jeep hit the two men in the road before they could raise their rifles. At the same time the remaining two men were raising their rifles at John. He loosed the remaining five rounds in his magazine and they also went down. John already had his second magazine in his hand and while reloading Marvin took out the remaining rifleman with a clean shot to the chest. As John closed the slide on his pistol sending a cartridge into the chamber he brought the pistol to bear on the observer at the edge of the jungle and fired four shots. This man went down but appeared to only be severely wounded. Marvin slammed the jeep to a stop, jumped out and leveled his pistol at the two bodies in the road. They were still moving and trying to crawl off the road while attempting to bring their rifle to a firing position. Marvin fired four more shots and was startled as John fired two more shots at the man in the jungle. The whole foray was over within forty seconds. Both men stood there shaking. They had taken out nine of the enemy with a couple of 1911 45's and the enemy probably only got off a couple of poorly aimed shots.

John finally spoke, "You okay, Marvin?" he asked.

"Yeah, I'm good. How about you?"

"I'm good. Had a couple of close ones but my guys never got off a good shot. Check the ones on your side and gather any papers you find. I'll check the ones over here. I'm particularly interested in the guy over there in the jungle. He looked like he was observing and not involved in the operation. Who do you suppose he was?" John wondered.

They both checked the bodies and searched their pockets for any intelligence. John started with the body in the jungle. In his shirt pocket he found a letter written in Chinese, which he believed to be addressed from Shanghai, China. In his other pocket was a pack of Chinese manufactured cigarettes. No other items of value were noted. On the other four men, who were obviously Filipino, no items were found. John made some mental notes on their dress and condition. Of the eight Filipinos only six were wearing jungle boots. The others were barefooted. He estimated their ages as ranging from 16 to 25. He had a strong suspicion that the man in the jungle was a communist Chinese agent who was teaching these men jungle insurgency fighting. John and Marvin dragged the bodies over to the side of the road and in talking agreed they should report this whole situation to the local NBI agent.

They climbed into the Jeep and headed down the road to the main highway. When they reached it, Marvin turned north towards Cagayan De Oro. As they reached town Marvin drove until he pulled up in front of the local law enforcement building. Here were the offices of the local police, Philippine Constabulary and local NBI agent. They jumped out and walked into the building. It was hot and muggy and the building had no air conditioning. All windows were open, ceiling fans were operating but the temperature was still just bearable. Things within the building were moving very slowly. There were few people working as most took a nap after lunch and had not yet returned to their desks. They found their way to the NBI office and upon entering ran into the field agent in charge. As luck would have it there stood Edgar Bond, one of the agents John had met at NBI headquarters when he was in the process of registering his pistol.

Edgar greeted John like a long lost friend and was glad to see a familiar face. "John, what are you doing here?" He asked.

"I flew my Admiral down for a speech but that's not what brings us to your office," he responded. Turning to Marvin he gestured, "I would like you to meet Marvin Johnson. He's the O-in-C of the weather station southwest of town."

They shook hands and John continued, "Edgar, we just had a gunfight with a group of gunman on the road down from the base."

"You better come into my office and tell me the whole story. Do we need to send any medical personnel out there?" he asked.

"No Edgar, they're all dead," John said.

"Okay, start from the beginning," Edgar said.

John and Marvin took turns filing in the blanks of what happened out on the road. At the end John pulled out the letter and cigarettes and gave them to Edgar stating that he thought him to be a Chinese agent or military officer who was training the insurgents. Edgar called in a couple of his agents and crime scene investigators and sent them out to the site of the attack. He then placed a call to Colonel Turkban at headquarters to report the incident and ask for guidance on how to proceed. Colonel Turkban instructed Edgar to continue to investigate and document the scene of the attack and to have John and Marvin sign a statement after it had been typed up for them. He also advised him to contact the Constabulary office to get them to provide some protection for the base and for John individually. He indicated that the insurgents would now place a price on the heads of John and Marvin, dead or alive.

Edgar called the Constabulary office and soon in walked Captain Bonnie Murrano. He too was surprised to see John and after greetings was apprised of the whole situation. Bonnie called his office and ordered a platoon of men to proceed out to the base and provide base security. Bonnie said his men would escort Marvin back to the base so he left and went over to Bonnie's office. Bonnie told Edgar he would take John out to the DelMonte plantation. Edgar told John to be in touch after he returned to Sangley Point. John and Bonnie departed for DelMonte.

The Admiral returned that evening and John went over to his cabin to brief him on the events of the day. The Admiral was shocked but expressed relief that John was okay. He made the decision that the golf outing would be cancelled and not worth risking John's life. They would depart for Sangley Point the next morning.

Sangley Point, Two days later

John was in his office when the phone rang. It was Colonel Turkban. "Good Morning, John," he began. "I just got a complete report from Edgar Bond and it isn't pretty."

"Well, Colonel, I didn't expect anything else. Give me the bad news," John said.

"Our investigation reveals the person you took the letter from, which was posted in Shanghai, China, was a Major in the Chinese army assigned to the Philippines and working in training revolutionaries in insurgency tactics. The others were members of Abu Sayyaf and that group has placed a bounty on your life. We are recommending that you transfer out of the Philippines as soon as practicable. There's no way we can guarantee your safety. Sorry about that, John."

"I got it, Colonel. I had suspected as much but now that you have confirmed my worse nightmare I guess I will work on a transfer. Thanks again for the update, I will be in touch."

John hung up the phone and immediately drafted a coded message to Commander Bates. He reported the status of the incident on Mindanao and the Chinese involvement. He relayed Colonel Turkban's recommendation on his transfer.

Within a day Commander Bates responded and advised John he would visit him in the Philippines within the week.

The following Wednesday afternoon Commander Bates boarded the Sangley, Cubi, Clark shuttle at Clark Air Base headed for Sangley Point. John had been alerted of his pending arrival and walked down to base operations to meet the shuttle. The Navy DC-3 soon appeared on short final for runway 08 at Sangley and after a short run out taxied over to base operations for unloading. The pilot shutdown the engines. After the wheels were chocked the passengers deplaned. John walked out to greet Commander Bates.

"Have a nice flight Commander?" John asked.

"It was okay, John, but I have been on the road for three days and that gets tedious," he replied.

They shook hands and John asked, "May I carry one of those for you?" he said referring to his luggage.

Commander Bates handed John a medium size travel bag which he picked up as John spoke, "I reserved you a room at the BOQ. Didn't know how many nights but we can correct that when you check-in."

The BOQ was just across the street and they were there within two minutes. Commander Bates checked-in and the two of them went down to his room.

"I am going to freshen up and then we can meet for dinner. How does that sound, John?" He said.

"That sounds good, sir. They serve dinner here at the BOQ or we can dine at the O'Club. Your preference, sir," John offered.

Pondering that for a moment Commander Bates said. "Let's try the O'Club tonight, John. We can probably get more of a variety there."

"Roger that sir. How does 6:00p.m. sound?"

"That'll be fine. I'll meet you in the BOQ lobby at that time," Bates responded.

John took his leave and went back to his office to finish a few reports he had pending. He walked over to BOQ in time to meet Commander Bates in the lobby. Together they walked the couple of blocks to the officers club. Once inside they were seated off in a corner of the dining room where they could talk freely and not be overheard by other patrons. The club was set in a grove of coconut palms with the dining room overlooking the runway with Manila Bay just beyond. It was a wide-open club with screens across the rear to keep out the mosquitos but allowed the beautiful tropical breeze to cool the place slightly.

They ordered drinks and dinner. Commander Bates asked John about his encounter in Mindanao. John told him the full story. They both agreed that it was a close call and not one that John wanted to experience again soon. John repeated the conversation he had with Colonel Turkban and Commander Bates stated that he agreed with him that John should transfer as quickly as it could be arranged.

"John, here is the situation as I have analyzed it. You have been with us now for a couple of years and at the 'company' we decided we would like to have you as a full time field agent. We know you wish to stay in the Navy and keep flying so here is the compromise we have arrived at. Admiral Reynolds, current Director of Central Intelligence, has directed me to have you transferred to Washington, DC, for temporary duty. He wishes to discuss your career personally so if you agree we will take care of the rest. What do you think?"

"Sir, I am ready to leave this place. The duty has been great but with the bounty on my life I believe it best to get out of here as soon as possible. So tell me what needs to be done." John said.

"The Bureau of Naval Personnel will send you a set of orders relieving you of duty here and transferring you to the Naval Administrative Command located at the Washington Navy Yard. Your assignment will be BuPers but you will be attached to the CIA. In the next week I will send you an envelope which will give you all the directions on how to proceed. Admiral Reynolds will have the final say on your next assignment after you complete some training. I would expect the training to last about seven months."

"That sounds like a good plan and is something I will like. I think that about settles the situation," John said.

"I'm glad we could get this done so quickly, John. Are you about ready to walk back to the BOQ." he asked.

John indicated he was, so they paid their bill and left the club for the BOQ.

The next morning John met Commander Bates for breakfast and he indicated they needed to talk to Murray Wright. They walked over to the administration building where Murray, as base personnel officer, had a private office. As they appeared in his doorway he greeted them and invited them to come in and sit down.

Commander Bates got right to the point. "Murray, I just wanted to touch base with you before I left for the states. John is being transferred from Sangley Point permanently and will be leaving here in a couple of weeks. You will become our primary DC-3 pilot and we will be sending you another copilot. Just wanted you to know you have done a great job under John and earned the Aircraft Commanders position. Nothing will change, except you will be responsible for all missions from now on. Congratulations." With that they shook hands all around.

Murray began, "Thank you, sir. I appreciate your confidence. John has been a great teacher."

The next morning Commander Bates met John for breakfast and after he checked out of the BOQ they walked across the street to flight operations where a DC-3 was scheduled to fly to Clark Air Base.

11

"TRAINING MODE"

Sangley Point, Philippine Islands

Within a couple of weeks John Walker received his new orders from the Bureau of Naval Personnel transferring him to the Naval Administrative Command, Washington, DC.

John had little in the way of personal goods but what he had he shipped to a holding company in Washington, DC.

It was a bright sunny and warm January day as John awakened for his last day at Sangley Point. The base officers had given him a wonderful going away party and he had said most of his goodbyes. He showered, dressed in his civilian clothes and went over to personnel to checkout. Murray was busy with his assigned duties and John stuck his head in his office and told Murray he was going to be on his way. Murray invited him in and they sat and chatted for a few minutes. Murray expressed his gratitude for what John had taught him about flying the DC-3 and how to survive in Southeast Asia. They had become close friends, been through a lot together and definitely respected each other. John arose, gave Murray a big hug and told him he would miss his great company. With that John grabbed his carry bag and walked out the door. He had a Special Services car at the curb to take him to the Manila Airport for the flight to Washington, DC.

His flight departed at 11:30a.m. He was at the gate by 11:00a.m. and took a seat in the waiting area. His flight was called and he boarded and began his new career. The first leg of his flight would be to Hawaii. It lasted about eight hours and soon was touching down at the Honolulu International Airport. It was Tuesday in Manila when the flight had departed. In Honolulu it was Tuesday but only 1:30 a.m. Since the flight had originated from a foreign country the passengers were required to clear customs and immigration. John retrieved his one checked bag and carried it over to the customs area for inspection. The immigration desk was in this area and he presented his passport to the agent. He had selected his green passport, as that was his official military one. The agent questioned him as to how long he had been out of the country. John responded, two years. Because he was an active duty military person he easily transited immigration and customs. He was soon back on the plane and headed for Washington, DC. The estimated flight time would be seven and one half hours so John settled down and took a long sleep. Traveling coach wasn't the easiest place but he managed to get six hours of sleep anyway.

On arrival at Dulles Airport he made his way to baggage claim and retrieved his bag. It was already 4:00p.m. and he was really hungry.

He had been instructed to check into the Holiday Inn located near Dulles Airport in Chantilly, Virginia, where transportation would be furnished to CIA Headquarters each day. He had been instructed to check into the Naval Administrative Command when possible. His orders allowed him ten days leave and he decided to use them before checking in with the CIA.

When he arrived in Chantilly he checked in at the desk of the Holiday Inn and found a reservation had been made for him for the next eight weeks. There was also a note from Commander Bates saying he would meet him in the morning for breakfast at 8:00 in the dining room.

John was up early and down in the dining room of the motel before 8:00a.m. At exactly eight, Commander Bates entered the room, spied John at a corner table and walked over to greet him.

The room was sparsely occupied and they could talk freely.

"Good Morning, John," Commander Bates said. John stood shook his hand and replied, "Good morning, sir. Nice to see you again."

As they sat, John offered, "I have not ordered yet, sir, except for my morning coffee. We have a couple of menus and I am sure the waitress will be back in a second to get you something to drink."

"Thanks, John. It's nice to see you again also. I'm glad you decided to join the company. We have a little bit of business to discuss before I send you off. Let's order first and then we can get too it."

The waitress brought Commander Bates a cup of decaf coffee and he and John ordered breakfast. The waitress quickly brought their order and they began eating.

Commander Bates began the conversation once again.

"John, this is probably our last official meeting as I will no longer be your handler. Do you have any plans for your 10 days leave?"

"Yes, sir, I thought I would visit my parents down in North Carolina. I haven't seen them for about three years," John said.

"That sounds like a good plan. After you return call this number," he gave John a business card, "and the person answering will make an appointment for you with the director."

John took the card, "Roger that, sir. I think I can handle that."

They finished their breakfast with little conversation and after coffee they arose and walked out into the lobby. They shook hands and John thanked him for all his guidance. Commander Bates acknowledged, turned and walked out the front door.

John called Enterprise Car Rental and made arrangements for a car for the next day.

Enterprise sent a car and driver to the hotel to pick up John and take him to their business address where he signed all the papers and picked up his rental.

It was a red Ford Focus and would be just fine for his trip to Flat Rock.

John returned to the hotel where he picked up his baggage and was headed off to Flat Rock. Before departure he dialed his parents number and on the third ring the voice of his father answered.

"Hello," he said.

"Hey, pop. Bud here. How are things?" he asked.

"Hey, Bud. We're doin' fine. Where are you?" Dad wondered.

"I just flew into Washington, DC, courtesy of the American Airlines. I'm going to be here for a while for some training and I was wondering if you are going to be home for a week because I would like to stop by and see you," John said.

"Yeah, Bud. We're going to be here. When can we expect you?" he asked.

"I'm leaving this morning and should be down your way by six-thirty. How does that sound?" John said.

"That sounds good. We'll be looking for you around suppertime then," he answered.

"Okay, Pop. See you then. Take care."

John hung up the phone. He was now a little excited as he hadn't seen his parents in about three years. They had moved from their little village in upstate New York to the mountains in North Carolina to get away from the bad winters they had been enduring for many years.

John pulled out of the Holiday Inn parking lot and headed for Interstate 66. Even though it was mid-winter he figured the scenery through the mountains would be pretty spectacular.

He was not disappointed. The Shenandoah was still beautiful and a little snow was present on the peaks and valleys. After passing Bristol, Tennessee, he took the exit onto Interstate 26 through Johnson City and across the mountains into Asheville, North Carolina. As he approached the Flat Rock area he took the exit and wended his way to his parents house. It was just about six-thirty when he drove into the driveway. His mom and dad greeted him. He thought they hadn't changed much since he last saw them.

During the next seven days he relived some of his youth and enjoyed mom's cooking. He and his dad talked mostly flying since both of them were naval aviators and they took a few trips to the rifle and pistol club where they fired off a few rounds. John's dad was still a pretty good shot as he had been a competitive shooter most of his life. He had passed on his love of the sport to John and taught him the fundamentals of rifle and pistol marksmanship.

The days went by quickly and it was time for John to head back to Washington. He packed his car, said his goodbyes had a lot of hugs all around and finally retraced his trip back to Chantilly and to the Holiday Inn.

The next morning he called the number on the business card Commander Bates had given him.

The director scheduled a meeting with him for this morning for 11:15a.m. in his office, and the lady on the phone said a vehicle would be at the hotel around at 10:30a.m. to pick him up and take him to headquarters.

John asked what his schedule might be for the next couple of weeks.

"The director will lay out his plans for you when you meet with him later this morning," the lady answered.

John returned to his room, put on his white shirt, naval aviator's tie and sport jacket, then picked up his briefcase and walked to the lobby where he awaited his ride to the CIA.

The white Nissan Pathfinder pulled up under the canopy at the entrance of the hotel. The canopy was built a little differently than most in that it was more like a tunnel, closed in on the far wall. John was unaware but it had been built for privacy. The hotel was completely owned, built and staffed by the CIA. The privacy was obviously to keep prying eyes from photographing guests coming and going.

John boarded the transport where he exchanged greetings with the driver who quickly headed out for the CIA headquarters in McLean. John noticed all the windows in the SUV were extra tinted probably to prevent photographing occupants and identifying anyone traveling in it.

When they arrived at headquarters John was let out at the main entrance. He entered and proceeded directly over to the security desk. He was asked to place his right hand index finger over the electronic scanner. The fingerprint was scanned into the security officer's computer, which caused it to be searched for in the company database. Very quickly John's personal information popped up on the screen and he was positively identified. He was issued a security badge, which expired in forty weeks. The officer gave him instructions on how to handle the badge properly, which would help him gain entry without having to check through security each day.

John was given directions on how to reach the Director's office on the sixth floor. He thanked the officer and proceeded through the security checkpoint where his badge was scanned and he then went directly to the elevator, entered and pushed the number six button. He excited at the sixth floor and proceeded down the long hallway to the Director's office. It was approaching 11:10a.m. which gave him five minutes to relax before he met the director.

As he entered the outer office, Judy, the director's administrative assistant, greeted him.

"You must be John Walker," she said.

John smiled, "Yes, ma'am, I sure am."

"I'm not a ma'am yet," she said as she sat down at her desk. "When I reach middle age you can call me ma'am, otherwise it's Judy. Have a seat," she directed. "The Admiral will be with you shortly."

John was flustered a little but gained his composure, "Thank you ma'am, er Judy. I didn't mean to be rude."

"You weren't. We're about the same age so I figured Judy was more in order than Ma'am," she offered.

John smiled once again and she knew he accepted her explanation. He fidgeted some from being in her presence, as she was a gorgeous woman with a knockout figure and a wonderful smile. It was tough being in the same room with her and not hitting on her, he thought.

The five minutes turned into twenty but finally Judy spoke, "The Admiral is free now, John. Please go right in," as she directed him to the Director's inner office.

As John entered Admiral Bill Reynolds came from behind his desk to shake his hand.

"I'm the director, John. Pleased to meet you," he said.

John responded, "My pleasure, sir. I'm proud to be on your team."

A quick glance around the room as he entered told John, here's an old Navyman, and an aviator at that, who's obviously proud of his prior service.

"Come have a seat in what I call my conference area, John. It'll be more comfortable."

John and the Admiral both took seats on sofas in an area away from his desk and sure enough it was more comfortable.

The Admiral began, "I wanted to meet you personally before you begin your training. I guess by now you realize my navy career is very important to me. I was CAG-7 on U.S.S. Oriskany during the Vietnam War and my aviators are important to me. You being an ex tailhooker and all I consider you as one of my boys. How many traps do you have John?" he asked.

"I have 346 traps sir, mostly on the Kennedy but some on the Lincoln, Intrepid and a few on Constellation." John said.

"I knew you flew Skyraiders but wasn't sure about your tailhook experience. Anyway let me outline what I have in store for you for the next ten weeks. I want you fully qualified as a field agent before I give you your assignment. For the next five weeks I am sending you to CIA University. It is located right near your hotel in the Chantilly area. I have set your studies as follows: I want you qualified in chemical weapons manufacturing, communication skills, dirty bombs, geography of critical regions, information technology, intelligence community, money laundering, project management, terrorism, weapons of mass destruction, and weapons proliferation. After that we are going to send you to the "Farm" down at Camp Peary near Williamsburg, Virginia. While you are there you'll get training in your defensive driving skills, interrogation techniques and weapons training. Not that you need that much after reading your reports of your escapades with Captain Murrano and the ambush you were in at Cagayan de Oro."

John smiled. "Yes sir that was one hell-of-a-confrontation we had with the Abu Sayyaf. My schedule sounds really interesting and I look forward to it. Will that schedule complete my training, sir?"

"That's all I have in mind for you here, John. After you have completed it, we will discuss your next assignment. Are you fluent in Tagalog?" the Admiral asked.

"Yes, sir. I have learned it fairly well during my assignment in the Philippines. Do you have any ideas about my next assignment?

"I don't have a firm grip on that yet, John, but with your language skill in Tagalog and your many contacts in the Philippines I think you may be comfortable in that setting. Presently the Abu Sayyaf is reinvigorating itself and looks to be a threat to the government itself. With your basic knowledge I'm thinking some assignment in that area would help us a great deal. We can discuss it further as your training progresses.

"That sounds like a great plan, sir. I will just play it by ear and await your decision," John said.

"Okay, John. I think that about lays out your training for the next ten weeks. Do you have any questions?"

"Yes, sir. When do I start at the University and how do I get there?" John asked.

"Good question, John. We have a class starting on Monday. There will be eight students in your class and company's SUV will pick you up each morning and drop you back at the hotel at the completion of classes. We know there are people who are trying to find out pertinent details of our students and the university so this is one way we can keep prying eyes from collecting any data. Just be wary of people you meet outside of normal business contacts. I hope that answers your question."

"Thank you, Admiral, that takes care of most of my questions. I'm sure my instructors will be able to meet my needs as they arise during my training."

"Good, John. Check with Judy before you leave as she may have some things for you to do before you leave the building. Oh by the way, congratulations on your promotion to Lieutenant Commander. I saw your name of the promotion list the other day. You will probably pin it on when you check into the Naval Administrative Command."

John rose, shook the Admiral's hand and walked out of his office. As he exited Judy spoke to him.

"John, before you leave the building you need to checkout with the personnel section and the Asian monitoring group. Ben Casey is in charge and I will get him up here to escort you down to his working area. Take a seat and relax for a minute. He should be up shortly."

Judy picked up the phone and punched in Ben's number. "Ben, I have John Walker here in the office. How about coming up and escorting him. He needs to be briefed by you as you discussed with the Admiral yesterday."

She turned to John. "Ben's on his way up should be just a couple of minutes."

"Thanks, Judy," John responded.

Ben showed up and escorted John to the Asian Section on the third floor. When they arrived they went into Ben's office where Ben offered John a cup of coffee. John accepted and soon they were sitting down discussing the Asian intelligence situation.

Ben opened his briefing folder and began, "John, our main goal right now is to document and follow the expanding influence of the Communist Chinese in Southeast Asia. Our second goal is to gather as much intelligence on Abu Sayyaf as possible so we can evaluate their intentions. We know that you have experienced some of it and have observed much of it based on your reports. You have good instincts, which will help all of us out in the field. Your judgment about the individual you ran into on the road in Cagayan De Oro was right on. We tracked down that individual's background and he was in fact an agent of Chinese Intelligence, trained in insurgency and assigned to help the Abu Sayyaf in the area you encountered him."

"Be aware the Chinese have been spreading their tentacles throughout Southeast Asia so you can expect it anywhere. Your previous reports have been more than satisfactory so just keep up the good work and keep sending them to us."

"You will learn this at the University but you need to begin keeping a daily diary. Recording who you met with, where you have been and any other details of your daily routine. Don't leave anything to memory, always put it in writing in your diary."

"Have you any questions, John?" Ben asked.

John responded, "Yeah, Ben, are we following the progress of the Chinese in Cambodia? I sent film and a report on their base building in northern Cambodia and I wondered if they had progressed any further?"

"Yes, John, we have been following that base with our satellite surveillance. The Chinese have it completed and are currently training Cambodian army troops in that area. It is with the knowledge of the Cambodian government leadership. That is one area we need to keep up to date on its development. Another hot spot at the moment is the Indian sub-continent including India, Pakistan and Bangladesh. We are also monitoring Nepal, Bhutan and Sri Lanka. It appears the Chinese are trying to get a foothold there working with Pakistan and Bangladesh. Recently they established a container facility in Colombo, Sri Lanka. India countered by signing an economic pact and antipiracy agreement with Sri Lanka and the Maldives.

"We probably need to concentrate on the goals of the Abu Sayyaf, as they are becoming more of a threat each day in the Philippines. I hope this answers your question."

"Thanks, Ben," John said. "I guess there is a lot to do once I get back in the field. The briefings before flying into these places will surely help on both ends."

"Your certainly welcome, John. I know you need to checkout with the personnel office before you leave the building so let me take you down to their offices on the first floor."

Ben led the way to the elevator and he and John entered. The doors opened quickly on the first floor and they walked briskly to the personnel office. Once there Ben offered his hand then departed.

The personnel office was efficient and had prepared all the necessary paperwork for John to sign. He completed it and was directed to the front entrance of the building where he would catch his transport back to the Holiday Inn.

The next five weeks passed very quickly and fell into a routine. An SUV picked up the eight students every morning about 8:30a.m. and took them some fifteen minutes away to the CIA University. Their building had a parking deck and was very private. The students were dropped off in this structure and then made their way to the classrooms within the building. This kept exposure to the public to a minimum and the prying eyes of the media. During their off-time these eight men became very close friends. Some were ex-military while others were just out of college.

John found the subjects quite taxing. All classes were very interesting and he soaked them up like a sponge. His Navy training had exposed him to some of the subjects on a peripheral level but the University went into them in depth. He especially enjoyed the weapons proliferation classes.

Week five came sooner than he would have wished, as he wanted more of what he was being exposed to. There were no final exams but each class ended with a roundtable discussion by the students and instructors with a critique of each course.

They were given a final briefing and instructions on what was scheduled for them for the next three weeks and how they would be transported to the "Farm." The farm was a secret CIA base located near Williamsburg, Virginia. Here they would take classes on how to conduct interrogations, weapons training and defensive driving.

12

"WEAPONS TRAINING"

Chantilly, Virginia

The eight students going to the Farm were waiting in the lobby for their transportation. At 8:36a.m. a ten-passenger Mercedes bus pulled into the driveway and stopped under the portico. Luggage was loaded and the bus turned out into Highway 50 headed east. To avoid the heavy traffic headed into downtown the driver turned off when he reached the Fairfax County Parkway. Some twenty miles down the road he came up on Interstate 95 and took the entry ramp headed south. Approaching Richmond, the highway split into Interstate 95 and Bypass I-295. The route took them on I-295 to Interstate 64. After turning onto the cloverleaf it would only be about 80 miles to Camp Peary, aka the "Farm."

The base was approximately a 10,000-acre reservation with 100 acres developed. Camp Peary was established in World War II as a training base for Navy Seabees. In 1951 it was transferred to CIA and redesignated the Armed Forces Experimental Training Activity (AFETA).

They turned off at exit 280 and headed east on the entry road to the base. It was only 200 yards until the bus came up on the security checkpoint. Two civilian security guard boarded the bus and asked everyone on board to show their CIA security ID. After everyone was checked the bus was cleared to continue onto the base and proceeded to the quarters where the students would be housed. After checking in at the main desk in the lobby John gathered his luggage and went down the hall to find his room. Each student was assigned a private room with adjoining bathroom. His room was 126 and soon he was unlocking the door. It was sparsely furnished with a bed, nightstand, armoire, and padded chair with desk and associated chair. He unpacked, hung up his clothes and carefully placed his casual clothes in the armoire. It was approaching the lunch hour so he left his room and decided to find the mess. It was in a connecting hallway running off the lobby. After lunch John inquired at the check-in desk about base transportation. He found out most people rode bicycles and that the quarters had them for rent. He checked one out for the duration of his stay. It would be a blast riding and keeping in shape.

The classes for new students were to begin the next morning. The class was to meet in the building across the street from the quarters so it was an easy walk. They were directed to report to classroom #2 where special agent Hector Martinez greeted them and gave them their schedule for the next three weeks. The first two weeks would be spent learning interrogation techniques with the last week split between defensive driving, weapons qualification and, finally, explosives.

The next morning they reported to the interrogation training building which was approximately two miles from their quarters. Some of the students gathered after breakfast and, after unlocking their bicycles, took off for the training building.

After settling into the lecture room Hector joined them. After a "Good Morning" he began his orientation lecture and covered the basics, which lasted about two hours. They took a ten minute break and reassembled outside an observation room. Hector led the way and they gathered behind a one-way mirror to observe an interrogation. This lasted some 55 minutes, after which they were excused for lunch to reconvene in the lecture room at 1:00p.m.

After lunch they reconvened where Hector led them through a critique of what they had observed that morning. They had been briefed on what techniques to look for and so they dissected the interrogation on what they had observed. Hector followed this training technique for the next week.

During his time off John had ridden his bike around the base just to get the lay of the land. He discovered the airfield and the defensive driving course on the southeast end on the base adjacent to the York River. He took particular interest in the airfield. It had one runway 5000' long heading 230º/050º. There was one hangar on the north side of the southwest end of the strip, which was capable of housing three medium aircraft. On one of his rides through that area he observed a Gulfstream 3, registered to Presidential Airways, land and taxi directly into the hangar where the doors then closed to obscure any passengers or pilots from outside observers. John knew from his research that the CIA was well stocked with airplanes and pilots. He would learn more as he worked for the company.

Beginning the second week of interrogation training the students took turns doing the interrogation, observing and once in a while participating as the interrogee. Dissecting each day's participation was always part of the learning process.

With interrogation training complete John would next be going to the range for weapons training. During his base exploration he had discovered the rifle and pistol ranges. He had estimated the three rifle ranges to be 300 yards maximum distance. It looked like pistol was fired out to about 75 yards. John reported to the pistol range the next morning. He was logged into the armory and issued a Beretta M9 pistol for his qualification. He had previously carried a Smith & Wesson Model 39 when flying the Skyraider during Desert Storm and had fired it many times so he was familiar with 9mm ballistics. John and his instructor moved out onto the firing line. Targets were already in place at 25 yards and John's instructor began asking him questions. His first question was whether he had ever fired a pistol before. He toyed with his instructor and said he had fired a pistol a few times. The instructor gave him the basic two-handed position and reviewed sight alignment and trigger control. He had John dry-fire a few times, which he found satisfactory. John was instructed to load his magazines and was given the course of fire. The rangemaster declared the range hot and John began the slowfire portion of the exercise. This was followed by timedfire and rapid-fire. After the practice round it was time for qualification. This time John paid careful attention to all aspects of this exercise. When the smoke cleared he fired a 396 out of a possible 400 score, which was well above the required score for qualification.

John's instructor broke out in a wide grin not knowing whether he was a great instructor or John was not revealing the truth.

"Just fired a pistol a few times, huh?" he asked.

"Aw I was just having a little fun," John replied.

"What kind of training have you had?" the instructor asked.

"A couple of years ago I went through police combat training at the National Bureau of Investigation in the Philippines. I usually carried my 1911 Springfield in. 45 caliber," John said.

"Have you ever fired a pistol in an actual combat situation?" he asked John.

"Yeah, had a little set-to with some terrorist rebels in the Philippines."

The instructor knew enough not to pry further so he continued, "Do you want to give the combat range a try today? We were scheduled for tomorrow and I see no sense in shooting any more fixed targets on this range. Do you have any preference in guns for the combat course?"

John smiled, "I'd prefer a 1911 but if you have none any .45cal will do."

"Let's go into the armory and see what we have on the shelf."

They cleared the weapon, and made the range safe then walked into the armory. After looking through the pistols on the racks for a few minutes the instructor picked one out.

"Here's a Glock Model G36. It's a long barreled .45 caliber which you might like."

He racked the slide back, checked it empty and gave it to John. It fit snugly into his large sinewy hand. "This one will do fine," he said.

They found a couple of magazines, which fit the Glock, and two boxes of .45 caliber hardball ammunition. John picked all this up and was headed out the door. His instructor reminded him he would need a holster so the stopped at the bin holding the holsters. John found leather, outside the belt concealed carry holster and after emptying his hands he strapped on the holster to his belt and mounted it just behind his right hipbone. This is where he usually carried his own pistol so it was a natural thing to do. He picked up the pistol, magazines and ammo and the two of them went out the door and to the right where the combat pistol range was set up.

The instructor began, "John, we have a set course of fire but why don't you fire the course you were trained in first. You will probably feel more comfortable doing that than trying to learn a new one."

As he was proceeding to the 50 yard line, John responded. "That sounds like a great idea."

John filled his jacket pockets from the first box of ammo. Twenty-five rounds in each pocket. He observed how the range was set up. A full man size silhouette on each side with half a silhouette to the center and another full size silhouette in the center. The right side was all open shooting while the left side was behind a barricade.

He loaded both mags and indicated he was ready. The instructor pulled out his stopwatch to time his firing. John ran over to the right flopped down at 50 yards in the open and fired five rounds. He moved quickly to the left and again fired 5 rounds, prone, from behind a log. He moved closer to the targets with each change in position firing sitting then kneeling. The next ten rounds were from behind a barricade, first strong hand and then weak hand standing. While still behind the barricade he reloaded both his mags and holstered his weapon. He reached the final firing position at seven yards in the open where drew and fired five rounds from the hip, reloaded and fired another five rounds then holstered his weapon.

His instructor had followed him down range observing his positions and firing. After holstering his weapon John turned and asked, "How'd I do, coach?"

"I think you forgot to holster your weapon when you moved from sitting to kneeling," he said. "We normally have our students do that when moving from one position to another."

John responded, "You're absolutely correct, coach. I was in a hurry and hadn't done this in some time and forgot."

"Not a fatal error, John. We do it on the range to make movement safer but you were okay with it. Let's check your hits and see how you did." They walked forward to the target line and checked each silhouette for hits. After counting hits on all targets, "Looks like forty-nine out of a possible fifty to me," the instructor stated. "Not bad for an amateur," He added.

"Well it felt good anyway," John mused.

"Want to try it again?" the instructor asked.

"Sure why not. We have plenty of time, don't we?" John asked.

The instructor nodded, "Go for it"

John prepared himself again and repeated the course of fire. He was careful not to make the mistake of not holstering his weapon when moving from yard line to yard line. His instructor followed him as he proceeded down range acting as a range safety officer. When he was finished they checked the targets for hits and forty-nine was once again the magic number.

"I think I pulled one off target kneeling in the open at thirty yards," John reported.

"I don't think most of our instructors could have repeated forty-nine twice in a row, John. Let's go back up to the armory."

Once they arrived John broke down the pistol and began cleaning it on the bench prepared especially for that operation. He and his instructor chatted during this process and when he was finished his instructor asked, "Normally our agents don't carry guns except in certain situations so how'd you like to have that Glock as your carry gun?"

The thought of having the Glock for a carry gun excited John, "You bet I would," he said.

"Okay it's yours. Pick a good holster from the new ones over in that cabinet." The instructor pointed to a wooden cabinet over on the far wall. The instructor completed the paper work and John slipped the holster and handgun into his gym bag.

"We're finished for today but tomorrow we are supposed to have rifle training. I don't suppose you have ever fired the AR-15 rifle?" he asked.

"I've fired it some on the range and had a little combat experience with it," John added. He recalled to his instructor how he and Bonnie Murrano had captured and killed the Chinese pirates in the southern Philippines.

"Damn, John. You sure have been a busy little beaver with your weapons," he said. "Tomorrow we will fire the combat rifle course including popups and moving targets. I'll get you an AR-15 equipped with an ACOG. I presume that's what you fired before."

"I took my initial training with metallic sights but Bonnie and I had for the operation I cited," John reiterated.

"Okay take off. I'll see you tomorrow," his instructor said.

It was mid-afternoon and John was a bit hungry. He stopped by the cafeteria, which was open 24/7, and had a little lunch.

13

"GROUNDED"

"Down on the Farm"

John arrived early at the armory. His fellow students were still receiving pistol training while he was assigned one-on-one rifle training with his instructor. He was obviously head and shoulders advanced in his handling of weapons and marksmanship. After he was issued one of the armory's AR-15s he and his instructor proceeded over to the combat rifle range. His instructor briefed him on his course of fire and the general layout of the range.

The first order of the day was to sight-in the rifle. This they did at 200 yards. In doing so it put the strike of the bullet about an inch high at 100 yards and 4 inches low at 300 yards. Next John took his place on the firing line in the prone position. The range master declared the range hot and John loaded a magazine with 15 rounds into his rifle. The idea was to place three shots into a pop up target at unknown distances. Once again the targets were man size silhouettes. Targets were scored by electronic means so it was not necessary to walk forward to score. John handled the pop ups with ease and after three magazines had 42 hits out of a possible 45. The final target was at 300 yards and was a side view of a man walking slowly. John had five rounds and received four hits. His instructor was pleased with his performance, as was John. When they finished the range went cold and they walked back to the armory. Once there John was debriefed on his weapons training and received a grade of excellent with comments that he was well qualified to handle weapons.

His next three days were spent at explosive training in the morning followed by defensive driving in the afternoon. John learned how to make bombs of semtex and detonate it with a cell phone. He also learned how to make IEDs from unexploded military ordnance.

Defensive driving turned out to be a snap as he had driven fast sports cars since joining the Navy so some of the defensive maneuvers were all he had to master. He enjoyed speeding around the hairpins turns and spinning his car around the track.

With their training complete the eight students were scheduled to be transported back to the Holiday Inn in Chantilly, Virginia.

On Saturday morning the eight-passenger Mercedes bus pulled up in front of their quarters where they loaded up and retraced their route back to Chantilly. When they arrived they were given one hour to clean up and board the bus to CIA headquarters where they were to have a small graduation ceremony and reception with the director.

The bus dropped them at the front door of headquarters where they made their way to the small conference room off the main lobby set aside for such ceremonies.

Admiral Reynolds entered and they all stood to greet him. He asked them to be seated and he took the podium. He congratulated all of them for successfully completing the training and welcomed them officially to the CIA as fully qualified field agents. He told them after the ceremony those who had not been assigned would receive their next posting. He ended the ceremony and stepped down and shook each man's hand congratulating him personally. His words had been inspiring while also telling them to always be alert and cautious. He then asked the men to join him in the anteroom for a little punch and cake.

As John stepped into the room he spied Judy. She was helping the food services people with the cake and punch which he was certain she had arranged. He walked back and greeted her. She was pleased to see him and she stopped what she was doing to spend a few moments talking with him. As that was happening the Admiral strode up and greeted John. He told him to come see him in his office the next morning. John acknowledged and said he would contact Judy for an appointment. The Admiral had taken a great liking to John and felt as though he was one of his family of past naval aviators whom he had herded through life. John appreciated the Admiral's affection and personal attention, which he valued greatly.

The festivities were over very quickly and the students found themselves headed back to their hotel and from there who knows where.

The next morning John boarded the white Nissan SUV for CIA headquarters. He had an appointment with Admiral Reynolds for 10:30a.m. He arrived at headquarters, cleared security and proceeded to the sixth floor and the Admiral's office.

As he entered Judy smiled at him,

"Welcome back stranger. I guess your training at Camp Peary went well?"

"Thanks for asking. Yes it went really well and I enjoyed it," John said. "Did you miss me?"

Judy giggled, "You know we missed you, John. The work here almost stopped."

"That's what I thought," John replied, laughing.

He knew she was kidding him as he had just done with her but it loosened up the atmosphere and kind of made him relaxed before he saw the Admiral. She was always pleasant to be around and John enjoyed talking with her.

Judy announced John on her intercom and the Admiral told her to send him in.

"Good morning, sir," John said as he entered the office. "I hope things are well with you today."

"Good morning, John," he answered. "Yes things are under control this morning for a change." Come in and sit for a few minutes. I want to discuss your future with us."

John took a seat across the desk from the Admiral.

"John, in reviewing your qualifications and experience I want to send you back to the Philippines. Not right away mind you but eventually. You can speak the language, have many contacts there who can be helpful to both them and us, have been to many of the main centers of activity and most of all you seem to understand the Filipino mentality. I believe I want you here for at least eight months, working with the Asian desk and learning all of what's currently happening in Asia. By the time we send you back to the Philippines a year will have passed since your episode in Cagayan De Oro. That is a good cooling off period. In this business you always need to be careful and the threat to your well being will have subsided to an acceptable level. How does that sound to you?"

"Sir, that sounds like a good plan and I would enjoy that. Where would I be working?" he asked.

"I will get you assigned as the Military attaché attached to the American Embassy. There will be an agent filling the station chief's job so you will be low visibility. The embassy has a DeHavilland Twin Otter for you to fly that will keep you in the flying game. I can see in the future the closing of all U.S. military bases so Murray would be available to be your Assistant Military attaché and copilot."

"That would make me feel even more comfortable, sir," John replied.

"Okay, that settles it. I will put you to work with Ben Casey at the Asian Section ASAP. Let me get Ben up here and I will brief the two of you on what we are going to do.

Ben arrived shortly and the Admiral briefed him on the plans for John. Ben acknowledged the Admiral's wishes and indicated he would make John a great agent.

They left the Admiral's office and headed downstairs.

Eight months later

John had been compiling and analyzing intelligence from Southeast Asia for eight months and he was sure he had learned as much as possible. He yearned for the adventure of fieldwork and being outdoors. Most of all he missed flying. That was his greatest love.

One day as they we discussing some intelligence from the Philippines the phone rang and Ben answered. It was Admiral Reynolds. He asked that John come up to his office that afternoon to see him.

Ben passed on the information to John. They had been in the middle of an analysis of a kidnaping the Abu Sayyaf had perpetrated. It was of an 18-year-old teenage girl just outside the U.S. Embassy in Manila. John was particularly interested in that she was from Sangley Point Naval Station, attending high school at the American School in Manila. Even now she was being transported to Mindanao to be sold or traded to the Datu of one of the Muslim settlements to be his concubine. The group transporting her was so clandestine that it was almost impossible to track. The Philippine law enforcement agencies were too slow to react and could not keep up with the route the Abu Sayyaf was taking. It would be impossible to get her back and everyone knew it.

After lunch John went up to Admiral Reynolds office. Judy was waiting for him and told him to go right in as the Admiral was free at the moment.

"John, come on in and have a seat," the Admiral said.

"Thank you, sir," John responded

"John, I believe you have had enough intelligence compiling and analysis to last a lifetime. It's time for you to get back in the field, which you seem to relish."

A big smile slowly showed on John's face.

"Sir, I thought you'd never ask. If anyone has ever been ready, it's me." John said. "What do you have planned?"

"I have talked with State and they have made room for you in the Philippine American Embassy as the Naval Attaché. Other good news and bad. Naval Station Sangley Point will close next month and Murray Wright will be available for transfer as your assistant and copilot. It is my intention that you be immediately processed for transfer to Manila. How does that sound?" the Admiral asked.

"That sounds perfect," John replied. "When can I get started?"

"Tomorrow morning you can report to personnel and start processing. I have already alerted them on what needs to take place. Remember you will have to check out of the Naval Administrative Command to maintain your cover as a Naval Officer. I hope you have had your uniforms brought up to date?" he asked.

"Yes, sir. I had my blues striped about seven months ago when my promotion to Lieutenant Commander was announced. I will wait to update the remainder of my uniforms including my mess dress in Hong Kong with Peter Chaing," John said.

"Give Peter my regards when you see him, John. I had suits made by him when I was CAG during the Vietnam War. I was on the Hancock then and we spent a week in Hong Kong," the Admiral related.

John smiled, "I can do that, sir. Peter is great to deal with and does great work."

John rose to depart and the Admiral came around his desk. They shook hands and John went back downstairs to the Asian Section. He ran into Ben and stopped to tell him that he would be leaving tomorrow and what the Admiral had planned for him.

Ben expressed a little sadness in hearing that news and told John they would miss him and that he was beginning to develop into a great analyst.

John thanked Ben for all his help and patience in helping him learn to analyze intelligence. He promised he would send him great weekly reports from the Philippines.

John reported to personnel the next morning and began his checkout. Within the week he had checked out of headquarters and the Naval Administrative Command and had booked a flight to the Philippines.

14

"TRANSPORTATION"

Manila, Luzon, Philippines

As John deplaned at the Manila International Airport the warm tropical air was a bit stifling after the cool airconditioned flight from Honolulu. He stopped at baggage claim to retrieve his checked bag, then caught a taxi to the embassy. It was located in downtown Manila and situated on the waterfront. He checked in with the personnel director who assigned him quarters in the restricted security compound located in Pasay City specifically for embassy personnel. Security compounds in the Philippines were necessary due to the large number of robberies, which would otherwise be perpetrated on unassuming Americans. It was a single bedroom bungalow with kitchen, living room, bathroom, dining area with a large lawn and garden. It was perfect for John as that was all he really needed.

He knew the routine from being stationed at Sangley Point so he asked personnel for the list of pre-cleared domestic help. These would be workers who already had a security pass to get into the compound. He indicated he would need a housekeeper and a gardener. He asked personnel to pick them for him and that would be acceptable. He felt he did not need to interview them for the job.

John settled into his office at the New Annex Building on the embassy grounds. He was welcomed by the ambassador and made contact with the station chief. In discussions with the station chief, headquarters had passed on instructions to investigate and report on suspected Hukbong Mapalaya ng Bayan, or "Peoples' Liberation Army", in the Mt. Ayrat area. They had originally been the Hukbalahap but with renewed Chinese influence had changed the name likely in emulation of the Chinese People's Liberation Army. John told the station chief he would look into it in a couple of days after he renewed communications with his contacts at the National Bureau of Investigation and the Philippine Constabulary.

Maria, a petite middle-aged woman, knocked on his door early one morning before he departed his quarters for the embassy. She showed him her security pass and a letter from the personnel section of the embassy indicating she was asked to apply to being his housekeeper. John spoke to her in Tagalog and she smiled widely. She was pleased as was John and after a short interview said she was hired. They agreed on a salary and John told her he needed to go to work but that she could leave at 4:00pm even if he was not home. She explained to him that was not necessary and she would wait until he returned. He bid her goodbye, once again in Tagalog, and caught the shuttle bus for the embassy. He figured he needed to get a good car soon to get around so he didn't have to depend on the shuttle.

When he arrived at the office he called Sangley Point and made contact with Murray Wright. Murray was pleased to hear from him and John invited him to the embassy for lunch as he didn't want to discuss matters over the phone. Murray accepted and said he could get there by 12:25p.m. since the launch from the base to the embassy didn't leave Sangley Point until noon.

After John hung up he dialed the NBI and talked with the director's secretary. He asked if he could meet with Colonel Turkban. She made him an appointment for 10:00a.m. the next morning. After that he called Philippine Constabulary headquarters and asked for Captain Murrano. He was told by the administrative assistant that it was now Major Murrano and that the Major would not return for a couple of days. She took John's number and said Major Murrano would return John's call.

It was 12:35p.m. and Murray knocked on John's door and stuck his head in.

"Hey stranger," he said. "What's goin' on?"

"Hey Murray," John replied. "Great to see you. How have you been?"

"I've been great," Murray said.

John set down the paperwork he was working on. "You ready for some lunch?" he asked.

"Yeah, I'm starved. Had breakfast early and no donuts today."

"Are you still on those things?" John asked.

"Naw, only once in a while," Murray said.

"Well, let's go to lunch downstairs in the cafeteria. Food's supposed to be good although I haven't been here long enough to make that call," John said.

"That sounds like a plan, old buddy," Murray replied.

They departed John's office and walked down to the cafeteria. The special of the day was beef stew with a side dish of macaroni and cheese. They both ordered that and took their trays to a table off in the corner. After they were seated John began the conversation. "Murray besides wanting to get together and see you there are a couple of things we needed to discuss. This information is still classified and not released yet to anyone but Sangley Point will probably close within the next six months. Having said that I want you to consider being my copilot here at the embassy as the Assistant Naval Attaché. You know we have the Twin Otter over on the military side of the International airport. I'll be honest with you I only took this job because the boss promised me I could have you as my assistant. What do you think?"

Murray looked really surprised but smiled widely. "You and me together again? I guess I would like that John. You can count me in."

"That's great, Murray. I apologize for having to spring it on you that way. Just keep it under your hat and when the base closes you will get orders to report here. Now tell me what you have been doing with my favorite DC-3."

"We have had a lot of flights down in the southern Philippines. Besides the increased Chinese presence, the Abu Sayyaf has been so active that we have been trying to pinpoint their bases. It has been difficult however as the jungle is unyielding to our photography. We have also spotted a lot of UFOs in that area also. Probably not related but noticeable anyway."

John inquired, "Have you put that in your weekly reports?"

"Yeah, we have, John."

"Good, Murray. That kind of stuff could be important down-the-road," John said.

The two men finished their lunch and John walked Murray out to the pier so he could catch the launch back to Sangley Point.

"Listen, old friend, be in touch and we"ll get together soon," John said as he sent Murray off in the launch.

John made some notes in his diary when he returned to his office. He would put his meeting with Murray in his weekly report.

Manila, next day

John had an SUV from the embassy take him over to the NBI for his meeting with Colonel Turkban. As he entered his outer office his administrative assistant announced John on her intercom. Colonel Turkban directed her to have John come in.

Colonel Turkban welcomed John as he entered. "Come in, John, and have a seat. I'm glad to see you once again."

"Thank you, Colonel," John responded. "It's great to see you also. I miss our mornings on the range."

Colonel Turkban took a seat. "Tell me what brings you to my bailiwick?"

"I don't know if you heard that I was assigned to the American embassy as the Naval Attaché. As part of my duties, I will be helping the U.S. Military personnel assigned to assist the Philippine military in their special operations especially against the Abu Sayyaf and Chinese influenced operations. We are seriously interested in helping to stifle the insurgents threatening your country, government and way of life. It is important to us that the Philippines remain a viable democracy and an ally of the United States. I wish to help you with the intelligence and will share anything we may discover in the course of our military assistance to your special forces."

"That sounds like a good proposal for a strong working relationship, John. I like that and I am sure we can work together to achieve the common goal. I know you have experienced the terrorist threat firsthand in your encounter with the Abu Sayyaf at Cagayan De Oro. It has been almost a year since then and I also think the threat to you personally has subsided. However I must advise you to keep a low profile so as not to put yourself in their crosshairs, so to speak."

"Thanks for the advice, Colonel. I intend to do just that and thanks for offering to work with us on the sharing of intelligence. I know it will help both our countries. Before I go however I have one favor to ask. My copilot, Murray Wright, will be reporting to the embassy in a couple of months from Sangley Point and I wish to get him qualified in police combat pistol. Do you think he could join one of your classes?"

"I'd love to have him, John. Just let me know when to expect him and I will accommodate him in my class.'

John stood to leave, "Thank you, Colonel. I will be in touch." He shook the Colonel's hand and departed.

John boarded the SUV and returned to his office in the embassy compound. He decided he needed a vehicle to drive so he called Ramon Guiang at the Mercedes production plant in Pasay City. Ramon had once worked at Sangley Point and John had colluded with him on a few projects.

Ramon answered the phone in his office. "Ramon, this is John Walker."

"Mr. Walker, how have your been sir?" he asked. "What can I do for you?"

"Ramon, I have been transferred to the embassy downtown and I need a vehicle to drive. Do you think you can help me?" John asked.

"Sure, I can help you. Why don't you stop by my office tomorrow and we can work on it," Ramon said.

"That'll be great. How does 10 o'clock sound?" John said.

That's good. I will be looking for you tomorrow at ten."

"Thanks, Ramon. See you tomorrow," John said as he hung up the phone.

After work he arrived at his quarters and was greeted by Maria.

"Hi, Maria," he said. "How did your day go?"

"It went fine, Mr. Walker. I worked most of the day in your bedroom and I will finish it tomorrow. I believe you need to go to the commissary and get some food for the kitchen. Also in about a week I will need a houseboy to polish the floors as it is too difficult for me to do."

It suddenly struck John, "Maria, I apologize. I forgot you need some food for your lunch. I will go to the commissary in the morning before I go to work. Besides rice what do I need to get you for lunch."

"I think you can get lumpia there and some veggies. Also I suggest you get yourself something for breakfast," she said.

"Sounds like a plan, Maria. As far as a houseboy can you ask some of the neighbors to help and see if you can get one of them for a half a day or for as long as you need him to do the floors?" John asked.

"Yes, sir. I will ask around. Also while you are at the commissary you need to get me some house-cleaning supplies including some hard wax for the floors."

"I will put those things on my list, Maria."

Having ended the conversation Maria picked up her purse and said goodnight.

Manila, next day

John was up early and out to the commissary, which was in the housing compound. The commissary delivered his purchases to his quarters and he was all set for Maria when she arrived at 9:00a.m.

Maria smiled as she spied the bags of goods from the commissary stacked in the kitchen. John told her not to wait for him that evening as he may be late. He also told her he had laid out his formal Barong Tagalog as well as his polo barong and shirt-jack barong which all needed washing and ironing. His formal Barong was made of Piña fabric that is hand-loomed from pineapple leaf fibers. He also had two Polo barongs that were short-sleeved version of the barong, made with linin. His Shirt-jack barong was cut in shirt-jack style and made of polyester-cotton.

The polo barongs would be suitable for his daily routine at the office and were worn by many of the embassy personnel.

John left his quarters, caught a taxi and was off to meet Ramon at the Mercedes production facility. He checked in at the reception area and the receptionist paged Ramon indicating he had a visitor. Within minutes Ramon stepped through the door from the district offices.

He greeted John with sincere warmth and invited him into the offices. They first stopped in Ramon's office where Ramon had laid out all the literature and advertising on their latest products. He went through them with John pointing out the specs and features of each of their cars. Ramon was in charge of production line troubleshooting and worked closely with the industrial engineers who set up the production. John finally spotted a white SUV he really thought he could live with. Ramon made a few calls and finally determined they had one that had just come off the production line and was being checked out by quality control. It would be available tomorrow if that's what John wanted. John and Ramon agreed that it was the car for him.

Ramon took John down to the district manager's office where he first consulted privately with him then summoned John into the office where he was introduced to him. They talked for a short time and soon the district manager said the SUV was worth about $29,000 but on Ramon's recommendation he had reduced the price to $6,000.

John was aghast at the discount, which he never expected, but never the less made arrangements to have a money order in that amount tomorrow when he expected to take delivery.

Ramon and John left the district manager's office and John kept thanking Ramon for getting him the discount. Ramon assured John he had done many things for him personally and the Philippine people in general and he felt he deserved it.

Ramon had one of his drivers take John back to the embassy.

When he checked back into his office there was a message from Bonnie Murrano inviting John to meet him at his office tomorrow. John made a call and confirmed their meeting and then secured for the day.

15

"NATURE CALLS"

Manila, Philippines

John was up early, had a light breakfast and was off by taxi to the Mercedes plant to claim his automobile. He met Ramon in the reception area and was ushered into Ramon's office. All the necessary paperwork was complete and Ramon gave John's money order to his assistant who walked the paperwork down to the financial office where it was credited to John's account and a receipt issued.

When Ramon's assistant returned he and John walked over to quality control where John presented his receipt. Within minutes John's new SUV was brought up where he accepted delivery. John and Ramon shook hands. John thanked him for his help and he drove off. Ramon had thought of everything including registering it with the auto license bureau. Before they had departed Ramon's office he had faxed John's car information to USAA insurance company in San Antonio, Texas, where his new car was put on his policy.

The GPS on his dash helped John wend his way back to the embassy grounds where he found a parking place in front of his building.

Manila, Embassy Compound, June 10th

John looked up the address of the Philippine Constabulary Headquarters and was now in the process of entering it into his GPS. He was going to need the GPS for a while until he found his way around Manila. John turned out onto Roxas Avenue where the traffic was bumper to bumper. John followed the GPS instructions and after a half hour was turning in the gate of Constabulary Headquarters. He cleared security after showing his military ID and communicating to the guard that he had a 2 o'clock appointment with Major Murrano.

He entered Bonnie's office on time. The first sergeant took his name and communicated with Bonnie in the inner office. Soon he was escorted into Bonnie's office where the two old friends greeted each other. "Walker," he shouted, "What have you been up to lately?"

"Not much, old friend. Just getting settled in my new job at the embassy. I am the new Naval Attaché," John said.

"That should keep you busy but I'm not sure out of trouble," Bonnie said.

"Have you been doing any target shooting?" John asked.

"Not since I won the National Pistol Championship last fall. How about you, John. Have you done any?" Bonnie said.

"No, Bonnie. I have gone through a bunch of qualification training with the pistol and AR-15 rifle but have not had a chance to do any serious target shooting. Listen, I came over today to ask you about your favorite terrorist group, the Hukbong Mapalaya ng Bayan. My state department and the military are concerned about American civilians traveling around Luzon. Tell me, what's going on around Angeles City? I am thinking about going up that way to find out what I can but I know you are the expert on that group."

"John, the Bagong Hukbong ng Bayan with the faction involving members of the HMB under Bernabe "Dante" Buscayno have launched a "protracted people's war". Their leader in the Angeles area is Beni Taruc, the grandson of the original organizer. We think he is being trained and supported by either the Chinese intelligence service or the Chinese Red Army. We have not been able to confirm this. However, we have an informer who hangs out at a bar called the 'Yellow Dogshead'.

His name is Ruiz Tarlac but just ask for 'Shivers'. He should be able to help you with some of the information you need. I suggest you take your pistol just in case of trouble. I'd go with you but I have a lot of things going on here at the moment which I can't leave, so be careful."

"Thanks for all the info, Bonnie, and you better believe I will be damn careful."

John departed the headquarters and made his way back to the embassy compound.

The ambassador had been in consultation with Admiral Calvin at Subic Bay as well as General MacTavish at Clark Air Base concerning the volcanic activity from Mount Pinatubo. There had been some minor eruptions of magma as well as ash and it was affecting base operations. Subic Bay was some thirty-four miles south west of Pinatubo but Clark Air Base was only 13.4 miles east. The activity at Mount Pinatubo had been on going and getting worse since March. Evacuations of people in the danger area on the volcano was now being stepped up as the scientists studying it predicted a major eruption within a short period of time.

On June 12th there was a major eruption. John had planned to go to Angeles City on the 15th but now it looked like that would be a stupid decision.

Admiral Calvin ordered the evacuation of all personnel at the communications station in San Miguel and also ordered the microwave relay station atop Mount Santa Rita closed and all personnel evacuated. Admiral Calvin reported to the ambassador that large amounts of ash were already falling on the base and could develop into a serious problem. He also indicated that he had been in contact with the Chief of Naval Operations and requested airlift be provided for military personnel and dependents out of the country as soon as possible.

The ambassador talked with General McTavish at Clark Air Base who indicated it was now too dangerous for aircraft to fly into Clark due to the excessive ash being deposited on the base. General Clark had ordered a complete evacuation of the base by road and he was mustering all the transportation he could to get the people out. He told the ambassador to expect air force transports to be diverted to Manila International Airport to evacuate his people. The only personnel remaining at Clark were a few security personnel to guard the classified material and the air traffic control center.

There were Americans at the consulate in Baguio and also some tourists who had taken refuge there. The ambassador had requested that John come over to his office and brief him on the situation.

As soon as John received the message he walked over to the ambassador's office. When he arrived he was immediately ushered into Ambassador Ross' office.

"Good morning, sir," John said as he entered.

"Good morning, John," the ambassador answered.

"Come in and have a seat."

As soon as John was seated the ambassador continued.

"I wanted to discuss the Baguio situation with you, John. We have consulate personnel and some American tourists there and I wondered if an evacuation was necessary and at all possible. Have you any ideas or information that might help me make a decision?" he asked.

"Sir, I have been trying to contact our offices in Baguio but with Admiral Calvin shutting down the microwave relay station on Mount Santa Rita no telephone communication is possible. I also talked with flight operations at Sangley Point and they tell me it is too dangerous to fly anywhere in that direction now due to the ash being deposited. You should also be aware that a typhoon is due to hit that area in three to four days that will also make flying in that direction dangerous. Sangley Point has grounded all their aircraft. My recommendation is to leave the people hunkered down in Baguio. I am sure they have plenty of food and water and are not in danger from the volcano except for the ash which is being deposited everywhere on Luzon north of Manila."

"Well that answers some of my questions in the very least, John. Thank you for being so thorough in your assessment," Ambassador Ross said.

"Sir, our military commanders are now isolated and we won't hear anymore from them for a while. I will monitor the standard high frequencies assigned to the military for any traffic that might be destined for us. I don't see that there is very much we can do to help them except what we may be asked to do by other activities and agencies. I will plan a trip over to Manila International Airport to talk with air traffic control and the airport manager and discuss the situation concerning military transports being diverted there for evacuation of American personnel. The United States Air Force had initiated a massive airlift effort to evacuate American service members and their families during and immediately following the eruption, named Operation Fiery Vigil. Most personnel will be initially relocated to Guam, Okinawa, and Hawaii, although I understand some personnel and dependents returned to the continental United States."

The ambassador arose to shake John's hand, "Thanks for your incite into these matters, John. I must say you have a good grasp of the situation and I appreciate your support."

John shook the ambassador's hand and departed his office. He walked slowly back to his office all the while looking to the north to try to assess the situation.

On the morning of the 13th a tropical storm warning came across John's desk. "Just what we need now," John thought. It was forecast to become a typhoon in the next day or two and would hit Luzon somewhere on the east coast and 20 to 50 miles north of Manila. The forecast track would take it across Luzon and out into the South China Sea near Linguyan Gulf. That would cause it to pass within 40 to 50 miles of Mount Pinatubo. Evacuation of personnel from Subic Bay and Clark Air Base would need to be done quickly because by the morning of the 14th it looked like ground and air travel would be nearly impossible. Ash was still falling heavily and reports from refugees in and around Angeles stated that it appeared as though night had fallen during the day. In addition, as if there weren't enough problems, small earthquakes were being experienced in Manila and ash was falling steadily.

John was getting edgy and sent a memo to the ambassador recommending closing down all services at the embassy and sending the people home and to the housing compound. If the winds picked up from the typhoon he knew the water in Manila Bay would rise and the embassy grounds could be underwater.

The ambassador took John's advice and the embassy staff was told not to report on the 15th. John felt duty bound to monitor the situation so on the morning of the 15th he took the shuttle bus from the housing compound to the embassy. If the embassy grounds were going to be under water he didn't want his new Mercedes damaged by saltwater.

He had made arrangements with the radio room operators for one of them to man the equipment. On arrival he made his way to the radio room where he expected to spend the entire day and probably the night.

High tide was at 12:01p.m. and he expected the winds to be out of the northwest by then, which put them blowing onshore and piling up water in

Manila Bay. John asked the radio operators to monitor the amateur bands as that was probably where some of their best updates would come from. They were also monitoring military communications as that was the only direct link to the Philippine bases.

All during the morning there were intermittent minor earthquakes and the wind picked up to 75 miles per hour. Wind direction was initially out of the northeast but was slowly swinging toward the north all morning.

At 11:54a.m. local time a strong quake was felt. It turned out to be Mount Pinatubo blowing its top in the second largest eruption of the 20th century.

The wind at the embassy was now 75 miles per hour and blowing out of the northwest. Water in Manila Bay was up four feet and almost over the seawall. The sky had darkened, rain was almost horizontal and ash was still falling and increasing.

The radio room monitored a message transmitted from Clark Air Base giving their status. The sky was overcast and was almost as if it were nighttime. It was as if mud were raining down.

Evacuation was almost complete from the area affected by the latest eruption of Pinatubo and in all some 60,000 people had left the area within 30 kilometers (19 mi) of the volcano before June 15th. Most people temporarily relocated to Manila and Quezon City, with some 30,000 using the Amoranto Velodrome in Quezon City as an evacuee camp.

In the days following, John focused mainly on the military situation at the three bases. U.S. military Special Forces manned the Military Assistance Advisory Group (MAAG) in Quezon City. John was aware that they could take care of themselves based on their training so he didn't pay much attention to them.

In the months following the eruption, Clark Air Base was eventually abandoned. Official reasons were due to the ash covering the entire base. Unofficially the local gang of criminals from Angeles City had looted the base and the cost to restock and repair Clark was too expensive. A survey had been done of the base. Offices and housing had been stripped of anything usable. This included toilets, sinks, bathtubs, kitchen appliances, household goods, copper pipe and personal items such as jewelry and electronic items.

One item, which peaked John's interest, was the 100,000 rounds of 5.56mm ammunition stolen from the ammunition bunker on the north side of the base. It was probably in the hands of the Huks but they were incapable of its use as they were armed with AK-47s provided by the Russians and Communist Chinese. However the Abu Sayyaf in the southern islands were armed with M-16s and AR-15s that were manufactured to fire that round.

John set out to discover where it was and where it might be going as that much ammo in the hands of the Abu Sayyaf could be a disaster. It would inflame the insurgency already being established in Sulu and Mindanao. John would need to contact Bonnie Murrano and discuss this situation.

Meanwhile negotiations on the leases for the U.S. military bases had broken down and the Philippine State Department was ordering all bases closed and turned over to the Philippine government. The communications stations at San Miguel and Tarlac had already been abandoned. Subic Bay Naval Station and the Cubi Point Naval Air Station were decommissioned and within a month were turned over to the Philippine government. All U.S. military personnel were withdrawn except for the MAAG personnel in Quezon City.

John's official duties were made a whole lot easier but unofficially a lot harder.

16

"TROUBLE"

Manila, Philippines

John had spent the previous two weeks trying to find out about the ammunition. He was working with Major Murrano in an effort to pinpoint its location and it appeared that a trip to Angeles City was in order. Intelligence gathering by direct contact was the only way to solve this problem. Bonnie once again warned John about the dangers of traveling to Angeles.

During all this flurry over the past couple of weeks Sangley Point Naval Station had closed and Murray Wright checked into the embassy as Assistant Military Attaché.

The following Tuesday John checked out an embassy car for his trip to Angeles. It was a white Nissan Pathfinder and had only about 6,000 miles on it. He asked Murray if he would like to accompany him on this trip. Murray jumped at the opportunity.

John asked, "Murray, do you have a pistol?"

Murray's response was, "Yeah, John, I do. Should I bring it?"

"It would be a smart thing to do. I don't know what the situation is in Angeles and we might need some firepower to extract ourselves."

John had his Model 36 Glock and Murray showed John his M9 Beretta in 9mm.

"Okay. Looks like we are all set to travel," John said.

The two of them piled into the SUV and headed north out of Manila on North Luzon Expressway. When they reached the Angeles area John turned off on Pandan Road. He finally ended up on Herndon Street in downtown Angeles. Murray spotted the "Yellow Dogshead" bar first and pointed it out to John. They parked across the street and walked over and entered the bar. It was a dingy place, not very well lighted or maintained with a number of call girls hanging around. There were a number of men seated at the bar and at tables. Some were playing Mah Jong and others were just sitting drinking San Miguel beer. John and Murray were dressed in casual clothes, jeans and a sport shirt, so they might better remain anonymous and not be pegged as American military personnel. John asked the bartender in Tagalog if "Shivers' was there as they were looking to talk with him. She pointed him out. Ruiz Tarlac aka "Shivers" was sitting at a table in the rear of the establishment against the wall. John and Murray made their way back to where he was sitting and John introduced himself. Ruiz spoke good English and responded to John's introduction.

"I'm Ruiz," he said as he motioned them to have a seat. "What can I do for you gentlemen?"

John began. "Ruiz, I spoke with Major Murrano and he suggested you might be able to help. We are trying to locate the 100,000 rounds of ammunition the Huks stole from Clark Air Base. Would you know anything about that?"

"I might," Ruiz said, "What's in it for me?"

John reached in his pocket and pulled out 600 pesos and placed it on the table in front of Ruiz. "This might buy a couple of San Miguels. What do you say?"

Ruiz reached to pick up the cash but John put his hand on top of Ruiz'. "How about some info first," he said. "Okay, I heard the Huks had the ammo hidden somewhere east of Angeles but within a couple of days were going to transport it to Orani where it is supposed to be loaded on a Banca and moved to Samar. The Huks supposedly have made a deal with Abu Sayyaf to trade the 5.56mm for 7.62x59mm ammo. The only rifles the Huks have are AK-47s provided to them by the Communist Chinese so the 5.56mm is useless to them. That's about all I know."

John removed his hand from Ruiz' and allowed him to pick up the money. About that time Murray tapped John on the leg and as John looked at him he silently mouthed the word "trouble."

As they had been transacting business with Ruiz, six men had entered the establishment and had taken seats at the tables up front. At the same time the clientele had quickly and quietly exited from both front and rear exits.

John stealthily pulled his pistol from under his shirt as did Murray and placed it in his lap under the table.

These men were obviously looking for Ruiz and meant to cause trouble.

Ruiz whispered so John could hear, "Huks."

One of the men arose and walked back to where they were sitting. He stopped and addressed Ruiz in Tagalog. "What are you doing Ruiz, talking with these Americans?" "They were asking about investing some money in sugar cane production here in the valley and wondered if I knew of any opportunities which may be available," Ruiz answered.

Since John could speak Tagalog he was following the conversation.

"And what did you tell them?" the man asked.

"I told them with the ash still falling on the area from Pinatubo it may not be a good time to invest," Ruiz said.

"That was good advice, Ruiz, but the license plates on their car tells me different. They have diplomatic plates so I know they are not businessmen, but are from the American embassy. I think you are a liar Ruiz," the man said.

John took a firmer grip on his Glock.

The man turned to walk away but suddenly wheeled with a gun is his hand and pointed it at Ruiz.

John raised his pistol from under the table and fired one shot. The man went down like a bag of rags. Now it looked like all-out war. The other five men, who had been sitting quietly, drew their guns and began firing from about twenty-five feet away. Murray, John and Ruiz hit the floor and tried to put as much furniture between the men firing and themselves. John instructed Murray to take the two on the right while he concentrated on the three on his left. The gun battle raged for about a minute or so and when the dust and smoke settled the five Huks were sprawled across the floor and furniture, mostly dead except for a few who were groaning.

Murray turned to John and asked, "Are you alright?"

"Naw, I took one in the arm," John said.

Murray looked at John's left arm. It was bleeding slightly but the round had only grazed his left forearm and made a small scratch. John holstered his weapon under his shirt and told Murray,

"Let's get the Hell out of here before there's more trouble." Meanwhile Ruiz ran out the back door while John and Murray made their way over the bodies and out onto the street. They walked quickly across to their vehicle and drove off.

Murray was driving and when they were some distance out of town John told Murray to pull off the road for a second. He exited the car and went to the back where he opened the rear door and retrieved more ammo and the first aid kit which was mounted in the rear door. He came back around, climbed in, and told Murray to get back on the N. Luzon Expressway bound for Manila. John opened the first-aid kit and treated the wound and put a gauze pad on it.

"You were one lucky son-of-a bitch, John. That could have been much worse," Murray said.

"Yeah, but it wasn't, so I'm hoping we're home free on this one. I didn't see much police action or upset citizens when we exited that place. I would bet nobody saw anything or won't report it if they did. They don't like the Huks anyway so six dead isn't going to get much play from the citizenry of Angeles."

"I guess you're right, John," Murray said.

He continued driving and soon was pulling into the embassy compound.

"Go ahead and turn-in the car, Murray. Just let me off at the annex. I'm going to the clinic and have the Doc clean this thing out and redress it," John said.

Murray dropped John off and continued to the garage while John made his way to the medical clinic in the annex. He told the Doc about the gunshot wound saying he was on a classified mission. The Doc acknowledged his fairy tale and finished dressing the wound. He told John to check back with him in a couple of days. John thanked him and departed. He found his car in the parking area and left for his quarters.

Next day, Manila, Philippines

John was in the office early. By mid-morning he had set up appointments with Colonel Turkban and Bonnie Murrano. He needed to pass on the intelligence he had gleaned from Ruiz Tarlac.

One o'clock found him entering Colonel Turkban's office.

"Good afternoon," John said as he entered.

"Good afternoon, John. Come in and have a seat." John took a seat and the Colonel continued. "What's on your mind today?" he asked.

"I wanted to bring you up to date on the ammunition reported missing from Clark Air Base," John offered. "I was in Angeles yesterday and I found out some pertinent information which I feel you might need to act upon as it relates to the security and safety of the Philippine people. An informant related to me that the Huks have the ammunition stored outside Angeles but have made a deal to trade the 5.56mm for some 7.62x39mm with the Abu Sayyaf. Word is that it will be shipped to Orani in a few days and then transshipped to Samar where the exchange will happen. I don't know how you want to handle things but I am available to do whatever is necessary to see that the Abu Sayyaf doesn't get it. I think if we can catch them during the exchange we can deprive both sides of the ammunition."

"Well that's interesting, John. I was wondering what the fuss was all about in Angeles yesterday. We heard about the shooting this morning which set off our interest but believe me we are not interested in prosecuting anyone. We are glad someone rid us of the six scum who ended up dead on the floor of the Yellow Dogshead. I see our pistol training has paid off. By the way how's your arm?"

"Thanks for the reprieve Colonel and yes the training did pay off. The arm is okay, just a little scratch, which brings me to a request for a favor," John said.

"I guess we can handle that," the Colonel responded. "What did you have in mind?"

"Colonel, my new assistant, Lieutenant Commander Murray Wright checked in. I would like to get him started on your pistol training we talked about a while back, if possible."

"John, I would be glad to have him. I have a new class starting next week. Send him over Monday. We'll begin our class at 8:30a.m. on the range."

John acknowledged, "I will do that sir. Now as far as the other issue is concerned, I have an appointment with Major Bonnie Murrano over at Constabulary headquarters later today to brief him on this same subject. I figure we are going to need all resources to catch these guys. Is there anything else I can do at present?"

"No, John. Not now. I am going to contact General Guzman who commands all Philippine military Special Forces and ask him to develop a plan to catch these bastards. When you see Bonnie ask him to call me and I will work out the details with him on coordination."

"Thanks, Colonel. I will be in touch," John said. He rose, excused himself and departed for the embassy.

Later that day found him in Bonnie Murrano's office. He retold the events of yesterday and of his meeting with Colonel Turkban. He passed the word that the Colonel wanted him to call so they could coordinate their efforts to catch these people and shutdown this operation.

Bonnie indicated to John he had some assets in Samar and would get them out snooping around to see what they could find.

John was happy with how things were progressing and went back to his office.

Two Days Later

John's phone rang and he answered on the second ring. It was Bonnie Murrano. "Good morning, John," he said. ""Here's the story from Samar. My assets report that the local Abu Sayyaf are expecting a rendezvous at the Tibiao River inlet sometime after tomorrow. My assets are shadowing them and checking as to where they are going to beach their Bancas. We need to send a force later today to Samar to intercept them. Unfortunately most of my Special Forces guys are in Mindanao but I am talking with the Americans at the MAAG in Pasay City to supply us with a couple of American Special Forces guys to help direct the ambush. I understand you have a Twin Otter at your disposal and might possibly be able to transport my attack force down to Samar. Is that correct?"

"Yeah, Bonnie, I have a plane to do that. We can carry only seventeen passengers safely so how many are we talking about?" John said.

"I have 15 men plus we will have three Special Forces from the MAAG," Bonnie replied.

"Drop one of your troopers and I will fill in for the 15th man," John said.

"Okay, that will be good, John. I plan to break up into three teams of five with one advisor for each team, so that will work out great. I plan to lead this operation so it will be just like old times for you and me," Bonnie said.

John chuckled, "Hey, just bring along a good M-16 for me and I will be happy. Let's plan on a 1600 departure time. That will put us in Iloilo at about 1730. I'll see you at the airport at 1500. We have the plane in Hangar 60 on the military side of Manila airport."

Bonnie responded, "That sounds like a plan, John. See you then."

John hung up the phone and immediately walked over to Murray's office.

"Hey old buddy, we have a flight this afternoon. Pack a bag for a couple of days. We are going to Iloilo. Plan is to depart about 1600," John said.

Murray looked puzzled. "What's on the agenda?"

John answered, "The Constabulary has an operation to intercept the ammunition we found out about the other day. Looks like it's leaving Luzon bound for Samar in a day or so. We are transporting the troops down there to participate in the operation. Will talk to you later, I have some things to do."

He turned and departed Murray's office and returned to his own. He sat down and wrote out a short memo to the ambassador outlining their trip and its projected duration. When he had it printed out he signed it and walked over to the main building where he left it with the ambassador's administrative assistant.

John and Murray had lunch in the cafeteria and afterward both departed for their quarters to pack and rendezvous at the airport at 1400.

John arrived home where Maria was still puttering around cleaning the house. John told her he would be gone for a few days and went into his bedroom to pack. He found his woodland camouflage uniforms and packed two sets for the trip. He had previously removed all identifying patches and insignia so he could not be identified as a U.S. military officer. He even removed his nametag. It would be against the status of forces agreement if he were to officially participate in any operation conducted by the Philippine forces but usually they looked the other way or had some excuse. All American forces carried loaded weapons in the event they were attacked directly so they could defend themselves. The last thing John packed was his trusty .45 caliber pistol. His motto was never leave home without it.

17

"MISSION SAMAR"

Manila Airport

By the time Bonnie Murrano and his men arrived, John and Murray had the Twin Otter pulled out of the hangar, fueled and ready to depart. They had filed a flight plan for Iloilo and were preflighting the aircraft when Bonnie pulled up in his staff car followed by a large truck with his men and equipment.

At about the same time a black Ford SUV with three American Special Forces arrived. All parties unloaded, introduced themselves and then went back to unloading their equipment and stowing it on the aircraft. Murray supervised the loading to ensure it was securely fastened down and was within the weight and balance limits of the aircraft.

When the vehicles were finished unloading, the Constabulary vehicles departed the ramp while the Americans parked their car in the adjacent parking lot. John indicated to Bonnie and the American Top Sergeant they were ready to load passengers. All-hands boarded while Murray and John manned the cockpit.

Engines were started and when they were ready, Murray called ground control for taxi instructions. Soon they were winging their way to Samar.

The flight was smooth and at altitude it was a cool 65ºF. At 50 miles out of Iloilo the flight was cleared for descent. After a visual approach and landing they taxied over to the Fixed Base Operator for parking and deplaning.

A Constabulary staff car and two trucks were there to meet them. After unloading all their equipment they were on their way to the Constabulary compound just north of the city. John, Murray and Bonnie were housed in the officer's quarters while the others were assigned berthing in enlisted quarters. Bonnie had instructed the men to meet at 0900 hours the next morning in his temporary office building which was right next door to the quarters.

After dinner Bonnie knocked on John's door and asked him if he would like to go for a walk. John indicated he would, and they both left dressed in their woodland camis. Bonnie knew one of his assets would be watching for his arrival and he had previously made arrangements for a meeting place. Bonnie and John walked down a deserted street until they reached the end where there was a small park with monkey pod trees, a lake and some benches. Bonnie motioned John to take a seat where Bonnie joined him.

They sat for a few minutes talking very quietly. Out of the woods behind them a young man appeared. He was dressed in casual clothes and sneakers, had no socks and wore a web belt. He looked like a typical, average native out for a stroll.

He sat down next to Bonnie and they began to talk quietly speaking Visayan. John was not fluent in Visayan so he could not understand the conversation. After some five minutes the young man disappeared into the night, just as quickly as he had arrived.

Bonnie sat for a second then started the conversation in English.

"My man tells me that the Abu Sayyaf sympathizers are moving out of the city and traveling towards Tibiao. He said he learned that the exchange would take place tomorrow after midnight sometime along the Tibiao River. Where exactly, he's not quite sure but indicated they have been looking at places west of the bridge where the Iloilo-Antique Road crosses the river. He says the water level in the river is so low that they will probably run their Bancas onto the sand just inside the mouth of the river where there is good cover by the trees and very few houses in the vicinity. The south side of the river appears to be the best place for their landing as there are more houses on the north side near the mouth of the river. They will need to haul food and fuel down there to refuel the Bancas in anticipation of their return trip. Let's walk back to our quarters. I need to get a good nights sleep as I think it's going to be a long day tomorrow."

John and Bonnie walked back to the quarters. "I'll see you in the morning, John. We will have a briefing at 0900 hours in the conference room next door."

They parted ways and each went to their quarters.

Next morning

After breakfast John and Murray walked over to the building next door and entered the conference room. It was just about 0900 and almost everyone was there already. John stopped to talk with the American Special Forces. He found the top Sergeant was a Green Beret and had come from Fort Bragg, North Carolina. He and his fellow Sergeants had been in country only about three months and were still getting acclimated to the country. They had been to the Army Language School and studied Tagalog but told John that these people here in Samar spoke a funny accent. John laughed and told them the people here were speaking Visayan, a completely different language. John also told them that he spoke Tagalog but there were thirtynine different dialects and this wasn't one of them.

Bonnie entered the room and asked everyone to take a seat. He began by repeating most of what he had told John the previous evening. When he was finished he asked the American Sergeant to come forward and help them plan the mission. He rose and approached the front of the room. "I am Sergeant Jones, these are my companions Sergeant Fitzpatrick and S`ergeant Tampani. I have studied the maps and terrain of the area. At the mouth of the river the country is all-flat farmland with scattered clumps of trees and on the south side there are very few houses within a half mile of the of the mouth of the river. The closest road is on the south side about a quarter of a mile from the riverbed. Depending on where the Major's assets lead us we will need to hoof it to our concealment places. I recommend we drop one team on the north side of the bridge and let them hike down the north bank to the mouth. We should park the vehicles on the road which forks off of Iloilo-Antiques Highway near the bridge after we travel about a mile down it towards Tibiao City. From there, the other two teams can maneuver down towards the mouth and (pointing to the map on the wall), take up positions here and here. If the Bancas try to escape we will then have them in crossfire. If they land on the north side of the bank we will have that covered but my best guess is they will choose the south side. I will leave the team assignments to Major Murrano."

Turning to Bonnie, "That's all I have, sir. Any questions?"

"Thank you Sergeant," Bonnie said. "Does anyone have anything they would like to add to the plan?" No one spoke up so Bonnie continued. "I will lead Team One, Lieutenant Dominquez will lead Team Two and Commander Walker will lead Team Three. Team Three will take the north side of the river while Teams One and Two will take up positions on the south side." Pointing to the map, "Team Two I want you to take positions in this clump of trees here on the river bank. You should have a clear view of what will probably take place on the beach, here just in the mouth of the river. Team One will take positions on and near the beach. After the Bancas have beached I will holler at them to surrender. John when you hear that you and your team fire a few warning shots to let them know we have them covered in all directions. If they try to escape to the sea, sink the Bancas but by no means let them escape. We will do the same. After you see we have them in custody you can trek back up to the main road and we will pick you up with the vehicles. Anyway play it as it unfolds. Any questions?" After a short pause. "I see none. Lieutenant Dominguez select your team. First Sergeant, you're with me." Bonnie selected his other three men and the remaining four would be part of John's Team Three.

Bonnie continued his briefing, "Men, we will be armed with rocket propelled grenades and M-16s. Be prepared with your grenades but only fire them to sink the Bancas if they try to escape. Let's try to capture them alive with their cargo intact. I want all headsets on channel 5. Right now we presume they will come in at night. The weather for tonight is forecast to be scattered clouds and a full moon so your ACOGs should be okay in that low light situation. Just in case we need them, each team will have one team member with night vision goggles. Are there any questions?"

While Bonnie had been briefing the troops, a person in civilian clothes had stepped into the room. As Bonnie finished he stepped up to Bonnie and whispered in his ear and quickly departed.

Bonnie spoke once again, "I have just received word that it appears the exchange will take place after midnight tonight in the area I just briefed you on. Here is the schedule. Let's gather in the armory at 2100 hours, check out our rifles and equipment then at 2200 proceed to the rendezvous point and get set up for the arrival of the Bancas. I recommend everyone get a nap this afternoon so you will be fresh when we go out this evening. If no one has anything to add you are all dismissed."

The room emptied quickly. John had been sitting in the front row and stepped up to say something to Bonnie.

"Well, Bonnie, looks like tonight's the night we catch those bastards," John said. "Looks like it will be a good mission."

"Yeah, I think so, John. The main thing is we can't let this ammo get into the wrong hands, and if we retrieve it, we will keep a lot of people from getting killed," Bonnie responded.

"You're right, old friend. I think I'm going to get some lunch and then take your suggestion and get a little shuteye," John said.

"Okay, John. See you this evening," Bonnie said.

John and Murray departed the conference room and headed for their quarters. They relaxed for about an hour then headed over to the base mess hall for a little lunch. After lunch they returned and both stretched out for a little nap. Murray had expressed his disappointment with not being included in the mission but he understood his position and knew that if something happened to John he would be expected to pilot the aircraft back to Manila. One of them had to remain safe and he drew the short straw so-to-speak.

Evening rolled around and the time was approaching for the teams to assemble at the armory. John dressed once again in his woodland camis with Murray tagging along dressed in his summer khakis without insignia. John had decided Murray could go on the mission, except he would have to remain with the vehicles while the teams were deployed to their positions along the river.

They walked over to the armory and arrived along with many other members of the teams. Inside the armorers were issuing rifles while an ammo specialist was issuing ammunition. John stepped in where he was greeted by Bonnie.

"Are you ready for this?" Bonnie asked.

"As ready as I'll ever be," John replied.

"Step over here, John, and pick out your favorite M-16. By the way they are all sighted in for 300 meters," Bonnie said.

John grabbed an M-16 from the rack and began checking it out. It had been recently cleaned and oiled. He turned on the ACOG mounted on top and put the rifle to his shoulder while pointed it at the far wall. The red dot was visible and pointed directly on the spot where he was focusing on.

He turned off the ACOG and asked the armorer if he had a spare battery. The armorer issued him one still wrapped in the shipping package.

John signed out the M-16 and then sat down and peeled the packaging off the battery then placed it in his upper right jacket pocket. If the damn battery failed while he was in the field he sure as Hell didn't want to have to search very far for the replacement. Next he stepped over to the ammunition issue and was given 100 rounds of 5.56mm ammunition. He exited the armory and sat down on the bench outside and began to load his magazines. He had been issued two-thirty round magazines and he filled them to the brim with ammo. The other two boxes of twenty rounds each he placed in his lower pants pockets. The two magazines he put into his upper pants pockets. He then pulled up his "Boonie" hat and placed it on his head. He was ready.

Bonnie called the troops together and gave then one final briefing.

"One of my assets is shadowing the Abu Sayyaf sympathizers and is on channel 5 on his headset. As soon as we are within range we will be getting up-to-date info on the situation. We are going to wait until they are in position on the beach before we move into our preplanned positions and await the Bancas. Okay everyone turn on your headsets and check in on channel 5. Once you have checked in, turn them off until we reach the debarkation point and then we will once again have a check-in."

Everyone's headset was working and the teams piled into the two waiting vehicles. Two members of each team were armed with an M-16 and A136AT4's. The other member had the night vision goggles and the team leader had a pair of binoculars and well as his M-16 and a .45 caliber pistol.

Murray climbed into the lead truck's cab and occupied the right passenger seat. He was armed only with his M9 pistol and two full magazines. At 2200 hours both trucks rolled off onto the Iloilo-Antiques Highway. It would be about a one and a half hour drive to the bridge.

18

"DEBRIEFING"

Approaching Tibiao

It was 2300 hours before the two trucks approached the Tibiao River Bridge. They crossed, turned right and pulled off at the end into a small grove of trees. Once parked, they turned off their engines and lights. That was the signal for all-hands to activate their headsets. Lieutenant Dominguez checked in first with Bonnie followed by John. Communications were loud and clear. John turned to his team and solicited a thumbs up or down of their headsets. All team members returned thumbs up.

Bonnie disembarked from truck number one and Team Three disembarked from truck two. The remaining teams remained hidden and quiet on their vehicles awaiting instructions. Bonnie walked over to John and whispered, "My asset says the bad guys are unloading their trucks on the access road about a mile from here and will soon be proceeding to the beach. He marked four of them. As soon as I receive the word they are on foot I will dispatch your team."

John acknowledged with a nod and a thumbs up. Using hand signals John directed his team to load their weapons. As soon as the weapons were loaded each team member gave John a thumbs up.

Within five minutes Bonnie looked over at John and gave him the signal to move his team out. Team Three moved across the road and down the bank and began to work its way toward the beach following the river.

Bonnie and Lieutenant Dominguez moved Team One and Two across the bridge and down the bank on the south side of the river and began their trek toward the beach. Within thirty minutes all teams were in their pre-designated positions. John picked a spot with some high grass and instructed his team to take positions there. They had crawled some 50 yards from a grove of trees to that position so as not to be spotted by the bad guys on the other side of the river.

The bad guys were in the process of building a large fire on the beach so it would be visible from the sea approach to the river mouth. This was probably the signal for the Bancas to proceed to the rendezvous. John's team was scanning the area with their night vision goggles and John had out the binoculars. John's team member reported movement behind the bad guys that he presumed to be Bonnie's Team One. It appeared everyone was in position. Now came the waiting.

Team Three members took turns scanning the area with the night vision goggles and binoculars. The full moon was very helpful. The South China Sea was particularly calm and well lit. John checked his watch. It was approaching 3:00a.m. The team member with the binoculars nudged John and pointed toward the ocean. In the far distance, probably a mile to a mile and a half, he could see a Banca approaching in their direction. They followed its progress until it loomed large while entering the mouth of the river. It was moving slowly with its engine almost at idle so as to keep the noise level low. As it approached the beach the four men there moved to meet it and assist in beaching. They could be seen shaking hands and talking but it was inaudible because John was located about 400 yards across the river from their position. John had indicated earlier that the A136AT4s rockets, if fired, would be almost at their maximum range and that their M-16s would be firing about 2" low at 400 yards.

Team Three continued to scan the South China Sea for the other Banca. At 4:24a.m. they spotted the Banca approaching the rendezvous. It entered the mouth of the river and those on the beach assisted it in beaching as close to the other Banca as possible. The ten men now on the beach all began to unload each Banca and transfer the cargo from one to the other.

Suddenly and with out warning Bonnie could be heard to shout, "Surrender your weapons and get down on the beach. You are surrounded."

Before John's team could fire a few warning shots as they had been directed, two of the men on the beach turned and began firing their AK-47s toward the shouted command to surrender. Just as quickly the other men grabbed their weapons and the firefight was on. John made a quick decision. He directed his team to concentrate on the Bancas especially the engine compartment that was located in the rear of the Bancas. His team probably fired 100 rounds into the Bancas, hopefully putting enough holes in the hull and rendering them unseaworthy and the engines unusable. They then concentrated on the men on the beach. John wished for his 300 Winchester magnum with a night scope. That would have made it easy but he had to deal with what he had, his M-16. After some 20 minutes of selected firing he told his team to ceasefire and listen. No longer could he hear the crack of the AK-47s and the report from the M-16s had diminished greatly. He observed no muzzle flashes coming from the vicinity of Team Two so he knew they had ceased fire. Once again he heard Bonnie shout for those on the beach to drop their weapons and surrender. Finally, two of the figures rose with their hands empty and over their head. The other eight men lay motionless on the beach. Team One moved forward slowly and carefully just in case there was more trouble. John observed Team One checking each position on the beach. He heard them call for Sergeant Tampani, who was a trained medic. He opened his medical kit and began to administer aid to two of those who had been shot but were still alive.

John heard Bonnie call for the vehicles to proceed down the road alongside the creek to a point closest to their position and to bring the body bags they had.

Team two had now moved down to the beach and allhands except the medic were gathering the ammunition cans in the Bancas and on the beach so they could carry it to the trucks.

John saw that his team was no longer needed on the beach and directed them to proceed back up the riverbank to the road and the rendezvous point. It took them about thirty minutes and when they reached the bridge they crossed to the south side at the road intersection and lay down in the grass to relax. Some of the team members dozed off but John and Sergeant Jones remained alert in case of more trouble.

The eastern sky was beginning to lighten before John heard the trucks' engines approaching their position. He rousted his men and they were all standing beside the road when the trucks pulled up.

Bonnie jumped down from his position and greeted John, "Nice work, John," he said. "We retrieved the ammunition and captured us a couple of terrorists. That was smart of you to disable the Bancas when the firing started. We didn't count the holes but here were plenty and the engines in them were destroyed. Put your team in truck number one. The other truck is a little crowded. We captured four of them. Two are seriously wounded and the other eight are dead. We also retrieved all the ammunition intact and the ammo cans are in truck two also."

John turned and directed his team into truck one. They turned onto the highway and were on their way back to their compound in Iloilo.

"Boy I could sure use a couple of beers right now," John thought. It had been a little stressful but nothing serious. Combat at 400 yards in the dark wasn't that bad.

The teams arrived back at the compound just after 7:00a.m. After unloading the bodies and wounded at the medical clinic they took the two other prisoners to a holding cell on the base and proceeded to the armory where they turned in their M-16s and hand held rockets. Bonnie directed all of them to get some sleep and everyone would meet again at 1800 hours in the conference room for a debriefing.

Murray dragged John back to their quarters where they crashed in their bunks for about five hours.

It was 3:00p.m. before John awoke. He lay there for a few minutes then jumped out of bed and into the shower. They had some dinner at the mess hall and then just before 1800 hours the two men walked next door to the conference room for the debriefing.

Everyone was there and took a seat. Bonnie arrived, walked to the podium and began the debriefing.

"Men, the only thing I can say is that this mission was a complete success. We achieved the objective and nobody was hurt or injured. Commander Walker could you give us your view of your teams part in this operation?"

John stood, "After we left the bridge we worked our way down toward the beach. We avoided any house that was in our path and tried not to attract any attention from the locals. As we approached our designated position, I'd say about 50 yards from it, we entered a small grove of trees. We could see the four men on the beach building a fire so we crawled the last fifty yards to a position in the high grass alongside the river. The night vision goggles were extremely helpful in spotting the Bancas approaching the river mouth and we followed them in from about a mile and a half.

After Major Murrano shouted at them to surrender we didn't have a chance to fire any warning shots as the two guys with their AK-47s, at the ready, began firing almost immediately. I made a decision that we should take out the Bancas as we were in the best position to do so and I directed the team to concentrate our fire against them. I believe we fired about 100 rounds into the Bancas. After that we used sporadic fire against the combatants and ceased fire after we observed little or no fire coming from that area of the beach. I think the plan came off as we had planned and was a great success."

"Thank you, Commander," Bonnie said. "That was a great decision to take out the Bancas to prevent them from escaping with the ammo."

Turning to Lieutenant Dominguez, "Lieutenant, is there anything you would like to add?"

"No, sir. Commander Walker has pretty much laid it out for us."

"Men, all I can add is well done. Oh, you might be interested in the bad guys and what we have found out. Of two we captured, one is probably a Huk from northern Luzon. We know that because he speaks only Tagalog while the other is a member of Abu Sayyaf from Jolo. The Huk is singing like a bird and has given us that much so far. We will continue to interrogate them and see what we can glean from them. Our Doc is performing autopsies on the dead right now and the documents we took from all of them are being studied as I speak. If no one has any further questions or anything to add you are dismissed."

John walked up to speak to Bonnie. "For planning purposes, Bonnie, what is the schedule for returning to Manila?"

"John, let's take one more day here and then depart early on Wednesday morning. How does that sound?" he asked.

"That sounds great, Bonnie. I am quite interested in what the prisoner has to say and also the identity of the other two people who were in the Banca that came in from Jolo. I'll see you in the morning for breakfast and we can plan our day," John said

"Okay, John, see you in the morning," Bonnie said.

John and Murray went back to their quarters hoping for a good night's sleep.

The next morning John met Bonnie at the mess hall for breakfast. They planned to observe some of the interrogation of the prisoners and read the report of what the interrogators had already learned.

They walked over to meet with some of the personnel conducting the interrogations. They learned that one of the men shot and killed, who was on the Banca from Jolo, was none other than Jainal Antel Sali, Jr. Early in January he had been put on the most wanted terrorist list by the FBI for crimes against American citizens in the Philippines. He had been responsible for the kidnapping of some Americans.

John commented to Bonnie that it was too bad they hadn't captured him alive, as The United States government, Rewards For Justice Program, United States Department of State, had offered a 5 million United States dollar (250,000,000 Philippine pesos) reward for Sali's capture, alive.

The interrogators had learned that the other prisoner who was being interrogated was from Jolo but was a low level member of the Abu Sayyaf. The two wounded prisoners were stable in the base dispensary and it was learned both were local sympathizers of Abu Sayyaf from Iloilo. Of the remaining five dead, two were Huks off the other Banca, one was from Jolo and two locals from Iloilo. There were very few papers recovered from the beach, Bancas or personnel killed or captured. It was going to take more than a few days to identify the dead, if ever.

Bonnie told John they should go over to the armory and see what they could learn about the weapons and ammunition they captured.

They left the interrogations building and walked over to the armory, entered and observed the armorers studying the captured weapons.

Bonnie spoke, "What have you men found out about the weapons?"

"Sir, we found out the AR-15s came from a purchase by the Kenyan Police from the Bushmaster Corporation. The M-16s were manufactured by the Colt Corporation and probably given to some country by the United States Army or State Department. We're not sure about the AK-47s because we haven't been able to tear them down and none of us has had training with them," an armorer said.

John stepped up, "Here, let me take a look."

He took one of the AKs and field stripped it down to its basic parts and placed them carefully on the workbench in an orderly fashion.

"I guess you might say I have had some training in this weapon," John said.

The armorer examined the AK and turned to Bonnie, "Looks like it was manufactured in China about ten years ago, Sir."

Speaking to the armorers, Bonnie reacted to the news, "Well, that takes care of the weapons now what about the ammunition. What can you tell us about it?"

"Sir, the 7.62X59mm came from China also. It was probably manufactured some eight or nine years ago. The 5.56mm was made by Lake City Arsenal three years ago." he said.

John chimed in, "we know the Lake City came from the United States Air Force, probably a government contract. The Chinese 7.62x59mm isn't worth a shit. Coupled with the Chinese AK-47 you probably can't shoot a three-foot group at 100 yards with it. I don't know about you Bonnie but it if were me, I wouldn't even take it back."

"What you say is true, John, but it is probably good for familiarization purposes. We can at least train our Special Forces in the use of the AK-47."

"I'll bet our American Advisors have had that kind of training and could provide it to your Special Forces. You just need to ask them," John said.

Bonnie thanked the armorers and he and John departed the armory. They discussed what they had learned as they made their way back to Bonnie's office. Not much more intel could be gleaned from the captured equipment or personnel. They would depart the next day for Manila as their job was completed.

19

"NEW ASSIGNMENT"

Manila, Philippines

John was back in the office and had made his report to headquarters on the Samar operation. He busied himself writing a summarized report of the Abu Sayyaf incidents in the Philippines as far back as he could find information.

Action against Abu Sayyaf was heating up and more action by the Philippine Armed Forces was imminent. John had reports that approximately another 100 advisors that were being sent by the MAAG to assist the Philippines in their operations. He had a report that Sergeant Jones had organized and conducted the required training of the Philippine Special Forces in the use of the AK-47.

That afternoon John received a special delivery letter in the diplomatic pouch. It was a personal note from Admiral Reynolds. He opened it and began to read. "John, I hope this note finds you well. Congratulations on your recent success operating with the Constabulary to retrieve the ammunition stolen from Clark Air Base. I know we have tasked you with gathering more information on the extent of involvement of the Abu Sayyaf, which brings me to the point of this note. I am going to assign you temporarily to the Special Activities Division (SAD). It is a division within the agency's National Clandestine Service (NCS) and is responsible for covert operations known as "special activities". Within SAD is the Special Operations Group (SOG), which is responsible for tactical paramilitary operations. I want you to operate with the MAAG and the 100 new Special Forces advisers. They will be helping the Philippine Special Forces conduct operations against Abu Sayyaf in the southern Philippines. We want you to target Khadaffy Janjalani, the current leader of Abu Sayyaf. From your research you have probably discovered he took over the leadership from his brother, Abdurajik Abubakar Janjalani who was killed on December 18, 1998, in a gun battle with the Philippine National Police on Basilan Island. You should be receiving a package via FedEx which will assist you in carrying out your task. Be well, John. Signed, Admiral Bill Reynolds."

John wondered what the package was but he could only guess at this point. He went back to his research on the Abu Sayyaf.

Manila, Two Days Later

It was after lunch and John was relaxing in his office when the mailroom clerk came by with a package addressed to John Walker. John signed for it and then closed the door of his office so he could open the package in private. The package was about four feet long, a foot wide and eighteen inches deep. He peeled off the outside wrapping and inside was a cardboard box. He opened the box and inside was a carbon fiber case. He set it down flat and opened the two catches on the side. When he opened the lid he was surprised but not shocked. Inside was a sniper rifle chambered in 300 Winchester magnum. It was built on an FN action (Fabrique Nationale), no serial number, with a Brux barrel, Picatiny rail for scope mounting and a Gissele trigger. The rifle stock was separate and was a McMillan carbon fiber stock. In a separate box was a Nightforce scope in 8.5-25-x 54mm scope. Also in the case were five twenty-round boxes of ammunition. Attached was a note listing the construction of the ammunition along with a table of sighting-in information. Now John realized what the Admiral had meant by "targeting" Khadaffy Janjalani.

John repacked his new toy and set it behind his desk. He would take it home that night to his quarters.

Manila, The Next Day

John called Lieutenant Colonel Bernie Davis, Commander of the MAAG and made an appointment that afternoon to see him. After lunch John drove over to the MAAG compound in Pasay City. He was cleared through security and drove up to the headquarters building.

As he entered the Colonel's outer office his admin clerk recognized him and told him he would let the Colonel know he was there.

LtCol Davis was a tall man about 6'-2" and a muscular individual, about what one would expect of a Green Beret. He was dressed in his Class A uniform.

Bernie Davis rose to greet John, "Good afternoon, Colonel, I'm John Walker."

"A pleasure to meet you, John," he replied. "I'm Bernie Davis and you can call me Bernie if you like. What's on you mind?"

"As military attaché at the embassy, I get a lot of requests from the State Department and I received instructions from them yesterday. They want us to take out Khadaffy Janjalani, leader of the Abu Sayyaf in the southern Philippines. The "us" eventually falls on me and that is what we need to discuss. I know from your reports back to DOD that you are going to beef up your advisors especially in Sulu. I need to blend into your unit and accompany them on one of the raids on Janjalani's camp. I would need a spotter as I do not have one available to me through the embassy," John said.

Bernie smiled, "The last part of your request is easy. I can have you work with Master Sergeant Jones. He is a trained sniper and is one of my best wind readers. He will make an excellent spotter. To fulfill your first part, I have a detachment of fifteen advisors going to Sulu next week. I have not been privy to the Philippine Army's operation scheduling but they are well overdue for a raid on the Abu Sayyaf. There was a recent attack on the town of Patikul in Sulu. Suspected Abu Sayyaf gunmen knocked on the door of a farm in Patikul and opened fire after asking residents if they were Christians or from another religion. Six people are confirmed dead, including a nine-month baby girl, and five others are seriously wounded. I also read about the bomb attack in the bar outside the gate at Camp Bautista which killed the American Security Advisor and wounded fifty Filipinos. I'm sure this put the Philippine Special Forces at Camp Bautista on high alert and they wish to retaliate. We can integrate you into our detachment and you can accompany them to Camp Bautista next week. Meanwhile let me put you in touch with Master Sergeant Jones." Bernie Davis leaned over his desk and activated his intercom, "Sergeant, get in touch with Sergeant Jones and have him report to my office ASAP."

"Roger that," the Sergeant snapped back.

Turning to John, Bernie Davis asked, "How about a glass of iced tea while we wait for Sergeant Jones?"

"That would be fine, sir. Make mine unsweetened," John replied.

Bernie waked over to a small refrigerator located in the corner of his office and retrieved a couple cold bottles of Snapple.

"Would you like a glass, John?" he asked. "No, a bottle is just fine, sir," John said.

While they were waiting the two men swapped stories of their military escapades and Bernie inquired about John's weapons training. The only part John left out was the CIA training he had received down on the farm at Williamsburg, Virginia. He had begun his high power rifle training at the Naval Air Station, Corpus Christi, Texas, with the small arms instructor there. Then there had been the Naval Emergency Ground Defense Force (NEGDF) training where everyone needed to be qualified with a rifle. Bernie was aware of their recent operation in Samar where they recovered the 5.56mm ammunition that had been stolen from Clark Air Base.

Sergeant Jones, who knocked on the Colonel's door, interrupted their story telling.

Bernie looked up and seeing who was at his door, "Come on in Sergeant. You of course know Commander Walker."

"It's good to see you again, sir," Jones offered. "Good to see you again, Sergeant, I hope you have recovered from our trip down south?" John said.

"Yes sir, I had a couple of days in Baguio for R&R. The drive up there was terrible however. The ash from Mount Pinatubo is still a problem in the valley around old Clark Air Base."

"Have a seat, Sergeant. We have a proposition for you," Bernie said.

After the Sergeant was seated Bernie continued, "The Commander here has an assignment in Sulu and he needs your help. State Department wants him to eliminate Khadaffy Janjalani, the current leader of Abu Sayyaf, but he needs a spotter and I recommended you for that assignment. What do you think?"

"I think that's great, sir. Anything we can do to eliminate that scumbag is fine with me and anything I can do to help him meet his seventy-seven virgins I will do."

"Okay, that's settled then. I will leave it to the two of you to work out the details. Plan on going south next week with the detachment we are sending to Camp Bautista," Bernie said.

John and Sergeant Jones left Bernie's office and took their discussion out into the hallway.

"Since we are going to be working so close together, Sergeant, let's forget the rank. My name is John."

"My name is Geoffrey but you can call me Jeff," he said.

"Great, now that we have that obstacle out of the way. The main thing I need to do is sight-in this new rifle I have. Can we get some time at Camp Crame rifle range?" John asked.

Jeff thought for a second, "We have a range party on Thursday, John. I'm sure we can get a little time at 500 yards to get that rifle sighted-in."

"That sounds good, Jeff. Give me a call on the time and I will meet you at the range and we can discuss this some more. I'll see you later," John said and departed the building.

When John reached his office he sat down and reworked his official report he had sent to headquarters on the Samar operation. He changed it enough so it would be acceptable for release to Colonel Turkban at the NBI. Colonel Turkban was responsible for Philippine intelligence and John wanted to keep him up to date on what intelligence he had on the Abu Sayyaf.

Later that day Jeff called and left a message that range time at Camp Crame would commence at 9:00a.m. on Thursday. John made a note in his schedule.

Murray broke John's concentration upon entering his office. "Just thought I would check in with you, John. I wanted you to know I finished a week and a half of my pistol training with Colonel Turkban. He said we would have another week and a half before we were finished."

"Well, don't keep it a secret. How are you doing?" John asked.

"The Colonel says I am an above average student but can do better if I concentrate harder. How the heck do I do that?" Murray asked.

"Let me give you a short lesson in mental discipline. Wipe your memory of all that is happening and focus on your current situation, the sights and trigger control. As far as your weapon is concerned, fire it the same every time. Remember breathe, sight alignment and trigger control. Of course you need to focus on what you are trying to hit. Just don't think about anything else. Are you using your 9mm for the course?" John wondered.

"Okay, I think I understand what you are saying. Focus is the key and yes I am using my 9 mil," Murray said. "What's going on with you?"

"I'm going out to Camp Crame on Thursday for some rifle training then next week I am going south to observe the MAAG people in action."

Looking frustrated Murray said, "What the Hell are you getting yourself into now?"

"Nothin' you want to get mixed up with, Murray, so let's just leave it at that."

"For cryin' out loud John be careful, will you?" Murray said.

"Will do, Murray. Anyway while I'm gone you should coordinate with the MAAG on their influx of new advisors. Find out their schedule and make sure they are taken care of on their arrival at Manila International Airport. Lieutenant Colonel Davis will be of great help so work with him whenever possible."

"I can handle that, John. How long do you intend to be gone?" he asked.

"I'll be leaving next week some time and should be back in about three weeks," John said. "Why don't you stop by my quarters this evening. We can have a good meal prepared by Maria and have a few drinks."

"Hey, that sounds like a great idea. I'll be over at about 6:00p.m. if that fits your schedule," Murray said

John smiled, "That fits perfectly. See you then."

Murray left John's office and John went back to finish his reports.

John arrived home sometime around 5:00p.m. Maria was just getting ready to start cooking dinner. He told her to expect one other for dinner. Maria grinned widely and acknowledged. She appeared happy that John would be entertaining that evening and went about preparing dinner.

Six o'clock rolled around and Murray knocked on the front door of John's quarters.

Thursday morning

John was already up and shaving in his bathroom when he heard Maria come in the front door. After he was dressed in his woodland camis he walked out into the kitchen where Maria was preparing breakfast.

"Magandang umaga," he said.

Maria smiled widely and replied "Magandang umaga." She was highly pleased that John would speak to her in her native language and made her all the more loyal to him.

"I think I need a big breakfast this morning, Maria. How about fixing me a small T-bone steak with two eggs over easy and some fried potatoes."

"I can do that for you," she said. "It will take a little time, however."

"That's fine, Maria. I have a few things to do before I will be ready for breakfast so take your time."

John went back to his bedroom to retrieve his sniper rifle and some ammunition. It was very compact in the case that had been provided and also had the necessary tools he would need to put it in the rifle stock and to mount the scope. After checking proper scope operation and the machine screws necessary to mount the rifle in the stock, he picked it up and carried it out into the living room and set it next to the front door. He picked up his morning paper, which Maria had placed on an end table next to his sofa, and sat down to read the Manila Times.

The headline blasted out at him, "Abu Sayyaf Hostage Released, Two Others Dead." He continued reading the story.

"Yesterday, in Mindanao, Philippine army troops conducted a rescue operation in which two of the three hostages held, Eddie DeBlasio and Filipino nurse, Macaria Taino, were killed. The remaining hostage was wounded and the hostage takers escaped.

Abu Sayyaf had conducted a raid and kidnapped about 20 people from Dos Palmas, an expensive resort in Honda Bay to the north of Puerto Princesa City on the island of Palawan, which had been considered "completely safe". The most "valuable" of the hostages were three North Americans, Eddie and Susan DeBlasio, a missionary couple, and Jason Futimo, a Columbian-American tourist who was later beheaded by Abu Sayyaf and for whom Abu Sayyaf had demanded $1 million in ransom.

The hostages and hostage-takers then returned hundreds of kilometers back across the Sulu Sea to the Abu Sayyaf territories in Mindanao.

According to author Charlie Menken the leader of the raid was Abu Sabaya. According to Susan DeBlasio, she had told her husband to identify his kidnappers to authorities as "the Osama bin Laden Group", but DeBlasio was unfamiliar with that name and stuck with "Abu Sayyaf".

After returning to Mindanao, Abu Sayyaf operatives conducted numerous raids, "including one at a coconut plantation called Golden Harvest; they took about 15 people captive there and later used bolo knives to hack the heads off two men. The number of hostages waxed and waned as some were ransomed and released, new ones were taken and others were killed."

Susan DeBlasio has been taken to the hospital at Camp Batista where her condition is reported as satisfactory.

John thought, "What savages these people can be. If ever there were terrorists these people fit that description to a tee."

Maria came into the living room and told John breakfast was ready. He set down his paper and followed her and sat down for his morning feast.

John told Maria she could take some time off as she saw fit as he would be gone later in the week and wouldn't return for about three weeks.

She smiled and told him she would look after things while he was gone.

He grabbed his rifle and stepped out into the carport and climbed into his Mercedes. He was off to Camp Crame.

On arrival at Camp Crame he stopped and parked at the Range Control office and waited for Sergeant Jones.

Jeff Jones arrived around 8:45a.m. with some of his fellow soldiers. There were 16 of them and all were Special Forces. They had M-16s along with a few scattered 7.62mm sniper rifles. Jeff was the senior NCO and organized them into teams. One would spot while the other would engage the targets. After the relay finished they would switch places and repeat the same exercise. Jeff instructed range control to raise the popup targets at 200, 300 and 500 yards. They were designed to fall over when struck by a bullet so no one needed to go down range. After a target was struck and fell over within 30 seconds it would reset itself and be ready to be engaged once again.

The firing line was just 100 yards to the west of range control so everyone took their rifles and equipment and proceeded over to their firing positions. John and Jeff set up on the high end of the range. In short order the range safety officer declared the range hot and cleared everyone to commence fire.

John had assembled his rifle and mounted the riflescope. He adjusted the elevation of the scope for 500 yards and put on the wind zero. Jeff set up behind him and asked him if he was ready to fire. John adjusted his bipod and turned his head and told Jeff he was ready.

Jeff gauged the wind and mirage and told John to put on two and a half minutes left windage and fire. John took aim at the silhouette set out to 500 yards and fired. Jeff was looking through his scope and observed the trace of the bullet to the target which went down and John turned and looked back and smiled at Jeff. "Not bad for the first shot," he said.

"That would have taken your target down but he would have survived." Jeff observed. "The hit was in the left shoulder. Come down one minute and right a minute and a half. That should center us up. Go ahead and fire the next shot."

Jeff checked the wind and mirage once again. He determined the conditions to be the same and said to John, "Take the shot, John."

That's what John was waiting for and within a couple of seconds fired his second shot. He unloaded the empty case from the chamber of his rifle and laid another round onto the loading tray.

Jeff reported a center chest hit on the silhouette. When the target popped up once again John closed the bolt and awaited the command to fire. Within a few seconds Jeff checked the wind and mirage and told John to take the shot.

John squeezed it off and the sound suppressor muffled the crack of the rifle. Target went down and Jeff reported a hit about one half inch to the right of the previous shot.

"I think two more shots should do it, John," Jeff said.

"That sounds about right, Jeff," John said.

The two men repeated the procedure two more times and the results were highly satisfactory. The group of hits were about two and a half inches with only the first shot in the left shoulder being out of the group.

I think this rifle is a keeper," John observed.

"That's one fine piece of machinery you have there, John," Jeff responded. "I'm going to check to see how my guys are doing."

"I'm going over to the rifle cleaning area and swab out the barrel," John said. "I'll see you in a few minutes."

John finished cleaning and oiling his rifle then met up with Jeff. The troops were just finishing their firing and Jeff told John they were going to the NCO club for a little lunch.

The two men met the others at the NCO club and sat down for a hamburger and a San Miguel.

20

"JUNGLE SURVIVAL"

Sulu Island

The Special Forces contingent arrived at Camp Bautista on Sulu after a long flight from Manila. Their uniforms had been sanitized of all miscellaneous insignia except for a black rank insignia on a tab, center chest and an American Flag on the right sleeve attached with Velcro.

John had no rank insignia and blended in with the other troopers easily. He and Jeff had gathered their supplies and equipment before they left Manila and were prepared to remain in the field for at least two weeks. MREs would be the main staple but living off the land would also come into play.

The mission of the Special Forces detachment was to participate in training and observing some of the Filipino Marine Special Forces, specifically their 2nd Battalion Landing Team attached to Marine Company One, currently located at Upper Kamuntayan, Talipao, Sulu, a small encampment located some 13 kilometers east south east of Camp Bautista. There was a contingent of the staff of the Philippine Armed Forces located at Camp Bautista. The Special Forces officers were to receive an intelligence briefing daily until they moved out to the advanced base. John and Jeff were invited to these briefings.

Major Ramon Vejho was the main intelligence officer who was responsible for the daily briefings. He was known to have a great network of Filipino civilians who were willing to report to him on the goings on within the Abu Sayyaf on Sulu. John was looking forward to his briefing.

The next morning all interested parties had assembled in a conference room next to the Major's office in the intelligence complex. There were coffee and donuts for the participants and John and Jeff availed themselves of the amenities. At 0935 Major Vejho and two of his intelligence analysts entered. He shook hands and introduced himself to all attendees, poured himself a quick cup of coffee, then stepped up to the podium. He introduced his two analysts and Master Sergeant Nunoz took to the microphone.

"Gentlemen, our briefing this morning will deal mainly with the activities of the Abu Sayyaf on Sulu." His assistant turned on the projector and an image of the island appeared on the screen at the front of the room. Sergeant Nunoz pointed to an area outlined by a white dashed line. He continued, "This is the province of Patikul and is the main area for Abu Sayyaf activity. Here is located the town of Patikul (he pointed out its location) where last weekend we had a raid which resulted in the deaths of 12 people. Suspected Abu Sayyaf gunmen knocked on the door of a farm in Patikul and opened fire after asking residents if they were Christians or from another religion. Twelve people are confirmed dead, including a nine-month baby girl and five others are seriously wounded. The perpetrators of this massacre retreated to an area somewhere between Patikul and our camp at Upper Kamuntayan, Talipao. It is an area of some 400 square miles and is mountainous. This area is to the east of a direct line between the town and our camp. We have not yet pinned down the exact location of their camp but we are closing in on it." The Sergeant next flashed up on the screen a picture of their leader Khadaffy Janjalani. "Just to remind you, this is Khadaffy Janjalani, the current leader of Abu Sayyaf. He does not stay at their camp but travels there about once a week to consult and plan with his Lieutenants on their tactical goals. We believe that this is the camp where they are holding the American hostage Charlie Schindler. There are approximately 45 Abu Sayyaf gunmen at this camp. We believe they are armed with only M16s/AR-15s and rocket propelled grenades. This estimate is based on the amount of food they are carrying out into the jungle each week. That completes my briefing."

Next the Major took to the podium. He thanked the Sergeant for his briefing and began his comments. "As we pinpoint this camp further as to its exact location, we are planning a raid to annihilate this cell of the Abu Sayyaf. We are hoping the raid will take place within the next two weeks and because of this I am sure you Special Forces guys will want to be there to help and observe. Gentlemen are there any questions or comments."

Captain Martin spoke, "Major that was a good briefing, thank you. In our advisory capacity we will probably be going out to Camp at Upper Kamuntayan, Talipao, to help with training and to observe the operation against Abu Sayyaf. John Walker and Jeff Jones are specialists in tracking and jungle concealment and I think if we send them out early they may be able to help pinpoint Abu Sayyaf's camp for you. Do you think you could arrange that?"

The Major smiled, "That sounds like a very workable plan. Let me check and see what we have scheduled in the way of transport going out there."

"That would be great, Major. Can we coordinate communications with them so they can keep your officers advised on what is occurring out in the field? Then if they discover the enemy's camp they can advise your troops for a quick response to take them down. Also can you give us some idea of the terrain and a general overview of any civilization out there?"

The Major turned to Sergeant Nunoz and asked, "Sergeant, can you give us an overview of the area where we suspect the enemies camp to be located?"

The Sergeant turned on his public address system and began his briefing, pointing once again to a topographical map. "In the eastern end of this target area we have rolling hills with some higher peaks and terrain. Just west of there a few civilians are located in isolated pockets. There are absolutely no roads or villages except near the coast and at Patikul. This area is dense jungle and very few trails within. It is rugged terrain with a topical rain forest and jungle cover of trees and shrubs. There are a few streams flowing through this area but be advised to stay out of them as the stream beds are soft and unstable and one could get caught in deep mud or quicksand very easily. Presently we are in the dry season but we usually have an afternoon thundershower. Does anyone have any questions?"

None were forthcoming and the Sergeant sat down.

It was a couple of days later before word filtered back to John and Jeff that transport had been arranged for them to proceed to Upper Kamuntayan, Talipao. Captain Martin briefed them on how the mission should be conducted. They were issued a satellite phone and also briefed on the communications frequencies for their headset radios. Their intercom between them was set to channel one while comm with the Filipino

Marines was set to channel two. Among the three of them they came up with a plan on how the enemy camp would be taken down.

With all their gear packed they gathered their rifles for the trip out to the jungle camp. John had his sniper rifle while Jeff was equipped with an M-14. Each also carried a Model 1911 .45 caliber pistol with two loaded magazines and a box of fifty cartridges.

Eventually they boarded a military 8x8 truck along with a few Filipino Marines for the ride out to the jungle camp. It was just over eight miles and a short 30-minute ride. The last mile was rough however; it was over a dirt road cut through the jungle and just wide enough for the truck. It reminded John of his encounter with the guerrillas on the road near Cagayan De Oro.

On arrival, they met the camp O-in-C, Captain Guayez, and his staff. After they stowed their gear in one of the Nipa Huts they had a meeting with all the Special Forces Marine officers where they outlined the plan for taking down the Abu Sayyaf camp.

Captain Guayez indicated the general area where they could expect to find the camp and stated he would support the operation to the fullest. The plan was to find the camp, coordinate the assault by the Marines and take out Khadaffy Janjalani. They set up a contact schedule for the satellite phone and double-checked the communications frequencies. When the meeting was finished they all went over to the mess tent to have some lunch and meet more of the assigned Marines.

John and Jeff decided they would set out early the next morning on their mission. They spent the rest of the day checking their gear and reducing the weight wherever possible.

After a good night's sleep and breakfast they put on their backpacks and slung their rifles, said farewell to the base O-in-C and headed north into the jungle. They followed the 1500' contour line for a short distance then began the climb up the mountain, which was 2575'. John talked it over with Jeff and they decided to take up a position just below the crest of the mountain. This would offer them better cover but allow for a wide scan of the area to the northwest through northeast. Within a couple of hours they had reached their goal and took up a position facing north just below the crest on the North Slope. Their position was in a grove of hardwoods but allowed them a wide scan of the area. After getting comfortable Jeff took out his binoculars and began the first two-hour scan. John would relieve him and they would swap every two hours so as to keep fresh eyes on the area. The main thing they were trying to observe was a large amount of smoke from campfires used for cooking. An encampment of 40 or so people would usually produce a couple of those kinds of fires.

It was into the 5th hour of scanning when John spotted newly lit fires about a half-mile down the mountain. He called Jeff's attention to the spot and Jeff also began to watch through his binoculars. It was approaching the dinner hour and they agreed someone was stoking the fires in preparation for cooking the evening meal.

A couple of MREs were opened and the two men settled down for a cold dinner. They didn't light a fire, to keep their position from being discovered. As they were eating, John noticed a grove of papaya trees about 100 yards to their right. He pointed them out to Jeff and they decided after dinner as dusk was approaching they would harvest a couple for breakfast the next morning. It was an easy task and soon they were back in their camp where they settled down for the night.

The next morning while Jeff scanned the area of interest John prepared the papaya. After consuming the papaya they both had a piece of dark chocolate enriched with sugar. This would help keep their energy level high. They saw the fires were once again stoked and it looked like preparation for breakfast at the camp they were watching. After breakfast the duo began stealthily inching their way toward the smoke. It was all-downhill which was easy but they stuck to the densest cover to remain hidden from the enemy. All the while they were moving they were looking for a place to camp with a good view of the enemy and good cover. Jeff stopped to survey the situation. He whispered to John that he believed there was a cave about 50 yards to their west. It was a very steep slope so they carefully moved laterally west towards that spot. As they approached the spot they could see there was an opening in the rocks. It looked almost ideal. The opening was about six feet across by three feet high. There were shrubs, bushes and a couple of fallen trees covering the opening. Jeff crawled in first followed by John. Jeff pulled out his flashlight from his pack and turned it on. He could see the cave went back into the rock at least fifteen feet and opened up to a height of about six feet. The floor of the cave was mainly level and Jeff could feel the air rising in the cave which meant there was an opening in the overhead. John scouted the view. The first thing he saw was that every man was armed with what appeared to be an M-16 or AR-15. He could see about half of the camp and had a good view of the area between a line of two rows of tents. There was a huge fire pit between the rows and appeared to be where the cooking was taking place. He estimated the distance to the fire pit to be 560 yards. What an ideal position he thought. They would be out of the weather and the observation and possible firing position was between a flat fallen log and another leaning against the rocks leaving an opening in between. The shrubs and brush also helped conceal their position.

Jeff came out from the back of the cave and sat down next to John.

"Well how does it look?" Jeff asked.

"I think it is going to work out just fine, Jeff. We have good concealment, a good firing position to take the shot and we'll be out of the rain if we have any. How do things look back there?" he asked.

"It looks like we have a good place to start a small fire. The cave has an air vent out the top so if we keep the smoke down we can get away with it. I think we will need to boil water and maybe cook a little meat if we kill an animal or two. Let's stow our gear and I'll take the first shift observing. Meanwhile you can assemble your rifle and scope and get ready to take the shot when the time comes. I'll set up my spotting scope and begin to get some idea of the mirage and wind from this position."

They stowed their gear and John broke out his rifle, scope and ammunition. Jeff had his M-14 at the ready with a loaded 20 round magazine and another 20 round magazine at his position. He set up his spotting scope and began to study the elements of wind, mirage and light. He agreed with John, the distance to the fire pit was 560 yards and about 200 feet lower in elevation.

John checked the action, set the elevation on his scope for 600 yards and laid the rifle in firing position across the log. Next he lay down a poncho to mark his firing position and keep him off the damp ground. He then set out a small canvas waterproof bag with five rounds of 300 Winchester magnum ammunition. He kept the remainder of the ammo in his knapsack.

They talked over what they were going to do after firing the shot. If they weren't discovered they would just hunker down and wait until the firefight with the Marines heated up and then they would hike back up the mountain and back to base camp. Meanwhile Jeff made a snare out of a strand of parachute cord and set it up on the fallen log. He put it high enough where it was out of their view. He hoped to catch a squirrel or two. When he finished he relieved John watching the camp and John set about checking out the satellite radio. Time was approaching 6:00p.m. which was their scheduled contact time with base camp. While maintaining cover, John set up the small parabolic dish just above the cave entrance with a direct line of sight to the satellite. He adjusted it with instructions from Jeff who was monitoring signal strength. When it maxed out he affixed its position.

Jeff picked up his headset and set it to channel one. John also turned his set on and switched to channel one.

At exactly 6:00p.m. Jeff called, "Wolf Pack, this is Stray Wolf One, over." They both listened intently for a minute, no answer. Jeff called again, "Wolf Pack, this is Stray Wolf One over."

Within a few seconds, "Stray Wolf One this is Wolf Pack Leader. Send your traffic."

"Roger Wolf Pack Leader. Believe enemy base located. No eyes on target at this time. Team condition A1. Will keep you advised of any changes, out." Jeff reported.

"Stray Wolf One. Copied all. Wolf Pack Leader out."

John shut down the satellite phone and retrieved the antenna.

"We need to pinpoint the camp on our map, Jeff. When we confirm this is the place and have eyes on our target we will be ready to send it to Wolf Pack."

"Yeah, we can do that tomorrow when we have some light in this place. I think when it gets really dark and things are quiet in their camp we can go out and get some coconuts. I saw a couple of palm trees off to the right of us about 200 yards. I also think there are some plantains in that general vicinity so we can scout it out. Let's check out our night vision stuff so we can be ready in an hour or so," Jeff said.

"I'll take my empty back pack with us, Jeff. We can probably fill it with some needed dry limbs to light a fire with when we get back. We should also scout for a water source while we are out. We are going to need some in a day or two.

"Sounds good, John," Jeff answered.

In about a half hour the men carefully crawled out of the cave and headed east along the contour of the mountain. They were very quiet and listened for any noise in the jungle as they crawled. Within a half hour they had reached the grove of palm trees and with hand signals Jeff won the toss to climb the tree and harvest a couple of coconuts. He was very nimble and within minutes three coconuts fell to the ground. He rejoined John and they decided to travel a little further for the plantains. Since they were off the steep slope they could walk so they moved carefully until they came across the plantain trees and harvested about a dozen plantains. There was some light in the jungle but the night vision equipment made it very easy to maneuver. On the way back to pick up the coconuts they collected some small branches, put them in John's backpack and continued. They picked up the coconuts and started back to the cave. As the terrain steepened the began to crawl and made the last 100 yards easily on their bellies.

Back in the cave they unloaded their harvest and settled down for the night. They would process their cache in the morning.

21

"JUDGEMENT DAY"

The routine in the cave had been pretty boring the past four days. It was mostly eat, sleep, stand two hour watch off and on and boil water. In the evening it was collect more food.

Currently Jeff was standing watch while John was back in the cave boiling and purifying water. It was approaching eleven o'clock and the temperature was beginning to rise above 75ºF.

Suddenly Jeff came alive and was very animated. He was gesturing to John to come and see what was happening in the camp below. John lay down on his poncho, picked up his rifle and stared through the scope. He had it set at the highest power so the image from the camp was very clear. Jeff quietly told John to observe what was happening in the jungle on the north side of the camp where the trail came into camp. John quickly picked up on the images and saw a party of about five men working their way up the trail into camp. They obviously were not military because of the way they were dressed.

The Abu Sayyaf on the north end of the camp spotted them first and they began to shout and what looked like cheering. Soon almost all residents of the camp were gathered and were excited with the arrival of these men. Obviously they were some of the leaders who were coming to visit.

The first one to greet them appeared to be the person who had been leading the camp in their daily activities and directing a few others who in turn directed the rest of the men.

John pulled a picture out of his shirt pocket and laid it on the ground between Jeff and himself. They discussed what they were seeing and soon agreed that the man dressed in Khaki pants and the Barong Tagalog with the close-cropped black hair was indeed Khadaffy Janjalani. Now both of them watched his every movement very closely. A couple of men took his backpack and stowed it in the first tent on the north end of the row of tents on the right. No one else's gear was stowed in that tent so this added credence as to how important this man was to the operation. A small contingent of the men brought campstools and set them down in front of the leaders' tent. It looked as though they were going to have a planning session.

While Jeff continued to watch, John took out a pencil and pad and began drafting a message. They would send it by satellite phone at their normal contact time of 6:00p.m. John wanted to make sure they got it right so he left nothing to chance. When he finished he handed it to Jeff and took up a position watching the camp while Jeff perused and edited the message.

The message read: "The package has arrived. Positive identification. Execute Operation Broken Spear. Objective located coordinate WC-9,000,000/125,000. Trails out all northwest through northeast. Recommend positions east and west of escape trails. We will handle all stragglers headed south. Will signal execute order on channel two. Expect one fired round prior to execute order. Will monitor your progress on channel two. Enemy estimated to be approximately 40 in camp at this time. Firepower consist of M-16/AR-15 platform. No larger caliber weapons noted. Some sidearms observed probably squad leaders and above. Advise when in communications range."

Jeff turned to John and gave him a thumbs up, "Looks good, John."

John nodded okay and gestured for him to put it in his pocket for the time being and until they made phone contact. "Take a break, Jeff. I'll take the watch for the next two hours. You might finish purifying the water. I didn't quite get it done before."

Jeff gave John thumbs up and went toward the back of the cave.

They rotated the watch every two hours and soon the hour was approaching 6:00p.m. John retrieved the antenna for the satellite phone and stood up placing it in the position they had determined was best for transmitting and receiving. Jeff monitored the signal strength meter and when John was pointed directly at the satellite he tapped John on the leg to let him know. John locked the antenna in place and Jeff picked up the phone.

At exactly 6:00p.m. Jeff called, "Wolf Pack, this is Stray Wolf One, over." They both listened intently for a minute, no answer. Jeff called again, "Wolf Pack, this is Stray Wolf One, over."

Within a few seconds, "Stray Wolf One this is Wolf Pack Leader. Send your traffic."

Jeff read the message they had written out earlier. Wolf Pack acknowledged with, "Copied Stray Wolf One. Message understood. Next contact will be on channel two, out."

It was a fitful sleep for both men. After completing the satellite phone call they had carefully packed their gear except for rifles, scopes and ammo. They knew a rapid withdrawal might be advisable after the shooting started. Both were wide-awake shortly before dawn. When the light was good enough to scan the camp below Jeff was already on his scope studying the personnel movements and the wind and mirage conditions. John finished his breakfast, which consisted of piece of fruitcake and a cup of tea he had made from the boiling water on the fire back in the cave. When he finished he took over spotting on the scope and Jeff had his breakfast. They had turned on their communications radios and set them to channel two. They checked their headsets to ensure both were in working order.

The sun had broken through the jungle and the temperature was on a steady increase. About 7:30a.m. their radio crackled to life on their headsets and Captain Gauyez called, "Stray Wolf One this is Wolf Leader. How do you read, over?"

Jeff responded, "Wolf Leader this is One. Read you loud and clear. State your position, over."

"Roger One. Approaching target coordinates, Leader and Stray Wolf Two will be in position within two zero minutes. What is your status, over?"

"Leader this is One. No eyes of target at this time. Will advise eyes on target, over," Jeff reported.

"Roger One. Break. Stray Wolf Two report your status, over," Guayez said.

"Leader, this is Stray Wolf Two estimate in position in one five minutes, over."

"Roger, Two, advise when in position," Guayez said.

John and Jeff knew that Captain Guayez and his men were taking a position slightly north and west of the trails leading out of camp while Lieutenant Mendez was taking a position north and east of the trails leading out of camp. This way they could catch the terrorists in a crossfire if they tried to flee the camp. It was unlikely they would try to flee south up the mountain where John and Jeff were because it would be more difficult and with less cover for them.

John shifted to his rifle and Jeff continued to spot through his scope.

He commented to John, "Looks like the mirage is light and the wind now is worth one minute left."

"Yeah, that's about what I estimated, Jeff. I doublechecked my elevation and I am set on 600 yards. That puts me just past the end tent where our target is staying. Since it is a downhill shot I am allowing two inches high for the impact of the bullet. If the shot is a little more than 600 yards I will be centered up on the impact point."

"That sounds good, John. I have my elevation set for 550 yards, one in the chamber and a full magazine of 20 rounds. I also have an extra 20 rounds in my spare magazine," Jeff said.

"I have nine extra rounds in my waterproof bag just in case we need to take care of stragglers coming our way after the shooting starts," John said.

After the conversation the two men were absolutely quiet. They were focused on the job at hand and were waiting for their target to appear. Down in camp there was some activity. The fires for cooking had been started and a few people were performing their morning ritual. Some were carrying their rifles while other were still too sleepy to know exactly what was going on. Two men had left camp with water camels and appeared to be headed for the stream about fifty yards north of camp to retrieve water. The Filipino Marines had skirted the camp far enough away that their chance of being discovered prematurely was practically nil. The two men returned with their water camels filled so that threat was avoided. Jeff next spotted their target exiting his tent where he began to speak with other members of the camp. John spotted him at the same time Jeff did. The target sat at one of the makeshift tables they had in camp. More of the camp personnel began to show up and soon they were all engaged in eating breakfast and talking with each other.

"Stray Wolf One, this is Wolf Leader. We are in position, over," Captain Guayez reported.

Immediately following, "Stray Wolf One this is Stray Wolf Two. We are in position, over," Lieutenant Mendez reported.

Jeff keyed his mic, "Roger Wolf Leader. Break. Roger Stray Wolf Two. Stand by for instructions."

Jeff looked over at John and asked, "Are you a go?"

Glancing up from his riflescope he answered, "Roger that," and gave Jeff a thumbs up.

Jeff gave John one more wind check, "Wind value still one left," he said.

John took a couple of long, deep breaths and squeezed the trigger. The bullet burst out of the barrel and with Jeff still on the scope, watched the trace of the bullet as it sped towards its intended target. It struck with a tremendous force and Khadaffy Janjalani crumpled into a heap where he sat at the table. Jeff could see blood squirting everywhere. He keyed his mic, "Execute, execute, execute," he said.

Down in camp things were chaotic. People were running in every direction. Some were trying to find their clothes; others grabbed their rifles and ammunition. The leaders couldn't seem to get things organized. About that time a few men had run into the jungle to find cover from the sniper. That's when all Hell broke loose. They were engaged by Captain Guayez' men. Rifle fire could be heard throughout the area. This seemed to focus the attention of everyone in camp. Many moved out while others took cover from the direction of the engagement.

John had backed off his rifle so the suppressor could not been seen from the camp. He still had a shot if needed. Jeff activated his radio and advised the attacking force what he was seeing and possible targets who might be moving their way.

Captain Guayez directed Lieutenant Mendez and his men to begin moving toward camp. This would put the defenders in a crossfire and force them to move towards Captain Guayez' position.

As soon as the camp defenders began taking fire from Lieutenant Mendez they started to retreat.

Suddenly a tall, large Caucasian male exited one of the tents and began running up the mountain in John and Jeff's direction.

"Don't shoot, John," Jeff said. "He is Caucasian and has no weapon that I can see. It may be the hostage, Charlie Schindler, who we heard about who has been a prisoner of the Abu Sayyaf for seven months. Let him go. We can track him later if we need too."

It appeared that two of the armed men from the camp had observed Schindler escape and began to follow him. When they reached a spot in Jeff's line of sight at about 300 yards, he nudged John and said, "Take the one on the right."

John nodded and fired. At the same time Jeff's M-14 barked and both pursuers fell in their tracks. Charlie Schindler turned and observed what had happened but had no idea where the shots came from. He proceeded up the mountain and passed within 100 yards east of their position.

From their position the two men could see Lieutenant Mendez and his men advancing slowly on the camp. There were a few stragglers who were soon eliminated and Mendez' men were clearing the tents. Jeff keyed his mic, "Stray Wolf Two, this is One. All clear on this end. Camp appears to be empty."

Mendez answered, "Roger Stray Wolf One. All secure here." He set up a position with his men on the north side of camp in case any of the enemy tried to infiltrate back into the area. Rifle fire could still be heard from Captain Guayez and his men but it was less and less as each minute went by.

Radio silence was broken as Captain Guayez reported, "All opposition neutralized. We are proceeding towards camp to join up with Stray Wolf Two. Cease fire unless eyes on enemy confirmed."

"Stray Wolf Two. Copied all. Break. All-hands ceasefire."

Jeff once again keyed his mic, "Wolf Leader, this is Stray Wolf One. We have one confirmed Caucasian prisoner who escaped during the firefight. He is headed in the general direction of our camp at Upper Kamuntayan, Talipao. We will track him and attempt a rendezvous."

"Stray Wolf One, this is Wolf Leader. You are cleared as requested. Will see you back at camp."

"Roger that. Stray Wolf One, out," Jeff answered.

John and Jeff crawled out of their cave and after attaching their backpacks and slinging their rifles began tracking the camp's escaped prisoner.

22

"HOME AT LAST"

Sulu Island

Jeff picked up the trail of the escaped prisoner heading up the mountain. Rather than climb up the mountain they elected to follow the 1500' contour of the mountain, which made walking easier and quicker. They soon reached a point on the south side of the mountain and began searching once again for the trail of the escaped prisoner.

After about a half mile of tracking John spotted the escaped prisoner. He was about 150 yards ahead of them headed south. John called out his name.

"Hey, Charlie. Stop. We are Americans."

He had disappeared into the thicker jungle and did not respond. They proceeded a couple of 100 yards further and John called out again, "Charlie, stop. We are Americans. We want to help you," he said.

About 50 yards ahead, Charlie Schindler stepped out of the jungle and just stood there exhausted looking at the two men approaching him.

By the time they reached him John had already pulled out his canteen of water. "Looks like you could use a drink of water," John said as he offered Charlie his canteen.

Charlie took the canteen and began to drink. Jeff motioned for him to sit down as he and John found a nearby log to sit on. "I'm Jeff Jones and this is John Walker," he said. "We presume you are Charlie Schindler?"

Charlie finished drinking from the canteen, "Yeah, I'm Charlie alright and who are you guys with?"

"We're military advisors to the Philippine Marines. We were observing and supporting their operation against the Abu Sayyaf camp you were held in. When the shooting started we saw you escape and we thought we had better catch up with you and help direct you to civilization," Jeff offered.

"I'm glad you did. I was about exhausted and not sure who was following me. I've been held prisoner for about seven months. They fed me pretty good but only once a day and I didn't get to walk around much so I am way out of shape physically. How far until we reach civilization?" Charlie asked.

John had been looking at his map and checking his hand held GPS unit. "We're about a mile and a half from camp. If you're rested, let's get on the trail. We should be there in about two hours."

John took the lead and headed off toward camp at Upper Kamuntayan, Talipao. After about an hour and a half they were approaching camp. They could hear the noises and smell food cooking. Suddenly they were out in the open and walking into camp. They were greeted by some of the Marines who asked them many questions about the operation they had just been involved in.

After unloading their gear and rifles into their assigned Nipa Hut they came back out and sat at one of the dinner tables. They had a long drink of fresh water and tried to answer all the questions.

It was only 2:35 in the afternoon and they expected Captain Guayez and his men to be returning soon. The Marines settled Charlie into one of the Nipa huts and then fed him a big lunch of meat stew and native vegetables. He probably drank two pitchers of fresh limeade the Marines had prepared from the fresh limes they had gathered.

It was late afternoon before Captain Guayez returned with his men. He reported all Abu Sayyaf resistance killed including Khadaffy Janjalani. The Marines had sustained only one wounded, not serious, and had stayed and buried all the Abu Sayyaf at the camp. Lieutenant Mendez had his photographer capture a picture of Khadaffy Janjalani that would prove to his superiors he was dead. Captain Guayez scheduled a debriefing for seven o'clock that evening.

Captain Guayez walked over to where Charlie Schindler was sitting and introduced himself.

"You must be exhausted after seven months in captivity," Captain Guayez said.

"Yes I am, Captain, but am happy to be free," he said "Get rested. We'll get you back to civilization in a day or two."

At seven, the officers and senior enlisted men gathered in front of Captain Guayez' quarters for the debriefing. John and Jeff were present as well as Captain Martin from the Special Forces advisors.

Captain Guayez called on Lieutenant Mendez to give his summary of what he and his men had done and what they observed. When he finished he went around the assembled group and offered anyone a chance to present what they had done and observed. Jeff spoke for himself and John and presented his observations. The only thing he omitted was the fact that they had taken out Khadaffy Janjalani. Lieutenant Mendez had reported that he presumed one of his men fired the fatal shot and Jeff left it at that. After all-hands had spoken, Captain Guayez summarized the operation. He thanked everyone for a job well done including the planning, which was superb. The coordination was excellent and probably was responsible for no lives lost in the operation. He reiterated the fact that they had taken out high leadership of the Abu Sayyaf and weakened their enemy to a great extent. He was pleased with all-hands performance. When all questions were answered he called the debriefing to an end and told everyone to get a good night's sleep. John and Jeff had their first hot meal in a week and, after the stressful situation of hiding and standing watch they both settled down to a good night's sound sleep.

In the morning, after breakfast, Captain Guayez informed Jeff, John and Charlie that a truck would be coming in around noon the next day and returning later in the day to Camp Bautista and they were welcome to take it if they desired. Jeff talked it over with John and indicated that since his job was done he would rejoin his fellow Special Forces guys and stay there to help do some more training. John told Jeff how much he appreciated what he had done and would be sorry to leave him but he understood the situation. John needed to get back to Manila and his job at the embassy. He told Charlie he would escort him back to Camp Bautista.

Next morning

The M-series 2-1/2 ton GMC truck could be heard for almost a mile before it reached camp. It brought needed supplies and some returning Marines from Camp Bautista.

John had been up early, packed his gear and rifle and finished breakfast well before 8:00a.m. He was ready to return to civilization. Jeff peeked out of the Nipa hut and John walked over. They spoke for some 15 minutes after which they said their goodbyes. The truck was already loading when John walked over and placed his gear and rifle up on the bed and climbed aboard. It was a bumpy ride and the heat and humidity was oppressive rumbling through the jungle on the narrow road. When they reached the highway they sped on at about 40 miles per hour and the fresh air spilling through the bed of the truck was refreshing. Within 30 minutes they reached Camp Bautista and John was dropped off at the Bachelor Officers Quarters where he was assigned a room. He threw his gear into the room and headed off to the staff headquarters where he made contact with the transportation officer. He inquired about a flight which might be going to Manila. The clerk in the office told them that a Fokker F-27 would be arriving that evening and departing tomorrow morning. He booked a seat for John for the 9:00a.m. departure. He thanked the transport officer and his staff and headed for his quarters and an afternoon siesta.

The base was a forward operating base with few amenities so after he awakened he put on his camis and headed for the mess hall and a hearty meal. It would be army food but plenty of it.

When he finished dinner John walked over to the tent set up for a club, walked in and ordered a San Miguel beer. It went down smooth and was nice and cold. He hadn't had a drink in about three weeks and the beer did him just fine. After two more he headed back to his quarters and a good night's sleep.

After finishing breakfast the next morning John grabbed his gear and rifle and headed down to air operations to await the departure of his flight back to Manila.

After boarding and takeoff the pilot climbed to altitude and headed northeast towards Manila. He leveled off at 20,000' where the outside temperature was about 20°F. The pilot cooled the aircraft and John relished in it. He hadn't been cool or in air conditioning for about a month and it felt great. He really enjoyed the four-hour flight but was glad to be back in Manila after such a long time. He flagged a taxi that he directed to take him to his quarters in Pasay City.

When they arrived at the housing compound, the guard recognized John and waved the taxi through the gate. At his quarters John paid the taxi driver and turned and carried his gear into his quarters. Maria was there, greeted him and inquired if he had a good trip. John answered in the affirmative and indicated he was going to shower and take a short nap. Maria brought a large glass of limeade and placed it on his night table in his bedroom. She went back to the kitchen and started to prepare dinner. She knew John would be starved when he awoke from his nap.

The dinner hour was approaching when John finally awakened. He had slept for two hours and felt really refreshed. After dressing in his usual casual shorts and golf shirt he walked out into the kitchen. As he passed through his quarters he noted that the house was in great shape and in good order. Maria was well worth what he was paying her.

As he entered the kitchen Maria spoke, "Did you have a good sleep?"

"You bet, Maria. It's great to sleep in one's own bed for a change," John said.

"That's good, sir, I hope you are home now for some time," she answered. "Why don't you relax in the den for a while. I will fix you your favorite drink and then I will have dinner for you at the regular time."

"Good suggestion, Maria. However I think I will work in my office for a while," John noted.

John went to his office, which was only an alcove he had converted into an office. Meanwhile Maria fixed John a Captain Morgan and coke.

John booted up his Mac and soon logged onto his email account at Earthlink. He had some three hundred emails to wade through and began that task. He had been offline for over three weeks and the backlog was terrific. He read each email subject line and if it had no relevance he deleted without reading. Some were from family members, which he read, then drafted and sent a reply. Some emails were embassy related so he read them and decided he would answer them when he went to the office the next day. One email in particular caught his attention. It was an intelligence summary of the operation Broken Spear originating from the Philippine military and forwarded to him by the MAAG. He smiled as he read it. The Philippine high command had taken full credit for all phases of the operation and never mentioned the U.S. Special Forces. That was great and as it was supposed to be. They rated the operation a great success and a blow to the leadership on Abu Sayyaf with the death of Khadaffy Janjalani.

Maria stuck her head in his office and told him dinner was ready to be served. He acknowledged and told her he would just be a minute. John logged off his account and shutdown his MAC. He stepped out into the great room of his quarters. The living room and dining room were actually one room divided by a rattan planter. Maria motioned for him to be seated at the dining room table where she had set one place for dinner. John noted the place setting with the best tableware, a placemat and a white linen napkin. The napkin was traditional for a Navyman as even on board ship officers dined with a white linen napkin.

John sat down and Maria served him his dinner. It consisted of beef lumpia, white rice and almonds and a large plate of various fruits Maria had prepared. For dessert, there was a dish of Flan with a sauce. This was a dish brought to the Philippines by the Spanish and passed down in Maria's family for a couple of generations. For a drink John had taught Maria how to make good southern iced tea and that was what he usually drank for dinner.

After dinner John moved into the living room and sat down in his casual lazyboy and turned on the television. Maria finished her chores and after the kitchen was spotless and dishes put away she came into the living room and asked John is he needed her anymore that evening. John told Maria to take off and go home and enjoy her family for a change.

John focused his attention on the television. A recent addition to the lineup was a news station called Fox News. It was right up John's alley, fair and balanced reporting. He watched for a while and during an advertising break went to the program schedule. On one of the HBO channels he came across a movie called "The Final Countdown." It was about an aircraft carrier whisked back in time just about the time of the attack on Pearl Harbor by the Japanese at the start of World War II. Just the thing to relax to, watching carrier operations. John missed that part of his career but didn't publicly admit it. The movie turned out to be great entertainment and it was over by about 11:30p.m. John turned off the television and went to bed.

23

"DESPERATE ENEMY"

U.S. Embassy, Manila

John had been back to work for about a week working with the station chief at the embassy to finish his report of the Sulu operation and help update their Abu Sayyaf file. From all their intel sources it was painting a picture of a more active and militant organization. Their forays were moving ever closer to Manila and Philippine intel organizations were becoming more concerned. In the past year they had taken many hostages and killed many villagers. The carnage they were leaving in their trail was frightening.

Word had leaked through Colonel Turkban's NBI that the new leader of Abu Sayyaf was Radullan Sahiron. During his past he had trained with Al Qaeda, had met Osama Bin Laden and been given six million dollars to help support his group.

Captain Guayez had collected some DNA from the body of Khadaffy Janjalani before he buried him in the jungle of Sulu and it had been shipped to the NBI in Manila for testing and verification. The NBI had gathered DNA from Khadaffy Janjalani's brother Abdurajik Abubakar Janjalani who had been killed in a gun battle with the Philippine National Police on Basilan Island. This would give everyone concerned final proof of Janjalani's death.

In the meantime John and Murray were flying their Twin Otter just to keep current. The Ambassador didn't like to travel much so flight time was scarce. One morning his assistant called and indicated that the Ambassador was planning a vacation in Baguio and wanted to fly there. John wrote down all the particulars and briefed Murray. They would depart Manila

International on Wednesday morning next week at 9:00a.m. and return the Ambassador to Manila the following Saturday by 4:00p.m. This made John extremely happy as he was starved for flight time.

John kept busy visiting all his intelligence contacts in the area and sending in his weekly report to headquarters. The trip to Baguio went smoothly and both pilots relished in finally getting some flight time not to mention a brief vacation in a beautiful location. Thursday morning rolled around when the office phone rang. John answered. It was Bonnie Murrano on the line.

"John this is Bonnie."

"Good morning, Bonnie. What's up?" he asked.

"I need a big favor. Our detachment in San Jose is currently under attack by an unknown force of about forty men, probably Abu Sayyaf. It has been confirmed directly by telephone but here's the problem. The Philippine military has no transport aircraft available at this time to get my Special Forces to San Jose. That's where I was hoping you could help?'

"We can probably get the Otter in the air in an hour, Bonnie, but I can carry only sixteen passengers. Is that going to be enough to repel the attackers?" John asked.

"I have twenty men stationed at Camp Winston Sibley Ebersole, which is our headquarters and about 700 yards off the end of the runway at San Jose. We believe the airfield has been evacuated and the tower unmanned but they can't have taken control of the airfield with the small force they have. We should be okay to land there. Sixteen men will have to do the job. Also I recommend you arm yourself for this trip."

"Okay, Bonnie, it's a go. I'll meet you at our hangar in about 45 minutes."

"Great, John. I will owe you big time for this one," Bonnie said.

"All right, see you in 45 minutes," John responded.

He hung up the phone and hollered for Murray, who was out in the hall at the moment talking with the station chief.

"Murray, we have an emergency in San Jose. It looks like a terrorist attack and the Philippine Constabulary has asked us to transport some troops over there. Take-off will be in 55 minutes. Where is your AR-15?" he asked.

"I have it in the safe in my office," Murray responded. "Okay, retrieve your weapon and some ammo and head over to the airport. I am going to call and have the plane pulled out and refueled. When you get there preflight and man the pilot's seat and be ready for departure. I am going to my quarters on the way to the airport and get my AR-15 and 300 Win Mag. I'll meet you there as soon as possible. Major Murrano will be arriving with 15 of his special forces for transport. They can stow their gear in the aisles because they are going to need to be ready to engage the enemy as soon as they step off the plane. I will brief you further when we get airborne. Get moving and I will see you there," John said.

"I got it, John. I'm on my way. See you at the airport."

With that, Murray departed for his office. John grabbed his keys to the Mercedes and headed out the door. He drove as quickly as possible to his quarters in Pasay City trying not to exceed the speed limit but getting there as rapidly as possible. When he arrived at the compound he was waved through the gate and proceeded to his quarters. Maria was there already and he quickly told her he wouldn't be home for dinner. He snatched up his AR and 300 Win Mag with plenty of ammo and headed out the door. The drive to the airport would take another 20 minutes and was a hectic drive. He didn't remember much of it, however, as his mind was racing on all the things he needed to cover and do before they touched down in San Jose. He arrived at the hangar, parked his car, and quickly took his rifles and headed for the aircraft. As he rounded the corner of the hangar and spotted the aircraft on the flight line, he saw two Philippine Constabulary vehicles pulled up to the plane and people off-loading gear and boarding the plane. Bonnie Murrano was supervising the operation as John approached.

"We're just about loaded, John. I talked with Lieutenant Commander Wright and he is supervising the interior placement of our gear."

"Okay, Bonnie, that's great. Let me talk with Murray a minute and I will come back and help you get loaded," John said.

He turned, climbed the forward, starboard stairway and boarded the aircraft. Inside Murray was supervising the loading. John caught his attention. "Murray, man the cockpit and read the checklist and be ready to start engines as soon as I can get there. I will assist Major Murrano in the loading."

Murray acknowledged, walked forward and manned the pilot's seat. He began executing the checklist as John had requested.

John turned to Bonnie with instructions.

"Bonnie, start getting your men seated beginning with the forward row. Once they are seated place their gear alongside them in the aisle. Let's load from the rear stairway. Have them save you a seat in the first row so you can talk to us in the cockpit while we are enroute."

Bonnie acknowledged and following John's instruction began loading his men and gear. They had all the standard gear for a Special Forces platoon and loaded it very quickly. The last man on the rear seat closed the rear aircraft door and retracted the stairway. The two vehicles parked by the aircraft retired to the edge of the flight line out of the way of any aircraft. Bonnie boarded the forward stairway, retrieved it and locked the door before taking his seat. John was already in the copilot's seat and Murray was cranking the starboard engine.

They completed all checklists while taxiing and as they approached the duty runway Manila tower cleared them for takeoff. As they departed the control zone from the airport, John told Murray to level the aircraft at 1500'. He had decided to go visual flight rules so they headed out of Manila Bay over Corregidor. They stayed over the water and headed for the North shore of Mindoro and then down the west coast to San Jose.

After they leveled off Bonnie stuck his head in the cockpit. He showed John his tactical map of the airport complex and surrounding area. The only runway was oriented east west with an elementary school about 500' off the east end of the runway. Southeast of that position was Camp Winston Sibley Ebersole. A large cemetery was oriented just west of the base with a lake in between. Bubog Road ran just north of the base in an east-west direction with the beach and South China Sea on the south side. Bonnie's intelligence personnel told him that the airport was abandoned and the attackers had shot up the place pretty bad. They had also observed three attackers heading towards the elementary school just off the end of the runway while six or more had established a command post in the cemetery. The remaining attack force was in the process of putting siege to the base. Knowing their modus operandi it was surmised that the intention was to kidnap 20 or so kids from the school and take them back to their base. The attack was not intended to capture the base but only to pin down the opposition until they could make their escape in Bancas they had beached just off the cemetery,

When they took off it was about 9:30a.m. and the flight would take about 40 minutes. The kids came to school about 8:30a.m. so it wouldn't be long before the terrorists would try to move them towards the beach. Bonnie traced the route he thought they might take, keeping to the streets rather than through the woods and backyards. If they arrived there before the terrorists moved the kids then he would send a team to the school. If they took only 20 kids no telling what they might do to the others including the teachers left behind. Bonnie wanted to prevent a bloodbath of school kids. He told John they would have a briefing when they landed and proceed from there. His 1st Sergeant at the base would be up on channel one and they could glean more intelligence from him once they landed. John acknowledged and Bonnie took his seat. He instructed his men to lock and load and be ready to fight once they exited the aircraft.

As the aircraft traveled down the west coast of Mindoro John briefed Murray of their approach and landing procedures. Murray descended to 100' over the water. As soon as John called airport in sight Murray retarded the power levers to flight idle and slowed the aircraft from 180 knots to 95 knots. As the passed 120 knots John lowered full flaps and completed the checklist. As they passed over the beach Murray further slowed to 85 knots. He was now descending and lined up with the duty runway one zero. He touched down 30' past the end of the runway and John cut the engines. Things were now very quiet as they wanted to be as stealthy as possible. At three thousand feet down the runway Murray took the angle taxiway and headed towards the terminal. He braked slightly and brought the aircraft to a stop heading east about 10' from the building. The rear exits were shielded from view from the east so the Special Forces could enter the terminal unseen by the terrorists if possible. Bonnie's men were out of the aircraft within three minutes followed quickly by Bonnie, Murray and John.

The group assembled inside the terminal and moved quickly to get the operation underway. Everyone had donned their headset and a radio check was done all around. Bonnie then made a call to his 1st Sergeant.

"Ebersole Base, this is Cobra. How do you read? Over," he transmitted.

Within seconds the radio crackled to life, "This is Ebersole Base. Read you loud and clear, Cobra. Sergeant Garcia here, sir," he said.

"Roger, Base. Loud and clear. Status report. Over."

"Cobra, Base, taking intermittent fire from north and south. Estimated casualties six enemy dead. Six enemy observed in the cemetery. Approximately 15 comprise the group to the north with 10 in the force to the south. There are three enemy reported holding children at the school"

"Roger, Base. Stand by for instructions," Bonnie said.

Bonnie turned to those assembled. "Sergeant Perez, your call sign is Habu. Take two men and clear the elementary school on the east end on the runway. Reports have three bad guys holding the children and probably waiting for instructions to move some of them to their Bancas on the beach. I recommend you move across the runway and use the road on the far side. There is plenty of cover and down here," pointing to his map, "There are plenty of houses. We are going to move into position behind the enemy and will wait until we hear you firing before we open fire or else that you have captured them. Use channel one for comm. If you have no questions, move out."

"John, Murray, your call sign is Boa. Murray, team up with my man in the terminal and provide security for the plane. If anyone approaches it, shoot to kill. John I want you to work your way over to the Sea Coast Hotel. See if you can find a view of the cemetery preferably a second floor position. This will give you a 600-yard shot if you get a chance. Do not fire until I give the word. We're all on channel one for this operation. Any questions?"

"No questions, Bonnie," John said.

"Sergeant Ocampo, your squad is with me. We will work our way down this hedgerow and take up a position in these woods on the north side of this pond. The enemy is entrenched on the north side of Bubog Road and this will put our position about 60 yards behind them. Sergeant Guiang, your call sign will be Python. I want you to take up a position on the west side of this road just short of the cemetery. We know there are about ten hostiles on the beach side of Camp Ebersole. As soon as the shooting starts all hostiles will try to move to a position towards the beach. Sergeant Guiang, I want you to booby-trap their Bancas so there is no escape by sea. When that is done have those men return to your position. Once the firing starts you can move forward to the edge of the cemetery. If there are no questions, let's move out." Bonnie ordered.

The men led by Major Murrano moved out the main entrance of the terminal on the south side. He took Sergeant Ocampo's squad along with John and began working his way down the hedgerow on the airport. As they passed the Sea Coast Hotel John peeled off and entered through the back door.

Meanwhile Sergeant Guiang took his squad and moved down the beach to his designated position.

John made his way to the front desk. Everyone was hunkered down in their rooms but John managed to find the desk clerk hidden in an office behind the front desk. He told him he needed an empty room on the east side of the building on the second floor. The desk clerk scanned his occupancy chart and gave him a key to the room on the southeast corner of the second floor. This was a perfect spot John found out as he entered the room. He had already rigged his rifle with the scope and bipod as he found a desk which he moved over in front of the glass door to the balcony. He swung open the doors and after placing his rifle on the desk found a comfortable chair and took up his firing position. He reported in on channel one, "Cobra this is Boa. In position, over."

The radio earpiece came to life, "Boa, this is Cobra. Copied," Bonnie said.

John scanned the cemetery through his scope. He could see four hostiles clearly and noted the position of the other two. He checked his distance. It was about 612 yards to the hostiles' position. Next he checked for any signs of the wind. It appeared to be blowing off the water from the south and judging by the smoke from people cooking he estimated the windage to be two minutes right. He checked his sights and cranked the elevation up to reflect 610 yards and put on two minutes of right wind. John took a couple of deep breaths and relaxed.

Habu team had worked their was down to the school. They entered the building from the northeast corner and began searching for the children. They searched the rooms toward the center courtyard and spied the three hostiles lining up about twenty of the kids. The teachers and remaining children were cowered in the corner against the far building. Habu queried his men and asked if they had a shot. They nodded affirmative. Habu leader told one to take the man on the right and the other the man on the left. He would take out the man in the middle. As soon as they had them in their sights he gave the fire order. The three rifles cracked at the same time and the three hostiles crumpled where they stood. Habu reported to Cobra that the school was secure and all hostages safe. Sergeant Perez moved quickly into the courtyard and found the school principal. He assured him they were friendly and the school was now safe. He recommended they all return to their classrooms and stay out of sight for a while and until the Special Forces could stabilize the situation. Once that was complete he and his men moved out to find Cobra.

Meantime Sergeant Guiang had moved into position and, after spotting the enemies Bancas on the beach, sent two of his men to booby trap their boats. They rigged them with grenades to go off once the engines were cranked. His two men returned and reported in with Cobra.

"Cobra, this is Python. In position. All hands at the ready. Enemy transportation is hot, over," he said.

"Roger Python, you are cleared to move forward to your next position. You are cleared to engage."

Bonnie then called base. "Ebersole Base, this is Cobra. Let's lay down some fire and get their attention."

"Roger. Cobra. Copied," Base replied.

The troops at Ebersole Base began firing three round bursts at the hostiles on both side of the base. Once their attention was directed towards the base Bonnie gave the order for his men to begin firing. Now he had them in a crossfire and he knew they would try to move west and south towards the cemetery.

John took the firing as a sign to commence fire. He took out the four-exposed enemy in the cemetery and waited for the other two to begin moving so he could get a clear shot.

The hostiles were now in full retreat. On the north side they were trying to cross the road towards the cemetery. Some were successful but Bonnie's men were taking a toll on the enemy. On the south the hostiles were making their way towards the Bancas. Sergeant Guiang and his men were taking heavy fire from the east and from the two remaining enemy in the cemetery. John still couldn't get a clear shot at the two in the cemetery so he kept watching the scene unfolding. Six hostiles on the beach were pushing their Banca out into the South China Sea. They were taking fire but managed to board it and one of them was seen cranking the engine. Suddenly the Banca went up in a brilliant ball of fire with pieces and bodies flying as high as thirty feet in the air. The remnants of the Banca burned to the waterline and what remained sank in about ten feet of water.

Sergeant Guiang turned his attention to the two hostiles remaining in the cemetery while Bonnie Murrano was advancing on the hostiles to the north as they continued to retreat towards the cemetery and the beach.

John counted seven enemy working their way through the cemetery and called Sergeant Guiang.

"Python, this is Boa. You have seven more hostiles moving your way through the cemetery," John said.

"Roger, Boa. Copied."

John took aim at one of the enemy and fired. He dropped and fell over a headstone. This seemed to slow the progress of the remaining six and Bonnie's men we moving closer toward them. They were now trapped in a deadly crossfire with no escape. The pond on their east left them no escape route and Sergeant Guiang had them trapped from advancing towards the beach. The battle lasted only a few more minutes before all the hostiles were killed. Bonnie had called out for them to surrender but more bullets flying only answered this. John had a front row seat for all the action and called Bonnie.

"Cobra, this is Boa. Over," he said.

"Go ahead Boa," replied Bonnie.

"Roger, Cobra. It appears that all hostiles are out of action. I see no movement in the cemetery at this time."

"Roger that Boa. Break. Python move into the cemetery from your end we will do the same from here," Bonnie said.

John could see that all hostiles were dead and accounted for so he broke down his position and went down to the lobby. Here assured the hotel staff and guests that the danger was over and exited the front entrance to join up with Bonnie and his men.

On the base Sergeant Garcia had been listening on channel one to all the action and hearing that everyone had ceased firing he took his jeep and an 8 ton truck and moved out from the base towards the cemetery. Once out on Bubog Road he had his men pick up the enemy bodies and stack them in the truck. He turned his jeep down the side road between the cemetery and the hotel and stopped about halfway where he saw Major Murrano and his men checking the fallen enemy.

He walked over, saluted and reported.

"Sir, Sergeant Garcia, we are in the process of picking up the bodies of the enemy and will take them back to the base for processing and burial," he said.

"Well done Sergeant," Bonnie answered. "Did you sustain any casualties?"

"No, sir. Just a couple of wounded from debris when they fired a few RPGs at us."

"That's great, Garcia. When you finish here there are three bodies over in the school you need to pick up. We'll help you with the bodies here. Once we get them to the base we need to search them for documents and any other information, which may help us identify them and with whom they are working. I suspect they are all Abu Sayyaf."

Garcia nodded that he understood and called the base for another truck to proceed to the school.

Bonnie directed Sergeant Guiang to have his men unrig the booby-trapped Bancas so no one else would get hurt. Once they finished processing the cemetery and surrounding area they would go over to the base and finish the mission with a debriefing.

John joined up with Bonnie and his men still working the cemetery.

"Nice shooting, John. Thanks for the support," Bonnie said. "We will be just a few more minutes then we are moving out to the base. Feel free to join us for the debriefing or you can go back to the airport if you wish."

"Thanks, Bonnie. If you don't need me for the debriefing I think I'll find me a San Miguel and cool down. I really need a beer."

"Sounds like a plan, John. We'll see you back at the plane in about an hour and a half.

John made his way back to the Sea Coast Hotel and entered through the front door. The desk clerk recognized him and greeted him, thanking him for what he had just done. John asked where he could get a San Miguel beer. The clerk went over to the bar off the lobby and returned with three San Miguels in hand. John opened one and stuck the other two in his backpack. He thanked the clerk, exited via the back door and headed for the airport terminal. When he arrived he found Murray and the Philippine Constabulary Corporal still alert and guarding the aircraft.

Murray walked toward John, "I guess you took out all the bad guys," he said. "Nothing stirred here. Things have been as quiet as a church-mouse."

As John handed each of them a beer, "the operation went smoothly, almost as planned. Bonnie is mopping up things at the base and should be here in about another hour. Did you observe any bad guys?" he asked.

"Naw, just a few locals crossed the runway probably going to work. We saw they didn't have any weapons so there was no threat," Murray responded.

"I'm going out to the aircraft and stow my gear. Should only take a minute. Let's see if we can get something to eat," John said.

The terminal was beginning to return to normal. Airline workers were returning as well as local people beginning to fill the streets doing their daily chores. The Philippine Corporal asked some of the locals where they could get some food. In a short time some locals arrived with some vegetable lumpia and fresh cooked wild rice. John returned from the aircraft and the three of them sat down at an outdoor picnic table and feasted on food set before them by the local people. Many came by and thanked them for what had just occurred.

Murray piped up, "Are the kids at the school okay?" he asked.

John looked up from his food, "I believe everyone is okay, Murray. Sergeant Perez had reported three hostiles neutralized and no children injured."

"That's good news. I presume all the other hostiles were neutralized?" he said.

"Let me put it this way. I didn't see any enemies who could be interrogated," John said.

They finished their lunch and went out to the aircraft where they prepared it for the return trip to Manila.

Bonnie and his men showed up about an hour later, loaded their gear and boarded the aircraft.

The tower was once again manned and power had been restored so John called them for takeoff instructions. The tower's reply was winds light and variable, your choice of runway, no atmospheric pressure available since power had not been restored to their instruments.

John told Murray and the tower they would depart on runway 28. Murray taxied out and down to the end of 28, swung the aircraft around to runway heading and added the power for takeoff. The flight was VFR and uneventful back to Manila.

On arrival in Manila there were Constabulary vehicles to meet them. Bonnie off-loaded his men and their gear and sent them on their way back to base. He was met by one of the vehicles on the ramp that turned out to be his commanding officer. Bonnie joined his CO in the car and debriefed him on the operation.

Meanwhile John and Murray secured the aircraft and instructed the company personnel responsible for managing the aircraft what was needed to be completed before it was hangared and readied for their next flight.

Bonnie exited the CO's vehicle, saluted and walked toward Murray and John.

"John, I can't begin to thank you enough for what you did for us today. We saved a lot of lives in San Jose because we were able to stop the enemy. Turns out as we expected they were Abu Sayyaf based out of Palawan. Stop by my office later in the week and I will fill you in on what we glean from all the captured material," Bonnie said.

They shook hands. "I'll see you then," John said.

Bonnie boarded his staff car and drove off.

24

"RELAXATION"

Saturday Morning

The weather was beautiful as John and Murray flew their Twin Otter across the valley passing Angeles headed for Baguio. They were both old hands at flying into the airport there as they had been doing it for five years. The Ambassador wanted to be back in Manila for lunch so they planned to depart Baguio around 10:00a.m. After landing John walked into the small terminal building and called the consulate. He told the duty officer they were at the airport waiting for the Ambassador.

Ambassador Ross arrived just before ten. John greeted him and helped him settle into his seat in the cabin. The Ambassador's assistants took care of the luggage and also boarded the aircraft for the flight to Manila. It was a two-hour flight and their scheduled arrival time was 12:06p.m.

John climbed into the copilot's seat and read the checklist. They were soon winging their way down the canyon and headed towards Manila. On arrival at the flight line at Manila International the Ambassador stuck his head into the cockpit and began a conversation with John. He thanked him for the nice flight and indicated he would like to have a conference with him on Monday. John responded he would be there at 9:00a.m. sharp. An embassy staff car arrived, loaded all the luggage and departed with the Ambassador and his staff.

John and Murray secured the aircraft and took the rest of the day off. Murray returned to his quarters. He had plans for later in the day to attend the Jai-Ali palace for dinner and watch the matches.

John drove his Mercedes out to Lake Taal. He was meeting his old friend Ramon Guing. Ramon knew a family that had a motorized Banca.

They would take it out to Taal Volcano Island and hike from the pier up to Crater Lake.

John turned off the Southern Tagalog Arterial Road onto Balete Road. This would take him over the mountains and down to the shore of Lake Taal. Ramon would also be driving his Mercedes and told John to turn north where he would see his car parked out front of the family home where they would catch the Banca out to the island.

John passed the Balete Family Farm and came to a T-intersection as he approached the lake. He turned north and within a half mile saw Ramon's silver Mercedes parked just as he had described. John pulled in along side and parked. The family children were the first to run out and greet him. They were all excited to have a visitor and all talked at the same time asking John questions in Tagalog. He asked them all their names and chatted with them for a few minutes as he made his way to the front porch of the house. He looked up and saw Ramon and his host in the doorway of the house waiting to greet him.

Ramon greeted John and then introduced him to Emilio Encito. Emilio shook his hand and, speaking Tagalog, invited him into the house. This is going to be an interesting day, John thought. The whole day would be spent conversing in Tagalog. He had changed into his hiking clothes before he left the airport and all he needed to do now was change his shoes. Emilio introduced his wife Monica who offered them a drink. They were a poor family but with much pride, and entertaining guests the proper way was a family tradition. John asked if they had any San Miguel beer. Monica went into the kitchen and soon returned with a San Miguel for both Ramon and John. As they savored their refreshments discussion of their upcoming trip to Taal Island dominated the conversation. Emilio told them he had a field of corn planted on the island as just one of the areas he planted for raising crops.

The men finished their beer and Emilio led them down to the water's edge where they boarded the Banca for the trip. The lake was deep blue in color, calm, flat and very beautiful. The wind was slight, less than 3 miles per hour. The trip took about twenty minutes and soon they tied up to a pier on the east side of the island. Emilio went with them as they began their hike around the island. He acted as their tour guide filling them with stories about almost every geological feature they were seeing. It was an easy climb to the edge of Crater Lake. This was the caldera of the now dormant volcano. John brought his camera and he knew the pictures he was shooting would be breathtaking.

In his description of Lake Taal and its activities Emilio told of the recent attack on tourists along the cliffs of the north shore. He told of the Abu Sayyaf attack on a tourist bus along the cliff road with five people killed and eleven wounded. Many more were saved because the Constabulary police responded so quickly. They had driven off the attackers who retreated to the north and west and only with luck some reached their Bancas on the shore of Manila Bay and made their escape. The attack had put a crimp in the tourist trade and fewer busses were making the trip to Lake Taal. John made some mental notes and would put them in his next report to headquarters.

The hike was refreshing but darkness was approaching so the party made their way back to the pier and the Banca for the trip back across the lake. They timed it just right as they arrived back at the Encito homestead at sunset.

As they entered the home, Monica greeted them with a San Miguel and some meat filled lumpia for snacks. She had prepared an evening meal for them consisting of a dish which was similar to a seafood quiche.

The kids had hiked over to Balaban Bay where they caught the saltwater crabs. Their chickens had provided the eggs and Monica's garden the veggies. It was a tasty dish and was enjoyed by all. Dinner was by candlelight and propane lantern. There was no electricity on this road with no home lighting and a propane stove for cooking. John marveled at this family's survival in such a harsh environment.

After an evening spent drinking San Miguel and discussing the Encito family life, Emilio showed Ramon and John to their sleeping quarters for the night. It was sleeping bags on the screened porch overlooking the lake. It was quite comfortable and John slept quite soundly. As the sun came up the children were the first awake and were playing in the yard. With no running water John put on his swimming suit and went down to the lake to get refreshed. The children crowded around him asking questions and talking endlessly. He really enjoyed the children. They all sat on the beach while he swam in the lake. This young blond-headed American intrigued them. John's hair was so blond it was almost white and the children asked him how old he was because of the color of his hair. When he finished his swim, he and the children made their way back to the house. Monica was already in the kitchen cooking breakfast. It would be eggs, bacon and some toast for breakfast. John greeted Emilio and Ramon who were sitting in the kitchen having a cup of coffee. John joined them and Monica served breakfast. It was a pleasant and relaxing time for John.

After breakfast he dressed, packed his small canvas handbag in his car and said his goodbyes to everyone. He was soon on his way back to Pasay City.

Monday morning

The aroma of baking coming from the kitchen awakened John. It was Maria. She had arrived around six and started baking some pecan rolls for breakfast, which she knew John liked very much. She also made a small pot of coffee and was already drinking a cup when John walked into the kitchen.

"You're up early, Mr. Walker," Maria said.

"Your baking smelled so good it woke me up," John responded.

"I thought you would enjoy my pecan rolls this morning since you hadn't had any, with your being gone so much," she said.

"You're right, Maria, I have been gone too much as of late. It will be nice to be home for a few days. Maybe you can spoil me with some of your good cooking. I don't have any trips planned for a couple of weeks," John said.

"I will do my best to have some good meals for you while your home. Here, sit down and enjoy your breakfast. "I will retrieve the morning Times for you," she said.

John sat at the dining room table and buttered a couple of Maria's pecan rolls. They were still warm and the butter melted quickly. Maria put the Manila Times on the table next to John's plate so he could peruse it as he wished. It was always printed in English so he had no trouble reading the latest news.

John finished his breakfast then took a shower and dressed for the office. Today he wore one of his fancy Barong Tagalog's. After all it was the tropics and a suit or uniform was called for only on formal evening occasions. He told Maria he would be home after five and she should plan on him being home for dinner. She acknowledged and he walked out the door, cranked up his Mercedes and drove off to the embassy.

It was approaching the eight o'clock hour and would give him some time to catch up on the intelligence postings. The chief of station and his assistant always put out a daily bulletin for the Ambassador on the local Philippine intelligence. John read through the last couple of days' summaries and noted that the Abu Sayyaf had been quite busy and bold in perpetrating their attacks closer to Manila. There had been an incident on the cliffs of Lake Taal and another in the town of Los Baños. He made a mental note to follow up on that raid with Colonel Turkban. As nine o'clock approached he walked over to the main embassy building for his meeting with the Ambassador.

As he walked into the outer office, the Ambassador's administrative assistant told him to go right in, that the Ambassador was waiting for him. John walked into the Ambassador's office where he was greeted.

"Come in, John, and have a seat. I was expecting you. Would you like a cup of coffee or something?" he asked.

"Yes, sir, thank you. A cup of coffee will do just fine," John said.

Ambassador Ross buzzed his assistant and asked for two cups of coffee. She soon returned with a sterling silver coffee server, sugar, cream and a couple of china coffee cups. She turned to John and asked how he would like his coffee. He responded black with one sugar. She poured one cup and placed it on the small table next to John's chair. She next poured the Ambassador's coffee and placed it on a linen doily on his desk.

"Thank you, Jane," the Ambassador said. Turning to John he began, "John, I wanted to brief you personally on what is occurring in the next couple of weeks so you can plan accordingly. Are you familiar with 'The Association of Southeast Asian Nations' (ASEAN)?" He asked.

"Yes, sir, I am," John responded.

"Good. There will be a summit of ASEAN held in Cebu on January 11th through the 14th. All heads of state and foreign ministers of ASEAN will be attending. Also Joseph McCarthy, our Secretary of State, will be speaking at the summit. He will be arriving in Manila on the 9th and plans to travel with the Philippine president to Cebu on the 10th. I am also going with the president to Cebu and that is where you come in. I need you to pre-position our aircraft in Mactan before the conference so the Secretary and I can return to Manila on the 12th. The President is staying for the entire summit but Secretary McCarthy wants to depart Manila on the 13th. The Secretary's security team also expressed concern about possible breeches in security while we are in Cebu so I need you to investigate that angle and also be prepared to pre-position the aircraft. Do you think that is doable?"

John thought for a minute then responded, "Yes, sir. I believe we can do that. From what you are telling me we will need to be in Mactan before the heads of state begin arriving at Mactan. I will plan on getting the Otter in Mactan on the 9th. As for the other matter, I can check all my local sources and see if there is any intelligence bubbling up about Cebu and the ASEAN summit. It appears we have about ten days to get things lined up, sir. I have no further questions but I will get back to you as quickly as possible."

The Ambassador came around his desk and shook John's hand, "I knew I could count on you, John. Thanks." John shook the Ambassadors hand, "You're welcome, sir, I will get back to you as quickly as possible."

John turned, left the Ambassador's office and went back to the annex. As he was entering his office, he ran into Murray. He invited Murray into his office, sat him down and briefed him on what the Ambassador had just laid out for them to do.

John had about ten days to find out what was happening, intelligence wise, but New Years Eve and the holiday on the first would cut into finding people at work. He would just have to work more efficiently with the workdays he would have.

New Years Eve was an enjoyable time. He had been invited by his friend, Commander Ramon Cruz of the Philippine Navy, to a party at his house in Pasay City. John had arrived about 8:00p.m. and was met by Ramon and his wife Julia. The party was in full swing as he stepped down into Ramon's sunken living room and was introduced to Ramon's four brothers. They were all drinking San Miguel so he acquired one and joined in the festivities. The discussion centered mostly on their jobs and hunting activities. The language was mostly in English with a little Tagalog thrown in along the way. John stepped away for a few minutes to sample the native Philippine food set out for all to partake of that evening.

It was quite different from Monica Encitos dinner menu. Obviously very much more expensive food but her's was every bit as tasty.

John rejoined the gathering in the sunken living room and noticed the brothers were all laughing, obviously at Ramon and Julia who were the brunt of the laughter.

"What's going on?" John asked.

Phillipe answered, "Watch Ramon and Julia for a few minutes and then I will tell you why we are laughing."

The brothers and John stood drinking their San Miguel all the time watching Ramon and Julia.

Ramon's parents were sitting on the left side on the room in a raised area with a wrought iron railing on two sides. Likewise on the opposite side of the room was a similar enclosure where Julia's parents were sitting. During the course of events Ramon would talk with his parents then come down into the sunken living room where he would converse with Julia. Julia would turn and go over to her parents and speak to them, after which she would return to the center of the sunken living room and once again engage Ramon in conversation. He would then start the cycle all over again with his parents. This went on for a couple of cycles before Philippe said to John, "Have you figured it out yet, John?" he asked.

"No, Philippe, "he responded. "Tell me what's happening."

Philippe began, "Our parents are asking Julia's parents a question. Our parents speak only Tagalog so Ramon speaks to them in Tagalog. Then he comes down and relays the question in English to Julia who speaks only English and Spanish. Ramon does not speak Spanish so the common language between Ramon and Julia is English. After that Julia goes up to speak to her parents who speak only Spanish. Julia's parents answer the question in Spanish and then Julia comes back to the center of the living room and speaks to Ramon in English. Ramon then goes back to our parents to relay the reply to the question in Tagalog. It is really funny to watch as the parents will keep it up all evening and when it's over Ramon and Julia will be exhausted and can't enjoy their own party what with all the translating they have to do during the evening."

"That is hilarious," John said.

The brothers just kept on laughing, as this was part of their entertainment. Soon the party in full swing and John mingled with the other guests. About 11:00p.m. all the guests and family sat down at the huge dining room table for a New Years Eve meal. It lasted for almost an hour until midnight approached when champagne was poured into the glasses at the table and Ramon stood and made a New Years toast. As midnight stroked twelve on the clock everyone wished each other a "Happy New Year." The party wound down around 3:00a.m. John said "Good Morning" and departed for his quarters. When he arrived home he crawled into bed and slept for a good eight hours. It was noon before he arose, showered, dressed and walked out into the kitchen.

Maria was fixing him a Bloody Mary, which would keep him going for the rest of the day.

25

"SUCCESS PERSONIFIED"

Manila, U.S. Embassy, January 2nd

It was back to work after a couple of days and John's first contact was a phone call to Colonel Turkban's office. He spoke briefly with the Colonel who invited him for lunch at NBI Headquarters.

John finished some of his paperwork and around 11:30a.m. he made his way over to the NBI's headquarters. When John was invited to enter the Colonel's office he looked up from the paperwork on his desk and spoke to John.

"Come in, John. I am just finishing up some work here and we can go over to my private dining room for lunch. I hope you are hungry as my chef has prepared us a special lunch."

It was a special seafood salad stuffed with fresh crabmeat from the South China Sea and a lentil soup made with fresh cooked native brown rice. Limeade was the preferred drink.

John and the Colonel sat down and the soup was served. John began the conversation.

"Colonel, my Secretary of State and Ambassador are both attending the ASEAN conference in Cebu on the 11th and I am inquiring on their behalf about any new intelligence you might have which could effect security at the conference. I believe they are traveling with your President to the conference and plan to attend the reception scheduled for the evening of the 10th."

The Colonel smiled and said, "Funny you should bring that up. I was just thinking of you and the intelligence situation." He then layed the bomb on John. "We have information that the Abu Sayyaf may be planning a car bomb attack on the conference. When or where is impossible to ascertain at this time but we are in the planning stages for imposing heavy security around the conference. As part of that, we have concluded that the President would be most vulnerable on the drive from the airport at Mactan to the conference center in Cebu city. We are trying to arrange for a helicopter to land in the city but it is impossible. There are no buildings with Helo pads and no open spaces either. Also transporting a helo to the Mactan airport is proving to be almost unrealistic. Our Air Force's C-130 is down for wing spar cracks and won't be available until February 1st. The range of the helicopters, which are available, is so limited that we can't fly one down to Cebu. We have the President's armored SUV being flown to Mactan on a Southern Air Transport but a helo is out of the question. It looks like we are saddled with a ground transport situation. Of course we will have all the streets blocked off on the route from the airport to the conference center but we will need quite a few snipers for rooftop support of the operation and right now we are a few short of covering all the possible sites. I hear you are a pretty good sniper yourself, John. The secret report we received from the Jolo operation says you did a fine job. Would you like to help us with this operation?" he asked.

I would be delighted to be of service, sir. Anything I can do to protect your President, my Secretary of State and Ambassador," John replied. "The outline of your basic plan sounds good, sir. I look forward to hearing the details of the security plan."

"We are looking at the details and assignments for all personnel who will be involved. I have talked with Major Murrano and he has six of his men assigned to our task force for this operation."

John smiled, "That sounds great sir, Major Murrano and his men are very capable. For your information I am flying our Twin Otter to Mactan on the 9th so we are in position before all the heads of state and their entourages begin arriving. I have room in my plane for any passengers you would like to transport on that date but I am limited to sixteen people. Also who will be my contact in Mactan?"

"I am planning a briefing here at NBI headquarters on the 7th for all concerned with this operation. If we find holes in it then that will give us time to patch it and make a correction to the plan. In this operation we need to be perfect."

"I agree 100%, sir. I look forward to working with all concerned," John said. "Keep me informed and I will be here on the 7th for the briefing."

The two men had finished their lunch, John excused himself and was back on the road for the embassy.

Next day

John made an appointment with the ambassador and briefed him on the situation. The ambassador was alarmed but remained calm and stated he would need to inform the Secretary of State of the situation. John left the communications with the State Department to the Ambassador. That was one can of worms he didn't need in his life.

January 7th

It was only four days since John had spoken to Colonel Turkban and time to countdown was moving very quickly. John arrived at the NBI's briefing room as all interested parties were gathering. There were many NBI agents, Filipino Marine Special Forces, three U.S. Army Special Forces from the MAAG, Major Murrano and four of his best snipers along with John. The Chief of Staff of the Philippine Marine Corp was also present with some of his staff along with the Commanding General of the Philippine Constabulary.

Colonel Turkban entered the room, took the dais and everyone took their seats. Colonel Turkban introduced his operations planning chief who took the podium and began the briefing. Security at the Mactan Airport was the responsibility of the Philippine Constabulary and would be increased with more men and bomb-sniffing dogs. They would also handle streets closures along with the Cebu City Police Department. The motorcade would consist of six black armored Nissan SUVs and Colonel Turkban's men would be assigned to them. One SUV would have President Aguinaldo, Secretary of State Joe McCarthy and Ambassador Ross embarked and the other five would be security personnel. All snipers would be assigned to a key building along the route of travel to take out any suspicious person or vehicle determined to be a threat to the motorcade. Radios would be issued to all participating personnel with channels to be assigned to each separate unit and supervisors being on the same channel so as to be able to communicate with each other. Sniper building assignments would be forthcoming the day of arrival of the VIPs motorcade. Once the VIPs were at the conference the NBI would assume all responsibility for their safety. The day before the conference ends another briefing will be held in Cebu City to ensure the VIPs safety back to the airport for the return flight to Manila.

After the operations officer finished his briefing some questions were asked and answered and minor adjustments were made to the plan. There were no major objections or changes required. It was a thoroughly thought out plan of action and all concerned agreed to it.

The meeting adjourned and John returned to his duties at the embassy. He briefed the Ambassador who in turn sent a message to the State Department relating the particulars of the security operation. State Security signed off and it was a go for the operation.

January 9th

John manned his plane at the Manila airport before the arrival of the Secretary of State. Colonel Turkban had asked John to carry twelve of his men to Mactan. They arrived, boarded the plane and soon John and Murray had their plane headed for Mactan.

On arrival John was parked in one of the upfront VIP spots, which was the plan. Later arrivals would be parked in less desirable parking spots. All personnel were transported to their respective hotels in preparation for the VIPs arrival the next day. The President's plane was due to arrive the next day at 5:00p.m. and the motorcade expected to arrive at the Cebu International Conference Center at 5:27p.m.

Colonel Turkban scheduled a meeting just after noon at the Marriott Cebu City hotel. As the time approached all concerned parties began gathering in an obscure meeting room for the briefing. John had conferred with the MAAG personnel and Major Murrano on the choice of weapons for this operation. It was agreed by all that their M-16s/AR15s would be sufficient as a shot of less than 300 meters would be the norm. John had mounted his 8x25-power nightforce scope with lighted reticles as his choice for the operation. He was using 80-grain hollow point Sierra bullets and putting them out the barrel at 3100 feet per second. The other snipers were similarly armed. During the assignments John was given the rooftop of the Mandaue City Hospital on the corner of Burgos and Soriano streets. This is the point where the motorcade would make a ninety-degree turn from Burgos Street onto Soriano and head directly for the conference center. Security would have both streets blocked so the projected travel route would be clear and easily traveled. Concrete barriers would be in place making it difficult for any vehicle to enter the projected travel route.

At 4:00p.m. John and others were picked up at the hotel and dropped at their assigned location to await the passage of the motorcade. John entered the Mandaue City Hospital and made his way to the roof to take up his assigned position. The motorcade would approach from the northeast and make then turn on the corner to a northwesterly direction. With his position on the southwest corner he had a clear view back up Burgos Street to the northeast and Soriano Street to the northwest. He had been issued a radio and he checked in on channel seven. Time was approaching 4:30p.m. so it was now just a matter of waiting. When the motorcade was expected to pass his corner it would be about four minutes from the conference center. John had his rifle sighted in for 100 yards so any shot up to 300 meters would put him within two inches of his point of aim. He had also calculated his corrected aiming point and adjusted his sights for shooting at a depressed target located on the street below.

Time was now approaching 5:15p.m. Channel seven on his radio began barking. A white Cadillac had just breeched a roadblock on Sanchez street and had disabled one of the motorcade's SUVs. Another had been run off the road by the accident. It was apparent the rear of the motorcade was unprotected. About that time a white Mercedes breeched another roadblock and was falling in behind the president's SUV. The motorcade had accelerated to the maximum speed possible and all snipers had been alerted to take out the white Mercedes at all costs. It was surmised that this is where the threat of a car bomb was now emanating from. The motorcade was reported passing the intersection of Burgos and Mendoza Streets. John knew this put the situation about three blocks from his position. As he was listening to the chatter he heard gunfire up the street from his position. It was other snipers trying to stop the white Mercedes. John sat on his butt and had already placed his rifle on the projecting wall. It was extremely steady and he sighted though his scope looking up the street in the direction of the motorcade. He quickly spotted the three remaining SUVs from the President's party that were hurtling at a high rate of speed towards his intersection. If John had to take the shot he determined it would be in the middle of the turn at the intersection. John estimated the distance to be 67 yards. The gunfire continued as if it were in a time warp. What seemed like ten minutes was only a minute and a half. The three black SUV's slowed, and swung around the corner and accelerated. John began tracking the white Mercedes. He couldn't make out the driver but knew exactly where he was sitting. As the vehicle braked severely and commenced a skidded turn the driver was exposed through the SUVs side window. That's when John fired. He expected the vehicle to explode immediately and shielded his face and head expecting the worst. The vehicle continued its skid and slowed noticeably. It ran straight ahead and hit a light pole on the northeast corner of the intersection. Pieces of the vehicle came loose and parts were flying in every direction. "Where's the explosion?" John thought. Everything came to a screeching halt and John wondered why there was no explosion. Normally the car bombers were armed with a pickle/plunger type switch and if he had it in his hand he more than likely would set off the bomb before he died. The Constabulary officers in the street hurried over to the now wrecked and burning car to assess the situation. If the bomb went off now it would kill a lot of people and demolish many buildings surrounding the intersection. Everyone involved knew the risk but they rushed headlong into danger anyway to try to defuse the situation. John stayed down behind his walled protection just in case the bomb was still active. "No sense in getting killed after the fact," he thought.

Soon a fire truck arrived and the firefighters began putting out the fire. John focused his scope on the bomber in the car. He could see him slumped in the front seat still holding the pickle switch in his left hand but no finger was visible on the button. The bomber appeared to be dead and no longer a threat to the situation. John quietly packed his rifle in his fiberglass carrying case and made his way down to the street. It was now jam-packed with vehicles, NBI agents along with Philippine Constabulary, Cebu City police, firefighters and spectators. The city police were trying to keep the spectators safe and away from the wreck. The firefighters had put out the fire and the agents were making an assessment of the situation. John made his way up the street passed the now completely blocked intersection looking for a ride back to the hotel. He soon came across a few other personnel who were part of the operation and they joined up and stood waiting for transportation.

It wasn't but a couple of minutes before a Constabulary vehicle stopped and they loaded their gear into it and headed up the street. In the next block they came across Major Murrano and the three sergeants from the MAAG. They too loaded their gear in the vehicle and headed for their hotel. The chatter on the radio was decreasing and everyone was assured that it was all over, that the car bomber had been sent to meet his seventy-seven virgins and the bomb defused.

Bonnie Murrano asked the question, which it seemed everyone knew except him, "Who took the fatal shot?" he asked.

Everyone turned to John and pointed and almost in unison said, "Looks like John did, Major."

That was all that was said as the code of the sniper was nobody wanted to talk about the shot so quickly after the target had been dispatched.

However John smiled and just said, "I'm glad I was able to save the President's life."

They all nodded in agreement and rode silently back to their hotel. When they arrived Bonnie invited them all to his room for a stiff drink. As soon as all-hands stowed their rifles they made their way down to Bonnie's room on the third floor and he broke open a bottle of Maker's Mark. It was a fine example of Kentucky bourbon, glasses were filled and a salute made to the fine work everyone had done that day on the street.

26

"REWARD JUSTIFIED"

Cebu City

John and Murray would not be leaving Mactan for another day. Colonel Turkban had called a meeting for that afternoon for a debriefing and critique on the operation.

At 2:00p.m. all concerned gathered in the secure meeting room and took their seats. Colonel Turkban and his operations planning officer took the podium and began the debriefing.

"Gentleman," he began. "We were successful the other day but just barely. Things had gone smoothly until we had a breech in the security perimeter with the first car smashing into two of our SUVs. Then the second car breeching security really put us in an extreme emergency and that's when things really got wild. We are investigating those two breeches and will ensure that never can happen again if we are able to prevent it. The bomber's body has been autopsied and it appears that he was killed with one shot. It penetrated just under his left armpit, missing the vest he had on with the bomb woven into it, and went through the heart and into his liver. Commander Walker can be credited with making that shot under very difficult conditions. It was a full deflection shot at 90 degrees to his position, penetrated the driver's side window just behind the windshield post. A remarkable, unbelievable shot. You are to be congratulated Commander for saving not only the life of our President but the United States Secretary of State as well as your own Ambassador."

There was a standing ovation and John was embarrassed for all the fuss over his accomplishment.

Colonel continued, "We still have the close of the conference to worry about and the transport of the President back to the airport. In the meantime we are doubling the concrete barriers closing off all streets to the route of travel. Sniper assignments will be made the day of the Presidents return trip. Commander Walker I understand you will be leaving tomorrow and won't be with us for the final day of the conference."

"That's right, Colonel," John said. "I am flying out tomorrow with the Secretary of State and Ambassador. We do not have a set time as yet but I will advise you as soon as I find out so you can assign the security detail for their trip back to Mactan."

"That's good. We will be using a couple of generic, non-descript cars for that trip so as not to attract any attention to the VIPs, we will be transporting. I don't think there will be any further attempts at a car bombing," the Colonel said.

"If there are no further questions, we will meet on Friday for a final briefing of the President's return trip to Mactan. For the departing heads of state we will use our standard security procedures. Thanks to all for attending. See you Friday."

The debriefing was adjourned and everyone came over to shake John's hand. He took it in stride and thanked everyone for their congratulations.

Next Day

The Ambassador's aide had called John early and said he and the Secretary would like to depart around 11:00a.m. John acknowledged and he and Murray packed. Before heading for the airport John made contact with Colonel Turkban to advise him of the planned departure. Colonel Turkban said he would contact the Ambassador's aide and make the arrangements for security to the airport.

The two Naval officers caught a taxi and were soon pre-flighting their Twin Otter for the trip to Manila.

The Secretary and Ambassador arrived about 10:50a.m. and after loading were on their way. For this trip John had the lounge seating installed so the Secretary and Ambassador could sit facing each other and carry on a discussion if they wished. The aides and remaining entourage were seated further to the rear in the forward facing seats. Three and a half hours later John was touching down at Manila International. Murray switched to ground control and they were directed to taxi up behind the Secretary's Boeing 757 parked at Gate 16 at the main terminal. John came to a stop at Gate 16 and Murray went back to assist the Secretary and his party with their luggage. The Ambassador's limo appeared and stopped alongside the Twin Otter so Murray assisted the Ambassador's party to get their luggage organized and loaded aboard the limo. Once finished and everyone was clear Murray asked and received clearance back to the hangar on the airport where they keep the airplane. After securing the airplane and writing up the maintenance report the two pilots headed for their automobiles and were on the road to their quarters in the embassy compound. John had invited Murray over for a few drinks and dinner so he was anxious to see Maria and brief her on what to expect for the evening.

As John entered his quarters Maria greeted him.

"Good afternoon, Mr. Walker. How was your trip?" she asked.

"It was interesting, Maria, and a little stressful," John answered.

"Why don't you sit down and relax and I will fix you a drink and some snacks," she said.

John picked up his backpack and rifle, "No, Maria. I need to get showered and cleaned up. I will have snacks and that drink after that. I invited Mr. Wright over for a few drinks and dinner. Will that be a problem?" John asked.

"No, sir," Maria said. "I will make a pitcher of Mai Tais. I know Mr. Wright likes those. As for dinner I will make sure we have plenty of food."

John acknowledged and stepped into his bedroom to get cleaned up. This was the first moment since his trip began that John had time to relax. Taking care of the Ambassador was always a chore but having the Secretary only added to the stress.

He stepped into the shower and raised the temperature of the water. It felt great on his body and he could feel the muscle tension ease. It was a good twenty minutes before he shut the water off and stepped out to dry himself. He quickly put on his golf shirt, shorts and flip-flops and walked out into the living room.

Maria spied him and quickly came out of the kitchen with a Mai Tai in her hand and some cheese and crackers. He sat down in his easy chair and flipped on the television.

Within a few minutes Murray came to the front door, shouted his presence and John invited him to in. Murray occupied the other easy chair and Maria greeted him with a Mai Tai.

"Maria, you always know my favorite drink," Murray said.

"Yes sir, Mr. Wright," she responded. "Mr. Walker and I keep track of what peoples' choices are."

"Thanks, Maria," Murray said.

As Naval Aviators are always prone to do they hashed over their last couple of days in Cebu and especially the flight back to Manila.

Murray bemoaned the fact that they hadn't chased any beautiful women while in Cebu. It had been all business and now they were ready to play. Murray and John planned to hit the town in the next few days and make up for lost time on the beach.

Maria came out of the kitchen and announced that dinner was served. She had been putting dinner on the table while they were talking and they hadn't even noticed her scurrying around. They took a seat at the dining room table and Maria poured each a glass of Cabrinet Sauvignon. The first course was a cold cucumber soup. It was superb and John complimented Maria. The appetizer was shrimp quiche and again the quality of food was superb. Pork loin was the main course and these Naval officers really appreciated Maria's cooking. After dinner they once again occupied the easy chairs in the living room and Maria served a Drambuie liqueur to each of them.

The evening for both of them was enjoyable as they seldom had the opportunity to socialize.

Three Weeks Later

John had received a private message from Admiral Reynolds. In it he told John that he was now in a position of greater danger from the Abu Sayyaf and that his transfer to a new station would be forthcoming shortly.

The Ambassador had a private meeting with John shortly after they had returned from Cebu and had thanked him for all the things he had done for him and the Secretary of State. John had settled back into his daily routine of gathering intelligence and had made a full report of the Cebu operation.

On this particular day the Ambassador called John over to his office after lunch for a brief conference. John finished his lunch and then sauntered over to the Ambassador's office. He was ushered right in as the Ambassador was expecting him.

The Ambassador looked up from his desk as John entered, "Come in and sit down," Ambassador Ross said.

"Thank you, sir," John said.

"John, I have had a call from President Aguinaldo's office and she has requested to meet you. The appointment is for this coming Friday at 10:00a.m. I have also been asked to attend so I would suggest a tropical summer dress white uniform for the occasion. Does that sound okay to you?" he asked.

"Sir, that sounds fine. What will be the transportation?" John asked.

"We will take the official limo over to the President's office. Let's plan on leaving here at 9:40a.m. That should give us enough time to get there at least five minutes early," Ambassador Ross said.

Friday, Manila

John met the Ambassador in front of the main entrance to the embassy. The limo was already there and waiting to take them to Malacañang Palace Complex. John entered the rear seat first followed by the Ambassador. The limo pulled away and began the 10-minute drive to the complex.

The limo arrived and stopped at the main entrance to the palace. A security guard greeted them and recognized the Ambassador immediately. The limo was flying the American flag on both front fenders and was the main reason for such easy access to the palace. Ambassador Ross and John exited the vehicle and climbed a few stairs to the entrance. As they entered the Entrance Hall an aide to the President met them and introduced herself as Sylvia Aquino. Sylvia asked them to follow her and she led them up the Grand Staircase and then into the Reception Hall. Once there she stopped and briefed them on the schedule. In a few minutes they would enter the Ceremonial Hall and would be assigned a space to stand. The President would then enter and would proceed with the ceremony. John was becoming intrigued by what was happening. He didn't have a clue but something was in the wind. He knew for sure as Colonel Turkban and some of his men entered the hall followed closely by Major Murrano and his men. All had been involved with the Cebu operation and it looked like the president wanted to thank them personally. Next the Philippine Military command staff entered the room. There were more Generals and Colonels than John had seen in a long time.

Everyone in the Reception Hall was invited to enter the Ceremonial Hall and take a seat. When John entered Sylvia placed him standing next to the podium on the dais. John knew for sure now that something big was brewing.

Within a minute the President Gloria Aguinaldo entered and stepped up on the dais. Sylvia stepped forward as the President stopped in front of John.

Sylvia began, "Madame President, I would like to introduce Lieutenant Commander John Walker, United States Navy."

John was at rigid attention. The President extended her hand and said, "It is a pleasure to finally meet you, Commander Walker. I have looked forward to this for a few weeks."

John shook her hand, "My pleasure, Madam President," John answered.

The president turned toward the audience, who took their seats.

President Aguinaldo began, "Ladies and Gentlemen, this is a joyous occasion which brings us together today. We have recently completed the ASEAN Conference in Cebu, which was extremely successful. Many of you were involved in the security operations. I wanted all of you here today so I could thank you personally for your dedication to my safety and the safety of all heads of state and ministers who attended the conference. I also wanted Ambassadors from those countries of ASEAN to attend today but due to restrictions placed upon us by the United States and in the interest of the safety, we have limited this occasion to this group now here assembled.

Today I want to honor one individual in particular who has contributed to the security of our country and to my safety as well. He is currently on the most wanted list of the Abu Sayyaf and his life is now in constant danger. He is directly responsible for my standing here today and has saved my life by his actions. Based on his action in Cebu I would like to read the following citation:

"For conspicuous gallantry even at the risk of his life to protect President Gloria Aguinaldo on the eve of the ASEAN Conference on 10 January 1999, Cebu International Conference Center, Cebu City. With extraordinary courage and presence of mind, Lieutenant Commander John Walker saved the lives of President Aguinaldo, the United States Secretary of State and other high ranking officials. During that fateful eve in January 1999, Lieutenant Commander Walker, while on loan to presidential security detail, did stop and render useless an Abu Sayyaf car bomber from attacking and detonating his bomb designed to eliminate the Philippine President as well as many innocent people of Cebu city. By his actions many lives were saved. His actions were in keeping with the highest traditions of the Philippine military service and the United States Navy.'

'It is my distinct honor to award Lieutenant Commander John Walker the Philippine Medal of Valor."

As President Aguinaldo finished, her military aide stepped forward with the medal. She picked it up, spread the attached ribbon and placed it around John Walker's neck. He was filled with emotion and could hardly keep from shedding a tear. The President shook his hand and thanked him for what he had done to save her life. She turned to the photographers gathered who snapped their pictures then invited John to join her. Sylvia stepped to the microphone and announced to all in the room that they were invited to join the President for the scheduled luncheon in the state dining room honoring the medal recipient.

John followed the President into the dining room and as the President was seated he was asked to sit next to her on her right. The Vice-president was seated on her left.

The luncheon was a blur to John. Things had moved very quickly and his mind was still trying to catch up with unfolding events.

After lunch the President arose, shook John's hand, thanked him once more and departed the room. The audience was now standing and many headed to the head table to shake John's hand and congratulate him on his earning the Medal of Valor. John was particularly humbled and proud when Bonnie Murrano shook his hand. Bonnie had earned the Medal of Valor during the Vietnam war.

John found out later that the U.S. State Department as well as Colonel Turkban were instrumental in keeping the ceremony extremely quiet. All special operative identities needed to be protected and both departments had been instrumental in keeping it under wraps. Admiral Reynolds knew John had become a target of the Abu Sayyaf and had arranged for a new assignment for John.

When John returned to the U.S. Embassy the Ambassador invited John to come up to his office with him. After they entered the office the Ambassador retrieved an official looking document along with a certificate. The ambassador gave it to John and extended his hand,

"Here is your meritorious promotion to Commander signed by the President of the United States along with a personal note from him commending you for your action in saving the life of President Aguinaldo."

John was so overwhelmed he was speechless but finally managed to say, "Thank you, sir."

He left the Ambassador's office and went over to the annex. Murray, who immediately spied John's new medal still hanging from his neck, met him.

"My God, John," he said. "What have you gone and done now?"

"I was just honored by the Philippine President with the military's highest honor, the Medal of Valor. I still can't believe it," he said. "And the President of the United States just promoted me to full Commander."

"Buddy, if anyone earned it you did. Saving her life and that of the Secretary should have been recognized."

John acknowledged what Murray was saying but was humbled by all the accolades. Honors continued for another week where John was the local hero. The only problem with all of this was that now he was known by everyone in the embassy to be an excellent sniper. His CIA cover was still intact as only a few were privy to that information.

John had another private correspondence from Admiral Reynolds. He indicated John would be transferred in a few weeks with fake orders from the Navy. He was instructed on what his actions would be and where his would be posted.

A few weeks later he was in uniform and winging his way to the United States on a U.S. Navy transport aircraft. They had a scheduled two-hour stop in Hawaii. When the passengers were called to board John Walker was not among them. At that moment, for the record, Commander John Walker, United States Navy, ceased to exist.